Acclaim for
The One That Got Away

"A great book! I devoured it. Taut, pacey and with a powerful sense of place, *The One Got Away* is an intelligent and astutely observed piece of American small town noir."
—Paula Hawkins, *New York Times* bestselling author
of *The Girl on the Train* and *Into the Water*

"Joe Clifford is a gifted storyteller with a knack for crafting characters who are entirely human. *The One That Got Away* is dark and unforgiving, a chilling crime novel with the perfect touch of tenderness that will keep readers turning the pages with haste."
—Mary Kubica, *New York Times* bestselling author
of *The Good Girl* and *Every Last Lie*

"With its sharply observed characters and setting and crime-thriller pace, its tough exterior belies a vast, unexpected tenderness. I cannot not quit thinking about this book."
—Emily Carpenter, author of
Burying the Honeysuckle Girls and *The Weight of Lies*

"It's not often that I read a top-notch thriller with layers of emotion buried within each page. *The On That Got Away* is by far Clifford's best and most fully realized novel to date, and might well be the most rewarding thriller I've read this year."
—Jennifer Hillier, author of *Jar of Hearts*

THE ONE THAT GOT AWAY

JOE CLIFFORD

THE ONE THAT GOT AWAY

Down & Out Books
3959 Van Dyke Rd, Ste. 265
Lutz, FL 33558
www.DownAndOutBooks.com

The characters and events in this book are fictitious. Any similarity to real persons, living or dead, is coincidental and not intended by the author.

Cover design by Zach McCain

ISBN: 1-948235-42-0
ISBN-13: 978-1-948235-42-6

*This book is dedicated to my mother Toni Lynn,
my grandmother Helen, my Aunt Patty,
and all my Upstate New York relatives.*

And I will always remember her this way.
Standing on the hill behind the football field,
her yellow hair shining like straw in the autumn sun...

THEN

She lost track of time, how long she'd been locked underground. Must've been several days by now. The pungent stench of urine filled the black, empty spaces like the alleyway behind the bus station. Her stomach gnawed, hunger panged, sliced at her guts, like a feral animal trapped inside her rib cage, mouth too dry to produce the spit to swallow. When she first woke, submerged in total darkness, she clawed at the concrete, beat her fists against the wall of whatever this prison was. She screamed until she couldn't hear her own voice anymore.

Then she slumped to the floor and waited.

She was going to die here.

But not before something very bad happened to her first.

NOW

CHAPTER ONE

On the overpass leading into Reine, the small Upstate New York town where Alex Salerno had grown up, some smart ass had spray painted "Abandon all hope ye who enter here." There was only the one road in off the 87, making the concrete billboard the perfect platform for free advertising. Mostly pissed-off punks who had been scaling the trestles since Alex was a little girl. Drunk on blackberry brandy, draped in black, tempting fate on midnight tracks where freight trains rumbled alongside the Hudson River all night long. Anything to mark territory, stake a claim. Make voices of discontent heard. Every spring the town sent in a cleaning crew. The following fall, another tag. As Alex drove closer to the bridge, she made out the hastily scrawled response: "You need hope to lose it, ass-hole." Point. Counterpoint. Alex imagined respectable suburban professionals, mothers with small children, housewives driving this same route every day, seeing the graffiti and wondering what was wrong with kids today because they had never been young and didn't remember what outrage felt like.

It took her a while to find the campus. Even when she lived up here, Alex hadn't spent much time at Uniondale University, the private college on the hill with its fake ponds and planted sod. Sitting on a bench burnished with names she'd never heard of, Alex took in the sprawling campus, the packs of giggling girls and cocksure boys. Alex had nothing against learning or higher education. She read books. In another life, she might've done well in college. But with each passing minute she felt increasingly uncomfortable among the rich kids shuttled in from Connecticut and the Hamptons.

Why had she agreed to this meeting in the first place? Because someone wanted to tell her story again, had offered to shine the spotlight once more.

The October sun lingered in a stubborn autumn sky, creating the illusion that there was time left. Late-afternoon clouds rolled in, the horizon growing darker. Alex pulled up her black hoodie and jammed hands in pockets. The college was a strange choice for an interview. Albany would've made more sense. Troy, Schenectady. Even Rensselaer. That's where the press was, the little big towns of Upstate New York. Which definitely did not include Reine. The longer she sat there, amid the quaint woodsy backdrop and postmodern metal sculptures, the more pathetic she felt. It had been years since she escaped that basement. Who would want to talk to her now? After all this time? Back then, they wrote stories about her. Back then, she was, if not national news, at least part of local lore. The girl who'd risen from the dead, emerged untouched, still pure. The one that got away. No one else would have to die.

Then another girl died, and Alex's story turned cautionary tale, an unpleasant reminder that promises get broken and nothing gold can stay.

Alex pulled her Parliaments, stashed them, pulled them again. A jogger stomped past and she flinched. She checked her phone. No missed calls, no unanswered texts. Opened her email. No update from Noah Lee, the reporter, saying that he was running late, no messages about crossed wires, a misunderstanding over what time or where they were supposed to meet. She contemplated heading back to her car, digging for his number among the clutter; it was in there somewhere, but she knew once she crossed the quad she wasn't coming back. She'd hit the 87 back to the city, where she'd do what she always did. Run off, find a party, score something to make her forget she'd ever been this needy.

A college kid with a backpack draped over his shoulder headed toward her, pleasant smile plastered on his smooth, youthful face like he needed to borrow something. Alex hid her cigarettes. Students were always bumming smokes at the bar, despite having way more money than she ever would. But the kid did not want a cigarette.

"I'm Noah," he said. "You must be Alex." He slipped the bag off his shoulder, dropping it between his feet and plopping down beside her.

She sucked on her smoke, biting the inside of her cheek, an anxious habit that had created a permanent nub, soft candy she chewed when nerves got the best of her.

Noah pointed at the tall light pole, a big sign with red slashes through all the things you weren't allowed to do. "Campus is smoke free."

"I thought this was an interview?" Alex dropped the cigarette, squashing the burning ember beneath the heel of her Chuck Taylors. "For a newspaper?"

"Yup. The *Codornices*. Uniondale's student publication."

The meeting had been set up via email, details arranged digitally. Why hadn't she taken six seconds to verify the name of the newspaper?

"I mean, I'm hoping they'll run it," Noah said. "No guarantee. Not too much competition though. I live in the same dorm as the editor. Mainly I need the interview for my final project."

"Final project?"

"Beats and Deadlines. It's a journalism class—"

"How old are you?"

"Nineteen."

"You got to be shitting me."

"I'm sorry. Did I say something wrong?"

Of course no mainstream press would want to talk to her now. Not after all this time. It had been years since Alex Salerno mattered. How many kids—girls, boys, teens, toddlers, babies—had been stolen over the past dozen years? Hundreds? Thousands? Hers was no longer even the latest abduction to come out of Reine. Certainly not the most infamous. Not after Kira Shanks went missing. The day Kira Shanks disappeared, Alex's fifteen minutes were up.

She stared at her old Civic across the quad, rusting in the metered section of the parking lot. A jangle of clipped wires barfed out a hole in the dash from where the stereo had been stolen. The prospect of driving two hours without music, back to a tiny rented room, sounded as appealing as playing freshman comp Q&A. She hated that sick part inside her that longed for the attention.

"Just ask your questions," she said.

"Sean Riley? The detective who rescued you?"

"What about him?" Alex leaned back on the bench. Just hearing Riley's name cracked the fragile parts inside her, unleashed the emotional shrapnel she'd learned to keep hidden. Talking about being snatched, imprisoned against her will? No problem. If she pretended hard enough, she could imagine somebody else's life. Dissociation, that's what her therapist called it, a strategy trauma victims employed to stay safe. Thinking about Riley made her feel things. Tender things. Vulnerable things.

Alex braced for what came next. Because just as she was inextricably linked to Riley, Alex was forever tied to that other girl. The bigger deal. The sexier story. The Mary Sue to her outcast. And if Noah Lee said her name right now, Alex swore she'd scream.

But of course he did.

"And, y'know, Kira Shanks."

There had been no reason for Alex to believe this interview would lead to anything beneficial. There was no money in it.

No prospective job offers. It was a long drive up from NYC, costing gas money she didn't have, shifts off from the bar she couldn't afford, time spent in a town full of painful memories. But at least the focus would be on her. Her struggle, *her* victory. The one good thing she'd done with her life: she'd survived.

Alex glanced around uneasy, trying to figure a way to bolt without looking smaller than she already felt. How do you explain you're sick of competing with a dead girl without sounding petty? What happened to Kira Shanks was terrible. Of course she felt bad for her. But by living, Alex thought she'd won. Turned out by not dying, she'd lost.

"Does it feel weird to be back up here?" Noah asked, pen in hand.

"No. Why would it?"

"Because it's not far from here where it happened."

"Where what happened?" Alex knew what he meant.

"Um," Noah stammered. "Do you feel, like, an affinity?"

"To what?"

"Kira Shanks. Because of her disappearance. Like you're both part of the same curse on this town. The other girls, too. But I can't talk to them. They're all, y'know, dead. You're the only one who's not."

Noah had been, what, seven, when Alex was taken? Twelve by the time Kira went missing? He knew the whole story or they wouldn't be sitting here. Alex Salerno had been the last of several young girls kidnapped by a man named Kenneth Parsons, who was currently serving several, concurrent life sentences far away without chance of parole. He'd die in prison. Kira Shanks had been murdered by a different man altogether. Five long years separated the crimes. Nothing tied the two cases together. Alex fought against her quickening pulse.

"When you wrote," she said, "it was to interview me. Why are you asking about Kira Shanks? Like I had anything to do with it?"

"I didn't mean you were involved."

"Wasn't even the same guy who took her. Everyone knows that. Parsons took me and killed those other girls. They arrested Benny-what's-his-name for Kira."

"Brudzienski. Benny Brudzienski."

"There's no connection between what happened to her and me."

"Some people think Parsons had help—"

"A rumor, something the media drummed up for ratings. Parsons and Benny never even met. That's been proven." Alex was repeating what the police and Riley had promised her. Even now she couldn't keep those wolves away.

"Parsons could've had a partner," Noah said. "They found other DNA."

"I know what they found. I was there, remember? Parsons confessed, copped to everything, pled out. Gave up every kill, every body. Hand-delivered detectives to each gravesite. Why would Parsons cover for anyone? His plea bargain with the DA is the only reason I am here." It had taken Alex a long time to squelch fears that another monster lurked in the dark, waiting to drag her back to hell. It was a never-ending losing fight. "Parsons is in prison because of me."

"Not exactly because of you."

"Excuse me?"

"He got time for the others. Technically. He didn't do anything to you."

"Didn't do anything to me? You know what that was like? Being locked underground, not knowing if I'd live or die, get raped, or something worse? I'm supposed to what? Feel lucky? Grateful? Because Parsons got picked up before he had a chance to do me like he did the others? Because Riley found me in that bunker, half-starved and nearly dead of dehydration? I was seventeen years old. Couple years younger than you are now. You have any idea how terrified I was?"

"I didn't mean—"

"You keep saying that, Noah. You didn't mean this. You're

sorry for that. Why did you want to interview me? If what I went through wasn't tragic enough for you?"

"I need to write this paper. It's very important to my grade."

"What's that got to do with me?"

"I messed up, okay? I jumped the gun and made enemies of your friend, Sean Riley. Detective Riley. This paper I'm writing accounts for seventy-five percent of my grade. I had this big idea for a real investigative piece because of how he doesn't think he did it and my prof loves frontline reporting—he worked with my dad—muckraker shit, undercover journalism. The sixties." He rolled his eyes. "I had the whole story mapped out. The cop who cracked the case changes his mind. Grants last-minute reprieve. Like the *Life of David Gale.*"

"What are you talking about? Who doesn't believe what?"

"Detective Riley?" Noah said, surprised. "How he doesn't believe Benny Brudzienski did it? Killed Kira Shanks? Riley's working with the Brudzienski family to get the murder charges dismissed. Although it's technically a disappearance, right? Since they never found the body. That's part of the enduring mystery, how they never found the body. Brings up all kinds of interesting legal ramifications. Don't you and Riley talk anymore?"

"Why would we?"

"I thought after…"

"After what?"

"Nothing," Noah said.

"Why do you care so much about Benny Brudzienski?"

"I told you. It's an exposé." Noah fished around his rucksack, retrieving a black and white composition notebook, the same kind Alex used to fill with the names of hard rock bands inside ballpoint pentagrams. He sat upright, clearing his throat, projecting confidence. "Seven years ago this November, Reine High senior Kira Shanks went missing, the latest in a string of horrific abductions to rock the small Upstate New York town. Benny Brudzienski, hulking man-child with a third-grade IQ, was sought in connection with the crime. Blood and DNA found at the Idlewild Motel just off the interstate where Benny worked as a handyman linked him to the scene. However, questions remain. Before police could swoop in and make an arrest, Benny had an 'accident.'" Noah did air quotes with his fingers. "Now Benny Brudzienski sits in a posh state hospital on the taxpayer's dime pretending he can't talk because he fell off his bicycle and hit his head after concerned citizens took matters into their own hands, unwilling to be victimized anymore. Some call it vigilante justice. But not this reporter. Where is the justice for Kira Shanks?" Noah closed his book. "Pretty good, eh?"

"I don't know. It's all right, I guess. A little pretentious."

"That's all I got." Noah's shoulders slagged. "A progress update on my paper is due and I can't get Riley to talk to me. I barged into the precinct and got tossed on my ass. Ordered not to come back. I kinda made a scene. That's why I reached out to you. You're right. I don't know what I'm doing. I got to write this paper, and it's a big deal, and Detective Riley won't return my calls. They almost arrested me."

"What do you want me to do about it?"

"I thought maybe you could hook me up with Riley."

"*Why* would I do that?"

"Look. My dad pays my tuition, all right? And he kicks down a lot of scratch for the day-to-day incidentals. Journalism's, like, supposed to be my thing? My father is Yoan Lee."

Noah waited for the reaction. Alex had no reaction.

"Yoan Lee, the columnist? The *Post*? *The* Yoan Lee?" Noah scanned the grounds, making sure no one else could hear him act like the spoiled trust fund kid he really was. "It's too late in the semester to change my topic now. And if I flunk Beats and Deadlines, I am screwed. My dad won't foot the bill if I get less than a three-point GPA. I live off that money. I'm not moving back home, and I'm *not* getting a job. I figure you can talk to Riley. You're still friends, right? I mean, he'll answer your questions. Maybe let you glance at his evidence, tell you why he suddenly thinks Benny Brudzienski is innocent? You get me his notes, snap a pic with your phone, provide me some quotes, I can pay you a little money. Like a finder's fee. An anonymous source. I ace this paper, it runs in the *Codornices*. People are reminded of who you are, your story, women's rights groups or whatever. A feature like this jumpstarts a career. It's a scoop. I might be able to start interning at the *Times* next summer."

"They teach ethics at Uniondale, too?"

"Couple hundred bucks ease your conscience?"

"How about you do your own homework?"

"Don't you think it's a little convenient?"

"What?"

"Benny Brudzienski not being able to talk."

"Not for Kira Shanks, it's not."

"She goes missing. The one guy who knows what really happened's already retarded."

"I don't think people call them that anymore."

"Fine. Mentally challenged, handicapable, whatever. Now all of a sudden, he clams up with some mysterious condition. The dude was hardly Mensa material but he used to hold down a job. Had to be able to follow instructions, right? From what I hear, after that bicycle accident, he just stares at walls and shits his pants. I think it's all an act. I want to know why your pal, Riley, thinks this dangerous predator is innocent. That's interesting, right? You say Parsons didn't have a partner—"

"For the last time, he didn't have a partner."

"Fine. He didn't have a partner. The two cases aren't connected, whatever. But there's still got to be a reason why the detective who broke both cases is now rushing to a killer's defense. I'd think you of all people—"

"Don't."

"What?"

"Play me. What makes you think Riley would let me look at case files?"

"Because of your relationship."

And there it was. Noah said it so brazen too, like everyone in Reine knew about their affair. The scandal they'd sought to avoid, a secret to no one. She loved Riley. So she'd let him go. But if Noah knew about it, everyone knew about it, so what difference did it make? They'd thrown away any hope of a future together. For nothing.

Alex gathered her things and left.

"Wait," Noah called after her. "How about two-fifty? Three hundred? Come back. Let's talk. Price is negotiable! Alex!"

Alex headed to her car. No matter how loud he called her name, she did not turn around.

When she came to the Interstate 87 split south, she didn't go home either.

CHAPTER TWO

She never wanted to hurt him. She knew the damage done if word spread, how it would destroy Riley's world, which in addition to the job and wife now included a new baby girl. The age difference alone would destroy his reputation. He might even go to prison. Alex had understood Riley's need to break things off. She never held that against him, and she believed him when he said he wanted to stay friends, have her in his life. And he tried.

It was funny. Riley's ending their affair wasn't what spurred Alex to leave town. It had taken Kira Shanks to do that. Not being in his bed hurt bad enough. Being rendered irrelevant was too painful to bear, the entire town consumed by Kira Shanks hysteria.

Alex had of course followed the story when it first happened seven years ago, was vaguely aware of the particulars. Noah's proposed exposé jostled loose the long-term, brought specifics back to the light.

Though they were no longer together, Alex watched Riley's star rise, albeit from a distance—his promotion to detective as he led the charge to find Kira, just as he'd done with Alex five years earlier. Only the hero was too late this time. Alex knew they liked Benny Brudzienski for the crime, which, as Noah Lee pointed out, still listed officially as a missing persons case since no body was ever recovered.

Benny Brudzienski wasn't much older than Alex. But he seemed a lot older. In part because he was such a permanent fixture in Reine. Like that hundred-year-old oak tree struck by lightning or the fire-scorched hall of records, you never remembered a time when he wasn't around. Alex could still picture Benny wandering through town—sloe-eyed, lumbering strides, aimless. Reine's very own George slouching toward Friendly's or the Pig 'n' Poke. Until one of his brothers would roll up beside him, load him onto the flatbed like some wayward, dopey cow that had broken through the fence. No one ever believed he was dangerous.

When word of Benny's involvement leaked, either via press or police, unidentified locals chased him down, ran his bicycle off the road, shook loose whatever remaining lug nuts were rolling around his junkyard oil pan. How much more damage could the accident have caused? Guy had the IQ of an eight-year-old to begin with.

Alex hadn't known Benny was in a mental hospital, but it made sense when she thought about it. Noah was the first to imply Benny was faking it. Alex didn't know if he was or wasn't. He deserved to burn all the same.

Sometimes Alex doubted her memory, especially during stretches where she partied too hard. There were a lot of stretches like that. It got worse after her ordeal, the pills she leaned on to make her forget, the holes in her memory that formed like Swiss-cheese excerpts of a hastily erased tape. There were times, late at night, when she'd wonder if what she and Riley had was as real and deep as she recalled. She knew she had a tendency to think in terms of black and white. Heroes, villains. Good guys and bad. When your hand is against a wall, you know where you stand, no matter how dark it gets.

Therapy helped. For a while. She liked the part about how Denise's rotating cast of abusive boyfriends hindered her chances long before Parsons came along. Loose mothers and tumultuous childhoods absolve most sins where therapists are concerned. Alex didn't appreciate the other interpretation though, the one about a seventeen-year-old victim infatuated with the young, handsome, married cop who saved her. Savior complex, the doctor called it. Alex hated that. Made her sound clingy, nuts, like some wacko trashy home-wrecker. She knew what she and Riley shared was real; she didn't need a diploma on a wall to validate it.

When Alex first left Reine, Riley checked in. Then that correspondence waned. Mostly because Alex stopped returning calls and answering emails. She'd never been one for small talk—how a new job is going, what are you doing for fun, how about this crazy weather we've been having. People move on. Alex hadn't spoken with Detective Sean Riley in at least three, four years. So why did the wound still feel so fresh, so raw? Why did just hearing his name make her heart yearn? Why had the need to see him come on so pressing, so strong, so relentless?

The Reine police station sat across the river in a squat brick building that might as well have been a video store in a strip mall. Reine had undergone a major facelift since Alex's last visit—more chain restaurants, renovated Hannaford, new Target—but the local PD hadn't parlayed the string of murders into bigger, better headquarters. Compared to the daunting NYC jails, the understated precinct projected junior league.

When all those girls went missing in the early 2000s, terror gripped the small town. You'd think local politicians would have been able to manipulate residents into footing the bill for more cops, shinier cars, state-of-the-art digs. Instead, everyone opted to ignore, pretend like it never happened, lock the doors and stay inside, turn a blind eye. Can't rationalize an evil you don't understand.

Maybe Noah Lee had been right about that part, too. At least in a broader cosmic sense. Like cheating death, escaping the noose meant for her. Didn't matter that the two cases were unrelated; that the man who'd abducted Alex and killed all those other girls, Ken Parsons, was locked up miles away in a maximum-security prison when Kira Shanks disappeared. Alex had traded one life for another, her unintended release creating a malevolent butterfly effect. Like one of those cheesy *Final Destination* movies. One child taken, another spared. Fate, a roll of the dice.

Alex parked her battered Civic around back beside a cruiser. Remnants of rainwater dribbled off the gutter overhead. Before her interview with Noah Lee, Alex hadn't known for sure if Riley still worked in Reine. She'd assumed so. Riley preferred to be a big fish in a little pond. Probably ran the whole show up here by now. Talking to Noah Lee had got her thinking, wondering...regretting? No, that wasn't the right word. But there was no reason why she couldn't stop by and say hello. They were both adults. In fact, given their history, be rude not to.

She tilted the mirror, sweeping the hair out of her eyes, securing an unruly lock of brown behind her ears. She retouched her lipstick and eyeliner, adjusted her shirt, tightening and tucking, grinning back at what she saw. Alex owed Denise and the father she never met that much.

"Can I help you?" the young desk sergeant asked.

Behind him, the small-town force scurried, filing speeding violations to make the monthly quota, or whatever they did to pass time up here in between kidnappings. Route 9 by the elementary school had always been a speed trap, stuffing county coffers since Alex was in pigtails. Denise had been popped there at least half a dozen times, providing her mother with yet another reason to feel like the whole world was out to get her.

"Miss?" the desk sergeant repeated.

"I want to talk to Sean Riley. Riley. Detective Riley."

"Is this about a case?"

"Yes," Alex lied.

The desk sergeant said to have a seat. Alex didn't sit, instead pulling her black hoodie over her head, jamming hands in her back jean pockets. She studied pictures on the wall. Certificates, awards, accommodations, handshakes with the chief, rewards for jobs well done. There was one of Riley being given his detective's badge. He faced the camera, stern expression betraying a solemn oath to serve and protect, but there was an undeniable glibness in his eyes, an inability to hide the joy. He deserved it. She could still hear the resounding cheer that erupted when they walked through the door that night. He'd wrapped her in a scratchy old wool blanket, his arm around her, pulling her so close she could smell the musk on his neck and feel the scratch of several days' growth.

"Alex?"

It felt like forever since she'd heard his voice in person. He had the same intense, soulful stare, and still looked younger than his years, except that he'd grown an actual beard, tight and trimmed. Faint crow's feet tattooed the eyes. Other than that, he was the same Riley.

"Surprise!" Alex said, feeling stupid the moment the phony exuberance escaped her lips. She'd intended irony. The exclamation came across as ridiculous, childish.

Alex pretended to be distracted by a sudden noise but the only startling sound was her own beating heart. She had a hard time avoiding that piercing gaze, which still possessed the power to disturb.

"What are you doing here?"

"In town. Visiting friends." They both knew that was a lie—Alex didn't have any friends left in Reine. Other than a cousin she seldom spoke to, no family remained since Denise died. Alex's mother passed, like most old alcoholics, going quietly in the night, unnoticed, unmissed, until the dogs next door smelled her and started barking and a neighbor alerted the police. Despite the town's best efforts at reinvention, Reine was still small enough that every death resonated, even that of the town drunk living alone above a bar.

Riley waited. Alex had seen enough cop shows to know the trick. Prolonged silence makes people talk, give themselves up, say anything to fill the void. And it worked.

"I talked to a reporter today," she said.

"Reporter?"

"Some kid with the college. Said you weren't returning his calls." The truth wasn't always Alex's first choice. Another coping mechanism, according to the doctors. The truth could be terrifying so victims of trauma often created their own realties. Easier to place pieces in advantageous positions that way. But Riley had always been able to throw her off her game. And this time the truth covered up the real, more substantive reason for her visit, the need to see his face, which came on without warning, relentless, like a rockslide, stones pressing on spine.

Riley creased his brow. "Noah something? Uniondale, right?"

"Yeah, that's him."

"Pain in the ass. Been calling nonstop. Stopped by couple weeks ago when I wasn't here. Caused a scene—" He stopped. "He's not a friend of yours, is he?"

"God, no."

Riley waited for more, but Alex didn't have anything else. There had been no reason to drive to the station.

"Are you okay?"

"I'm fine. It's just that reporter, Noah. He was talking about Kira Shanks, and I guess it got me thinking."

"About what?"

"Us. Not us-us, but that time. In my life. What happened when I was seventeen. How if you hadn't found me..." Alex let the words trail off, choking back a laugh. "I don't know why I came here." She thumbed out the glass door. "I'm going to get going."

"You want to grab dinner?"

No one recognized Alex at the Double Y, the twenty-four-hour restaurant near the interstate on-ramp. Why would they? Several years had passed, and her star had long faded. A couple regulars waved hello to Riley.

After they sat, he tried to sell her on the burgers, like a dad implying she was too thin. Alex asked for a beer.

Riley ordered a Number Twelve, salad instead of fries, dressing on the side, with a water.

"How's Meg?" Alex glanced at the space on his left hand where a wedding ring should be. "And Sam? She's got to be, what? Almost in middle school by now?"

"This year." Riley gestured out the window. A bigger Exxon had been erected beside the Vitamin Shoppe. Chain outlets lit up the dreary night sky. The new and improved Reine. "How long has it been since you were back?" he asked.

"When did my mother die? Two and half, three years ago?"

"You didn't tell me you were in town."

"I wasn't actually in town." She nodded into the dark. "The morgue in Albany. Just long enough to ID the body. I made the cremation arrangements when I got back to the city."

The waitress brought her IPA. "Quite a change," she said, referring to the widened roadway and added eats, superstores, and general increased bustle.

Riley unwrapped his silverware from the tight, taped napkin, tapping his butter knife off the tabletop. Quiet conversation murmured among regulars along the counter. Cars spat back ground water as they raced along the busy boulevard.

"What? Aren't you happy to see me?"

"It's always nice to see you, Alex. But I haven't heard from you in four years. You stopped responding to emails. I left more than a few unanswered messages on your phone. Till your number changed. We haven't had a real conversation in ages. Then you pop in out of nowhere." He ran his fingers through his thick hair, the same way he always did when she got him flustered. Strange how it all came rushing back. He kept tapping the butter knife, trying to grin away the awkwardness they both felt. "Maybe I'm rusty."

Alex brushed the hair out of her eyes. "Didn't realize you missed me so much."

"Of course I missed you."

Since she was a kid, Alex had the ability to flip switches, like she was turning off a light. If she didn't want to deal with something, an emotion came on too strong, the timing wrong, inconvenient, she could check out, go somewhere else. One more survival technique. Her shrink could rationalize away every tic and shortcoming. Part of the reason she liked Dr. Amy so much. At first. All faults forgiven, Alex's life had been one forged from necessity. A drunk for a mother, no money, no sense of security, ducking landlords, fleeing with meager possessions in the middle of the night, this sense of uncertainty and instability exacerbated after Parsons. Alex could do it on the drop of a dime, check out of a situation, the choice to be physically present but mentally removed. Except when it came to Riley. His mere presence commanded she be with him. And when the feeling was good, like right now, she didn't want to be anywhere else. Everything she wanted, right there in front of her.

It's why she had to leave, move all the way down to the city. Out of sight, the only way to keep him out of her mind. Sitting across from him again, Alex ached for the sensation of his skin against hers one last time.

"I'll always feel..." Riley trailed off.

Alex leaned in. "What?"

"An obligation."

"An obligation." Alex eased back in the booth, watching the trucks and trailers zip past, gather speeds for the on-ramp. She swiped her beer. Took a pull, then another, then tipped back the whole bottle, sucking down the rest.

"What would you like me to say?"

"No, it's fine. Don't worry about it." Alex held up the empty bottle, waving it for the waitress to bring another. "Like I said, it was stupid of me to stop by—"

"Did this college reporter say something to get you upset?"

"I'm not upset."

"You look upset."

"I'm not upset."

Riley glanced around, fumbling for the answers she herself didn't fully grasp. "I guess I don't understand why you'd drive all this way for a college newspaper interview. Why put yourself through that? It was so long ago, Alex. Why would you want to revisit that time?"

She wanted to tell him it wasn't *all* bad, that after it was over, in a strange way, it might've been the happiest she'd ever felt. At least in the beginning. Denise briefly cleaned up her act, so glad to have her daughter back. Strangers treated her like she mattered. Everywhere Alex went she received celebrity treatment. And she had him. Which made the whole experience worth it. No, it wasn't perfect. He was married. She was still seventeen, if barely. But their time together was real. What they shared was real.

Her arms goose-fleshed, the walls coming down, and she hated being so vulnerable. Hated that Riley could stay so cool, like they'd never been more than cop and vic.

The waitress brought her refill. Alex took a long, hard slug, waited for the buzz, a fleeting reprieve from the constant pressure. When it came, she set the bottle down hard enough to draw stares from the staff and customers.

Riley's pinched expression twisted. "This isn't about that bullshit Parsons had help? We've been over this. You're safe. Kira was an isolated incident. Totally unrelated—"

"Then why are you trying to get the charges against Benny Brudzienski dropped?"

"Who told you that?"

"Noah Lee. The reporter. Is it true?"

"It's a little more complicated than that. But I promise you, it has nothing to do with you or your case."

"What does it have to do with then?"

"I can't discuss private police matters."

"Oh, fuck that."

"You can't trust reporters. And everything you read in the papers isn't true. At least not the whole truth. There was more to it than the media reported. Misinformation got out, the public ran with it. There were inconsistencies with the Brudzienski case, okay? Some of Kira's friends—" Riley stopped himself. "I don't want to talk about this. Let's talk about you. What have you been up to? What are you doing for work down there? Fun?"

"Can you give me a ride back to my car? It's getting late."

"Alex, please—"

"Great. I'll be outside."

Alex smoked a cigarette underneath the awning while he waited inside for his takeout. A light rain started to fall. She pulled her hoodie, bunched her bomber she didn't bother zipping up. Cars sped behind her, tires slick on the wet roadways, making sucking sounds. How could he still do this to her? After all this time, disarm her so readily? She resented him for how weak he could make her feel.

Ten minutes later, Riley met her beside the car, toting a greasy white sack. Good. Let him take it home to Meg and eat it cold.

Driving back to the precinct, Alex watched the naked trees, stripped of their cover, zipping past, bare and exposed. Some things had changed about their hometown, it was true. But in between the new Chili's, Arby's, and PF Chang's was the same rundown crap she'd grown up with, the package stores and hole-in-wall bars, the impersonal behemoth stone churches, the bland, two-toned duplexes. Slapping on a new coat of paint didn't conceal the blight or erase the ugly. A while back Alex, stumbled across clickbait on the web. The Ten Most Depressing Cities in America. No surprise, seven of them were located in Upstate New York. The only reason Reine didn't make the cut was because it was too small, too insignificant to matter. There was a barren quality, an ache and emptiness germane to the region. Maybe it was the architecture, drab and uninspired, or the weather, stifling in the summer, bleak and gray the rest of the year. Most likely, it was the people, with their abysmal posture and sallow complexions, men and women who walked without purpose, resigned to their fate, knowing they'd never leave this place.

Back at the police department, they sat silent in the car, Riley waiting for her to get out, Alex trying to find the right moment to do so on her terms. She kept her gaze locked straight ahead, out the windshield. The precinct lights haloed through the raindrops.

"Why do you care what I think about Benny Brudzienski?" Riley said. "Did that reporter give you a list of questions to ask me or something?"

"This isn't about a reporter or any questions. I have a right to know."

"It's an ongoing case, Alex."

"So you *do* think Benny is innocent?"

"Like I said," Riley reiterated extra slow. "I'm not allowed to talk about an open police investigation with civilians."

"Civilians?" Alex grabbed the handle.

Riley reached for her but she was already outside.

She leaned in before closing the door.

"It was nice seeing you."

Alex stuck her hands in the back pockets of her jeans.

"You sure you're okay to drive? The city is a long haul. Maybe you want to come in, rest for a few."

"It was two beers. Besides, I'm not driving back tonight. Going to see my family. What's left of them."

Riley thought a moment. "Your cousin Linda still up here?"

"Yeah."

"Are you staying with her?"

"No. I'm renting a room." She nodded through the tree line. "The Royal Motel. Next door to the Pig 'n' Poke." She'd seen it on the drive in. Even now she couldn't abandon the urge. "I'll be there all night. Alone."

She slammed the door and walked away, wondering if he was watching her ass or if he'd come after her, grab her by the hand, turn back time. The driver's side door opened and shut. She resisted temptation to turn around.

Then she heard footsteps beat a path in the opposite direction.

CHAPTER THREE

At the Royal Motel, Alex plunked down the fifty-four dollars and change, spelling her name nice and neat in the registry in case anyone wanted to find her. She requested a room on the second floor. Reine still possessed enough squirrely sections that you didn't stay on the bottom one. The clerk passed along the key card, tucked into a little envelope with a long series of numbers stamped on back.

"What's this for?"

"Wi-Fi code."

"Why do I need it?"

"The internet?"

"I don't have a computer."

The clerk pointed behind her, at a tiny desktop cramped beside the empty pot of coffee and container of powdered creamer. "You can use that one. It's complimentary for guests." He glanced up at the clock on the wall. "But not now. The lobby is closed."

"I don't need to use the computer." She nodded at her name next to the make and model of her car. "You can read that, right? Salerno. E r n o—"

"If you're expecting company, you'll need to put their name down."

"What for?"

"Motel policy. We get a lot of college kids from Uniondale wanting to party up here."

"Do I look like I'm in college?"

"No."

The clerk hadn't taken any time to think about the question before answering, which, even though the right response, still pissed her off.

In the room, Alex peeled her clothes, stepping in the shower. The hot water felt good against her skin and face. Alex hadn't planned on spending the night and didn't bring along any toiletries, let alone a change of clothes. She'd have to make do with the complimentary soap and shampoo. Sliding hands over her naked body, Alex reached the faint scars on the undersides of her forearm and wrist. No one ever noticed them unless the light was just right. Usually the morning after. Tangled in sheets, bodies still entwined. Only a few guys pointed them out, and even then a shrug was enough to stop follow-up questions. She used to blame the scars on a fictitious car accident. Then she realized the one-night stands she picked up after her shift ended at the bar didn't give a shit. There were a hundred conclusions to draw before self-mutilation. The scars had faded over the years, and it was hard to pick out the small white crosses beneath the tattoos she used to cover her past. But she knew they were there. To her they bore a permanent part, evidence of when she thought pain should be stamped like a badge and presented for the world to see.

The knock on the door coincided with her turning off the water. Of course a part of her was hoping he'd come, it's why she'd told him where she was staying, but now that he was actually here that other part, the one not wanting complications, kicked in, causing her to panic.

She wished she'd had the chance to make herself look pretty, or at least brought the black panties she wore when she knew she was getting laid.

Alex whipped down a towel from the wire shelf and wrapped it around her long, lean body. The by-product of poverty. She didn't have the disposable income to piss away on taxis or Uber.

Parking in the city is a pain in the ass, so you end up walking everywhere. Keeps you hungry, fit.

The knock sounded again. More frantic, urgent, aggravated.

In front of the mirror Alex combed back damp hair with fingers, swiveled the towel lower. For as mixed up as she was feeling right now, as vicious as the conflict warring inside, she knew when she opened that door everything would be okay. She wasn't asking for longer than tonight. Just a little relief, a break from the norm. Like a drug, she needed the reprieve from reality.

She pulled open the door. It wasn't Riley.

Another man, much bigger, more gruff-looking, stood on the landing in plaid flannel, rolled-up sleeves and sun-bleached trucker's cap, heavy-duty work boots caked in mud. He leered at the free view. Alex said hold on, slammed the door, and pulled on her jeans and tee. She slid the dead bolt before opening this time. The man had pulled the cap lower, making his eyes tough to read, but the smirk lingered.

"What do you want?"

The man gestured over the railing, at Alex's old Civic in the parking lot. "That your car?"

Alex didn't answer. There were no other cars down there, at least none in the immediate vicinity.

"Your headlights're on."

"No there're not." Alex saw they weren't, the whole lot blanketed in darkness. Not a glimmer from the Pig 'n' Poke, lights unable to penetrate the dense forest.

"They *were*," the man said. "I turned them off for you." He looked back at the car. "In case you saw me opening your car door. I was turning off the lights. That's what I was doing. Locked the doors for you too."

"Thanks." Alex didn't know what else to say but the man remained, so she added a second thank you.

He touched the brim of his hat, like a Southern gentleman, tipping his head sideways so he could steal a better look as she shut the door.

Alex waited until he was gone and slipped on her sneakers, heading down to the parking lot. She unlocked her car and turned over the motor. Coughed to life, no problem. She did a quick search of the floors and console, popping the glove compartment, nothing missing, nothing worth stealing. Entire car wasn't worth three hundred in parts. She killed the engine, shut the door, and inserted the key to lock up—which was the only way to lock the door. Wasn't any other way...

A gentle breeze hushed through the bare birch orchard that led downslope to the highway. Alex strained through the chain-link, panning the grounds. Inhaling the rotting compost of dead leaves, she couldn't see a thing.

The bedside clock read a little after midnight and Alex hadn't been able to fall asleep. There was nothing on the motel's limited cable. By now she'd accepted Riley wasn't stopping by. She tried to convince herself she was relieved but mostly she felt like a fool.

She scrolled through her contacts, surprised to find her cousin, Linda, had made the cut after so many lost and stolen phones.

"Alex? Alex? That you?" Raucous barroom chatter bled over the line. "Alex? Is everything okay?"

She walked to the front door, pulling her Parliaments, ignoring the No Smoking sign by the keyhole. She poked her head outside. The light in the lobby was off and rain slicked the rail. She closed the door and slid the deadbolt, grabbing the empty Diet Coke can for an ashtray. What were they going to do? Charge her credit card? Good luck. There wasn't fifty bucks left to cover a cleaning fee.

"Alex?" Linda hollered, plugging an ear, mouth-breathing.

"Yeah. Everything's fine. I'm here."

"Here?"

"Reine."

There was a long pause while her cousin mulled over what that meant. Linda wasn't the swiftest boat sober. And at this time of night, that dinghy had drifted way past the breakers.

"Where?"

"Royal Motel."

"On Cutting?"

"By the Pig 'n' Poke."

Another long, uneasy pause.

"I'm leaving soon," Alex said.

"Oh, next time call me earlier. I would've loved to see—"

"Want to grab a drink?"

The Fireside Pub spilled over with Uniondale students, who outnumbered the locals three to one. Everyone was playing nice. Back in the day it would be a cold day in hell before you caught the two groups mixing, like Greasers and Socs. But here they were, sharing pitchers of beer, racking games of nine ball, laughing, talking sports, and getting shitfaced together.

Alex spotted Linda and her longtime boyfriend, Tommy, sitting in a booth by the pool table, their regular spot. The two of them had been coming to the Fireside since graduation, probably had their names carved inside a heart somewhere. Hard to miss them. Had to be carrying five hundred pounds between them. Alex always had a soft spot for Tommy. Good guy, big heart, giant teddy bear. After Alex and Linda fell off, Tommy was left navigating the worst fights, those drunken brawls where they really went at it, viciousness that kept escalating until Alex finally split town. Time apart had repaired some of the damage. Pretending nothing was wrong took care of the rest.

A couple other guys sat with them. One of them wasn't bad looking, almost cute, in that lost puppy dog sort of way. A cross between a young John Cusack and Izzy Stradlin.

Alex dragged a chair to the edge of the table, the queen's seat as her mother called it, a thought that made Alex laugh out loud and everyone else stare. Tommy took her order, which translated to another pitcher of beer and round of shots for the table. When Tommy got up, he left behind his permanent indentation in the cushions. Alex glanced around the bar, not relishing fond memories.

She couldn't understand how Linda still stomached the place. The cousins had grown up at the Fireside, back when their mothers, Denise and Diane, worked the room, letting strangers buy them drinks, kick down pills and powders for the privilege of playing Daddy for a week or two. Sometimes that experiment lasted a month, once or twice six, but never longer than that. The money always ran out, the party always ended, then the sisters were back on the hunt for new meal tickets. Why no one called the cops on a couple kids hanging around a bar at all hours, Alex had no idea. Then again, it was a different world in those days. Alex could still see the cigarette smoke ribboning through the sea of old timers with huge schnozzes, gin blossoms, livers on last legs, ballooned, swollen organs so jam-packed with waste and poison they hung over belts like colostomy bags, fierce testaments to self-destruction and the pursuit of darker causes. No one smoked inside the bar these days, the air clear as mountain skies. Frat packers in maroon and gold jackets clasped the backs of factory boys still dressed in their issued grays. If anyone was dealing coke, it was on the sly. Two different ball games played on flat-screen televisions mounted above the bar, tables stacked with baskets of deep-fried pickles and jalapeño popper combos. The Fireside, once a bastion of degeneracy, had turned into a goddamn sports bar.

"Why you up here again?" Linda had always been a big girl but she'd put on considerable weight since Alex had last seen her cousin, face ruddier, puffy bags under her eyes. She had that crocked, inbred look everyone around here gets if they're pissed enough.

"Work," Alex said.

Linda didn't know enough about what Alex did or didn't do to risk embarrassment by asking what exactly.

"What's your name?" one of the boys, the not-cute one, asked.

"What's yours?"

"Mikey."

His buddy glowered at her. "I'm Nick," he offered without provocation. "Nick Graves," the last name punctuated like an accusation.

"Good for you, Nick Graves."

Linda licked the rim of her shot glass. "How's that detective boyfriend of yours? Still married?"

Alex ignored the dig, turning around to see Tommy standing behind her with a pitcher and five more shots. He must've cast Linda a look because her cousin clamped up after that.

Nick Graves continued to leer. Maybe Alex misunderstood and he was trying to hit on her and doing a lousy job of it. Women like Alex didn't often come into the Fireside. Sure, some of the girls from Uniondale were as pretty, but those university girls kept to their own kind. Shooting pool was one thing but they weren't going home with boys like Nick Graves.

"When you headed back?" Linda asked.

"You're Alex Salerno!" Mikey said, beaming, like he'd found a clue in the picture book. "I know you!"

Nick Graves backhanded his chest. "Shut up, Mikey."

"Remember? The girl. The one that got away? Shit. That was like, what, ten years ago?" He poured another beer, suds slopping over, slipping down the side. "Always wondered what happened to you. Such a fucked-up case. They caught the perverts who did it, right? We went to different schools but how could anyone forget that? How you been?" Mikey looked to Linda. "I didn't know you guys knew each other."

"Cousins," Linda muttered.

Alex pounded the shot, followed with a chaser, and bolted for the door. From the corner of her eye, she saw Mikey try to stand and Tommy plant a big bear claw, keeping him in place.

In the cold parking lot, the whiskey and beer hit at once, eyes momentarily unable to focus, ears ringing, ground shaky beneath her feet. She scoured her surroundings trying to remember where she'd parked her car.

"Don't mind Mikey," Linda said, coming up behind. "He's a dumb shit."

Alex waited for the rest of an apology she knew wasn't coming. Linda had never been good with words. The harder her cousin tried to think, the more confused she looked. Then again, she had a point. What *was* Alex doing up here? Still seeking cues from the Universe?

"You all right?" Linda asked.

"I'm fine." Alex spotted her Civic. "I should get going."

"You just got here," Linda said, feigning enthusiasm. Alex knew her cousin would be glad to see her leave, but blood dictated she at least make the effort. "Come on, I haven't seen you in, like, what? Four years? You haven't made a dent in your beer. Is it Nick and Mikey? I'll have Tommy tell them to take a hike."

"I couldn't care less about those two. Been a weird day, weird night. Weird life." Times like this Alex could use a friend but it had been a while since she could call Linda that. It had been a while since she could call anyone that. "Don't pretend you're happy to see me."

Her cousin huffed, wriggling her fat fists into tight jean pockets. "Why did you come back? You hate this place. No way you're relocating for a job."

"A reporter called me. For an interview."

Took a second to click. "Because of what happened? Back with Parsons?"

Linda wrenched free a bright pink hand, holding it out for a smoke.

Alex passed along a lit Parliament. "Anyone got anything?"

"Up? Down?"

"Weed? Something to take the edge off?" At this point, Alex would take anywhere but sober.

Linda nodded back at the bar. "Come inside. Let me ask around. You know the Fireside. Someone's always holding something."

Alex considered the likelihood that any of those frat boys had anything worthwhile, and more importantly what she'd have to do to get it, and decided it wasn't worth the effort. "I think I'm going to hit the road. Got a long drive."

Linda tried to act disappointed. Unable to hide the relief, she reached in for an awkward embrace. "Don't stay away so long next time, okay?"

Over Linda's shoulder, a man exited the bar. He brushed up the sidewalk, close enough for Alex to catch a glimpse of his face, before angling through the parking lot to his truck, where he stopped, turned around, and stared right at her. A chill cut to the marrow. It was the same man who'd come to her motel room earlier, the one claiming to have turned off headlights that hadn't been on.

Alex disentangled from Linda, motioning at the man, who'd already climbed into his cab. "You recognize that guy?"

Her cousin squinted. "I think that's Dan Brudzienski. Benny Brudzienski's younger brother. Remember him? Retard that killed Kira Shanks? Or it might be the other one, the middle brother, Wren."

Alex had taken a step toward the truck when the Fireside doors burst open, sounds of celebration erupting. At the mouth of the bar, Tommy dragged Nick Graves by the scruff of his neck, his buddy, Mikey, running alongside, trying to break them up, onlookers egging them on. With all the effort of taking out the trash, Tommy flung the smaller man into the dirt lining the walkway. Nick scrambled to his feet, lowering his head and charging to pile drive, but Tommy swatted him back down.

Tommy dropped to a knee and pressed Nick's head into the pebbled sidewalk, his beet-red face turning redder. Nick squirmed, sputtered, arms flailing wild. Sweet, good-natured Tommy who'd sooner trap a mouse under a salad bowl before breaking its neck. Alex had never seen him riled like that.

Mikey pulled at Tommy's arm, shouting for him to stop,

Nick couldn't breathe, but Tommy was too big to budge. Mikey kept grappling, tugging Tommy's shirt, which earned an elbow to the gut. Mikey doubled up, gasping for air.

By now Linda had hoofed over, demanding Tommy let Nick go. Tommy wasn't letting go. The cheering crowd grew in size. The Fireside wasn't a sports bar anymore. This was a return to the old days when nights ended with black eyes and broken bones, a gash in somebody's head, a pair of drunk and disorderlies stuffed in the back seat of a cruiser.

In the darkness behind them, a truck sped out of the gravel lot, kicking up dust in the moonlight.

When Alex turned around the barman had managed to break up the fight. Linda had hold of Tommy, whose head drooped in shame, a misbehaving mutt caught peeing on the rug. Nick and Mikey limped off in defeat in the other direction. Nick glanced back, blood smeared across his battered face.

"What were you thinking?" Linda said to Tommy. "What would your PO say?"

Parole officer?

Tommy didn't offer an excuse, no matter how much Linda badgered him. Not that you needed a reason to get into it if you were that loaded. Alex had seen fights break out at the Rat and Raven, the bar she tended in the city, over nothing more than dirty looks and misunderstood song lyrics.

Alex snuck off. There wasn't anything worse than getting stuck in the middle of a couple fighting, especially when alcohol was involved.

Even after Alex got in her car and shut the door, she could still hear her cousin berating Tommy in the parking lot. What happened to make him flip out like that?

CHAPTER FOUR

Alex got back to the Royal Motel a little after two. The lobby door was locked but a fuzzy gray light flickered around the corner. She tapped her key card off the glass door until the night clerk popped his head out. Acting irritated, he didn't look like he'd been sleeping. He cracked open the door.

"I need to use the computer."

He turned over his shoulder, toward the desktop sitting atop the small table. "You can't. I mean, it's for daytime use only."

"Why?"

The clerk hadn't thought that one through. When he couldn't come up with an adequate response, he let Alex in.

Settling in the folding metal chair, she wiggled the mouse until the screen fizzled to life.

"Hey," Alex called out. "I need a password or something?" The clerk didn't respond. She muttered "asshole" under her breath as she opened a search engine, typing with one finger. Was that one of Benny Brudzienski's brothers at the Fireside tonight? Linda thought so. Why would Dan or Wren Brudzienski be following her? She didn't know much about the two brothers or the rest of the Brudzienski clan, other than what you learn about any family in a small town.

The Brudzienskis owned a large farm on the outskirts, which they inherited after their folks died. The family liked their privacy. Even when Mom and Dad were alive, you rarely saw the whole brood together, probably due to Benny's condition. Considering the circumstances surrounding Alex's return, what were the odds he'd picked her motel room at random? Less. None. Maybe she just had the misfortune of coincidence in a small town where people liked to drink. No, the timing was strange. Then again, what *hadn't* been strange since she'd been back? It was two in the morning and she was sitting at the Royal Motel, a roadside dump she'd passed countless times and never imagined herself in, no matter how dark days with Denise got—and they got pretty dark—rooting around newswire archives, looking for what exactly? A draining day had morphed into an exhausting night, dragging Alex past the point of delirium. Something danced beyond the fringes of her mind's eye, taunting, gnawing, clawing the back of her brain like mice scurrying beneath floorboards, which rounded out the recipe for another sleepless night.

There were countless webpages and newspaper sites dedicated to the Kira Shanks disappearance. Most of the details Alex already knew, small bits lodged into her subconscious, so even the parts that appeared foreign created a fleeting sense of déjà vu.

What had Riley meant about the media not reporting the whole story? Why was Noah Lee so amped to write this piece in the first place? Why did she care about any of this? What did she hope to gain rubbing dirt in old wounds? When Noah launched his pitch, preaching about collusion and injustice, she thought he was just another white college kid calling for equality from his privileged perch. Alex knew Riley better than that. A cop through and through, Riley would never advocate for the release of a killer. After his chilly reception at the Double Y, maybe she'd gotten it wrong. Like Tommy's hothead act back at the Fireside—how well did she know the guy? People change. Maybe Riley had waylaid concerns, lied to make her feel safe. He insisted Parsons acted alone. Benny and Kira had nothing to do with her. No killers roamed free. Or maybe Alex only heard what she wanted to hear.

Truth was, by the time Kira went missing, Alex had already

checked out of Reine, cutting most ties, the big one being Riley, but Linda too, and anyone else who reminded her of the past. Which was everyone. Alex followed the case. With one eye on the door. Denise was still alive then, but that wasn't reason enough to stick around. Ever since Alex was a kid, their roles had been reversed. And the child had grown sick to death of taking care of the parent. Kira Shanks didn't force Alex to leave. She just made the decision easier.

Goddamn Noah. Posing his bullshit questions, suggesting a lunatic was still on the loose, asking Alex if she thought her abduction contributed to a curse on this town, the idea laughable. She knew what he really wanted: someone to do his homework for him. Entitled jerks like that think everyone is for sale. Alex didn't get to go to college. Why should she help someone else earn his degree? For a few hundred bucks? Not that she couldn't use it.

But there was no denying Noah Lee had rented space in her head, because here she was doing his homework for him.

No one knew what happened to Kira Shanks, except that she was certainly dead. The only question was whether Benny Brudzienski raped her first before he buried her somewhere in the deep, dark wood. Whatever Benny had done to her body, wherever he'd hidden it, her end was not a pleasant one. Alex didn't know Kira. Not personally. She may've been aware of her presence, the way everyone knows everyone in a small town. But they weren't friends. Answering these questions now wouldn't make any difference.

If this sudden preoccupation with the missing girl was an effort to establish community with the suffering, Alex could've picked any of the half dozen girls whose bodies were dug up beneath Parsons' lake house property, all of which showed signs of sexual abuse, over long periods of time, enduring hells unknown. Their bones had been found, damage measured, quantifiable, evidence tangible. *That* was supposed to be where she ended up. In the cold, cold ground. Alex had something in common with those girls. She shared nothing in common with the perky cheerleader who'd gotten too close to the village idiot.

Alex skimmed the headlines, brushing up on details, digging deeper, curiosity and coincidence too formidable an opponent to ignore. She avoided the conspiratorial, shock-jock blogger bullshit. Every mainstream source offered the same version.

Kira Shanks hadn't been seen for several days when her parents reported her missing. Now not seen in seven years, she'd been declared dead, foul play strongly suspected if unproven. Papers mentioned Kira's friends as having been questioned but they'd all been cleared. The names of these friends didn't sound familiar. One name, however, Sharn DiDonna, stood out, but that was only because it was so odd. Alex was older, not part of that scene. Blood found at the motel, along with semen and additional samples, put Benny Brudzienski in the room with her, guilt preserved on bedsheets. No other serious suspects were even hinted at. One day a hard rain would unearth Kira's earthly remains in the forest behind the motel. Depending on how deep Benny dug that hole. Clear-cut as it gets. The only thing better would've been a confession.

Which they'd never get.

A week or so after Kira went missing, authorities had found Benny Brudzienski in a ditch, barely breathing, run off the road by a lynch mob, thrashed to a pulp. The timeline didn't exactly match up. The police speculated Benny had most likely been hiding out in the vast woods behind the Idlewild Motel.

The papers quoted Wren Brudzienski as saying Benny never returned home, and that he and his brother, Dan, had been looking for him for days. If a man knows enough to hide, he knows what he did was wrong. Good enough for Alex. Already brain damaged, Benny was rendered nearly comatose by the assault. The men who'd run Benny Brudzienski down had never been identified. No one had looked that hard to find them. And since Benny wasn't talking, the case was effectively closed. Benny had been sent away. Problem solved. So why the renewed interest?

In the back room, the volume cranked louder. The clerk cleared his throat, coughing. Alex got the hint and headed up to her second-floor room.

Turning on her TV for the background noise, Alex stripped out of her jeans and slipped beneath the top blanket. As usual she left the lights on. Bathroom fan, too. Not that it helped. The terror came back; it always did.

Alex's nightmares weren't the outright horrific kind with lakes of fire, horns, and snarling teeth. The devils that haunted her sleep were suggested rather than fully realized, subtle, implied, the haunting gray-scape of unease preferred to straight-up hellfire. Faces without eyes, words without sound, the shiver beneath flesh that can never be warmed. She could still see the dirty light, the way it tried to negotiate basement cracks. But the threshold was impenetrable, blocks of kaleidoscopic ice blunted through the bottom of a Coke bottle, reality distorted beyond horizons. The memory still tormented. Three days locked underground in a tomb isn't easily shaken.

No one had thrown her into the car; she'd gotten in of her own accord. He hadn't been that good looking or charming. Parsons' greatest trick? He'd been willing to pay attention, listen to her, pretend what she said mattered. How pathetic was that? And so like a foolish child chasing the promise of magic beans, she'd allowed herself to be taken. And that's how it should've ended. No one would miss her. Oh, Denise would fall apart, because that's what Denise did. Her mother's entire life had been a desperate search to justify the misery. Alex should've been laid to rest in the hogweed and ox-eye with the others.

Except Riley got to her first.

Bright, cold sunlight raked through the blinds breaking the morning in two. Even when the knocking on the door stopped, the thumping inside her skull hammered on. She didn't remember drinking that much, or even falling asleep. Her mouth parched, body sapped of hydration, no different than a three-day bender. Except this wasn't a hangover, this was something else, a judgment cast. This was a reckoning.

Sitting on the edge of the bed, she slid on her jeans as the knocking started back up.

"Hold on! I'm coming!"

Had she slept past checkout? What was their deal? How bad did maids need to clean this hellhole?

She jerked open the door, and blinding, bitter sunshine slapped her in the face, casting an unflattering light.

Riley looked like he'd been up for hours, black hair combed, parted, short beard neatly trimmed without a speck of grey. Alex could feel the rat's nest atop her head, the sleep in the corners of her eyes, that filmy, white paste gumming her mouth, and she resented him for the power play.

"If you wanted to grab coffee, you could've warned me first." Alex shielded her eyes and covered her body with the door as if she were naked, even though she was fully clothed. "What time is it?"

"Have you been harassing the Brudzienskis?"

"Who told you that?"

"Never mind. Have you been following Benny's brothers?"

"Following *them*?" Alex tried an exaggerated laugh, but morning breath aborted efforts midway. The result came out as an awkward snort. Disheveled and unprepared, she felt like a little girl.

Anyone else she would've told to get lost. For Riley, she let go the door. He caught it with his foot before it closed. She needed a cigarette. She swiped her pack off the table, shaking the hair out of her eyes, leaning against the dresser, trying to appear relaxed, feeling her whole body go rigid. Riley took a step in the room, then backed out, like testing the waters in a cold pool. Good. Let him be the one to feel uncomfortable for a change.

"Are you going to answer me?"

"Since when did you become such a Benny Brudzienski supporter?"

"You don't know what you are talking about."

"I might not be living here, but I know what he did to that girl. Everyone does. It was in all the papers, all over the news, across the internet." She struck a match. "Maybe you should spend more time at home with your wife and daughter and less time helping killers." That was the best she had in the bag.

"I'd appreciate it if you'd leave the Brudzienskis alone. They've been through enough."

"*They've* been through enough. What happened to you? I thought cops cared about the victims? Why are you defending a murderer, Sean?" She never used his first name. That had been the first thing he said to her in the back of his patrol car twelve years ago. "My friends call me Riley." So she'd call him Sean. "Well, what is it? Can't have it both ways."

"Come on," he said. "Let's go."

"Where are we going?"

Riley looked off to the side, the bored detective tired of explaining rudimentary basics to someone below his pay grade. He wound a hand to speed things along, a gesture that grated on Alex's nerves endlessly.

She snatched her hoodie and bomber off the bed. Not like she had anywhere else she needed to be.

CHAPTER FIVE

The changes to her hometown were subtle and profound, major and no big deal. Unless you'd grown up here, come and gone, been someone else before, you wouldn't notice an improvement. Redone Shop Rites, a Walmart, new strip mall, double-decker fast food restaurants. Fancy ones that combined all the cheap eats into one convenient pit stop, a Taco Bell *and* a KFC, a Pizza Hut. In a town like Reine, these alterations mimicked progress, and were a distraction from limited job opportunities and stagnant pay rates. A Krispy Kreme goes up around here, and the line extends up the block to be first in line. Alex recognized the push toward gentrification: bike lanes added, better bus routes, duplexes all painted that same shade of green. But Reine was still a poor man's town, the same one she'd escaped. They could erect all the skyscrapers on the horizon they wanted, even change the name; Reine would always be Reine.

Sugar maples and red oaks shed their skin, burnt orange and deep, dark maroon falling from crooked bones. They hit the interstate. Dented metal guardrails and rocky barriers zipped past. Staring out the window, Alex couldn't believe she still let herself get swept up in the romance of it all. There are no star-crossed lovers, no casualties of circumstance. This wasn't the movies. They were just two people in a moving car; and she hated herself for ever wishing they could be something more.

The currency of sympathy in the face of tragedy is a strange thing. There were a million girls like Alex when she was growing up. Lousy mother, absent father, no money, no one cares. Alex's day-to-day existence went by unnoticed. No one saw a damn thing. Not the teachers in school. Not the priests at church. Not the pillars of the community, the same respected ones who would later cheer her resurrection as proof that miracles happen. Growing up, Alex didn't enjoy many happy days. Few friends, she led a solitary life. When she grew into her looks, the boys came around, but not the kind of boys you wanted coming around, not the boys who stayed. There were plenty willing to use you for a night. They'd say what they had to, be as sweet as they needed to be until they got what they wanted, then they'd throw you away like yesterday's trash. No one saw the real her. No one really tried. Until Riley, and that only happened because of Parsons.

As bad as those three days and nights locked in the basement were, as frightened as she was, Alex could list fifty memories that had hurt as bad, had inflicted as much damage. But no one cared about those. They weren't as sensational. No one notices a life lost in the cracks. People can see physical injury. Busted arms and black eyes are tangible, quantitative. Emotional wounds are abstract, subjective. Broken bones heal. The other kind of pain lasts a lifetime. Her tenth birthday, having to drag Denise out of the Tic-Tac Club because there was nothing in the fridge but a wilted head of lettuce, some mustard, and plastic beer rings. The week she spent alone when she was thirteen, after Denise and some guy (Ron?) headed to Atlantic City for the weekend, leaving twenty bucks for food, money she spent on pizza and soda the first night, surviving on rice and Ramen for the next six, wondering if her mother was coming home, and not knowing if she was better off one way or the other. Parsons? Parsons was a bruise among scars.

She'd been scared when she woke up on that cold concrete. She could taste the chemicals burning her throat. She was hungry and alone, and she knew horrid things awaited her. But Parsons never came for her, never touched her. Of course she had no way of knowing he'd already been picked up, having traded her whereabouts for leniency. In the end, time had undermined the fear she felt. With so much trauma packed into such a short span, it made the denial easier. After a while, she'd checked out, gone somewhere else, somewhere far away. There's only so much torment the mind can withstand. Maybe that was where she'd honed the ability to separate space and time. Alex could divorce herself from the situation, pretend it was just another episode of *Law and Order: SVU*.

And, when it was over, there had been an unexpected benefit, a perk. To the town of Reine, Alex Salerno became a celebrity. Her life changed when she rose from that bunker. Alex Salerno suddenly mattered. To the town, its people, an entire region. She personified hope.

Until Kira Shanks.

If Alex had been hope, Kira Shanks came to represent something else. The mystery surrounding her disappearance, the horror that had latched onto Alex by proxy. After Kira Shanks, when people saw Alex, they saw a dead girl walking. Triumphant tales rewritten, no one emerged victorious; there could be no happy endings. There were only the ghost stories told by parents to frighten children about boogeymen who waited in the dark to snatch unwitting prey from the safety of their beds. So behave, eat your vegetables, listen to Mom and Dad, go to sleep on time, or what happened to those girls will happen to you, too.

Riley said something that snapped her out of her head. As was often the case, Alex had lost a huge chunk of time, unaware of how long they'd been driving. Could've been ten minutes. Could've been two hours.

They now sat parked in front of a large, brick building. Towering, institutional, white. A hospital.

"What are we doing here?"

"You're so interested in Benny Brudzienski," Riley said, pointing up at the high windows. "Thought you'd like to say hi."

Outside the car, she patted down her bomber for cigarettes, scanning the grounds. No tall fences. No razor wire. Not even an overweight, middle-aged security guard holding a peashooter. Just doors people could walk out of any damn time they pleased.

"This is where they keep a man guilty of murder?" Alex cupped her hands and struck a match. "Must be nice."

While Alex scrambled between bartending jobs in the city, fighting off drunken come-ons, cobbling together a livable wage by walking dogs, selling pills, any other part-time gig she could land to make rent on an undersized, overpriced room in someone else's house, a monster like Benny Brudzienski got to spend his days in a furnished pad, courtesy of the state. Three squares a day, a warm bed, free housekeeping, probably cable TV, too.

"Put that out," Riley said, pointing at the sign that forbade smoking within twenty feet of the hospital entrance.

Alex took a last, long drag and flicked the butt into the lot, even though there was an ashcan by the automatic doors.

Riley handled sign-in, exchanging IDs for visitors' badges. Alex meandered around the lobby, which wasn't much different than any other waiting room. Like they were visiting Grandma at the Sunnyside Retirement Home. Old *People* magazines and *National Geographics* with original addresses torn off the front spread across bleached-wood tables in between cushy chairs and fake ficus trees. Department store artwork hung on walls, askew. Maybe she should feel lucky. At least the man who kidnapped her had been put in a regular prison where inmates meted out their own brand of justice. Alex heard Kira's parents left Reine after the tragedy. It couldn't have been easy knowing the man responsible for their daughter's death had copped to an insanity plea, enjoying all the spoils of hospitalization over incarceration.

Riley called Alex's name—she'd drifted to the other side of the room, debating whether to re-center a photograph of a sunflower. He was directing her to the elevator, doing the hand-winding thing again, which made her want to beat her fists against the wall.

He stood at attention, holding the doors open. Stepping inside, Alex could feel his anger directed at her. What had she done? She had been the one wronged, not him. He'd abandoned her, not the other way around. Now he was more concerned with Benny Brudzienski catching a bad break?

They waited to be buzzed in at the set of locked taupe-colored doors. All the walls were painted similar unthreatening hues. Light pinks. Soft tans. Rounded corners instead of sharp edges. Nothing too jarring to incite the lunatics.

"You're taking me to see a bunch of psycho killers? Sure know how to treat a girl."

"This isn't a date." Riley punched the buzzer and pulled the door.

Another checkpoint waited for them. An orderly in white sat secured behind a cage. He sifted through a large ring attached to his belt and unlocked the gate. There was a loud metallic clang as the heavy steel door caught rollers, cranked open and disengaged. Even the Royal Motel had key cards. The jangling metal harkened back to the days of shock therapy and lobotomies, *One Flew over the Cuckoo's Nest*, an ice pick jammed between the eyes to quell hysteria.

On their way in, a nurse was walking out. Her night shift over, she handed off a chart to a young, black man.

In the large, communal area, sedated patients slumped over tables bolted to the floor. Some fumbled with their hands, rolling one over the other in a never-ending game of baker's man. Others pulled at tufts of hair like they were plucking lint from the carpet, fleas from a dog, monkeys delousing. You could smell the crazy soon as you stepped on the ward.

"Is everyone like this?"

"It's a psychiatric hospital." Riley pointed across the room, where a large, bald man slouched in a chair propped by the window. A long scar rivered the back of his skull, punctuated by a sizeable divot in the center. He watched big black birds perched on power lines. As Alex drew nearer, she saw he wasn't watching birds. Head lolled to the side, he stared beyond them, over the pasture, into the distance, at nothing.

Alex turned back to Riley. "That's him?"

"Say hi to Benny Brudzienski."

She took a tentative step closer, like you might a wounded wild animal, unsure whether stillness was a ruse, a ploy before the beast pounced. But Benny Brudzienski wasn't going anywhere. He looked different than the man she recalled shuffling around town. Older, of course, but moreover his body was losing its containment, years of inactivity collapsing form into a gelatinous blob. Alex waved a hand in front of his face. No response, not even a blink. His face remained a blank slate, eyes glassy, lifeless. The light was on but nobody was home.

Sticking her hands in back pockets, Alex turned to Riley. "They have him pumped full of meds. I knew a girl like that down in the city. Schizo. Overdosed on Thorazine. She looked like this."

"They found him like that," Riley said. "After that mob came after him with pitchforks."

"What's wrong with him?"

"Catatonic."

"From the beating?"

"Possibly. Even the doctors aren't sure. They say sometimes a person can experience something so disturbing, it pulls them under, into an abyss, where they are lost in the fog forever."

"Disturbing? Like maybe witnessing rape and murder, firsthand?"

"Maybe," Riley said, not baited by the sarcasm.

"Or maybe he's a big, fat faker?" Alex peered over her shoulder to see if her jab registered but Benny Brudzienski did not stir.

"Benny's mental state was already compromised."

"Compromised?"

"Stunted, slowed. Mentally deficient. Whatever you'd like to call it. He wasn't playing with a full deck. Had a fifty-six IQ. Doesn't matter how you classify the condition. The attack didn't do him any favors. He hasn't said a word since whoever it was took a run at him."

"Didn't they find Kira Shanks' blood all over his clothes?"

"They found her blood, yes."

"And his?"

"Yes. They found his blood, too."

There was no point in Riley denying what Alex read in the papers; it was public record. But she knew Riley wasn't giving her anything else.

"So, what?" Alex said. "He was all messed up in the head before Kira Shanks goes missing, now he can't talk? Great. They wheel him up to the window, let him look at the pretty scenery. That it? Gets to sit in this place instead of a prison? Access to free food, water, shelter. Doesn't seem like such a bad deal, if you ask me."

"No one asked your opinion."

"Why did you bring me here?"

"You come back to town, out of the blue, start harassing the Brudzienskis—"

"I was not harassing anyone—"

"Asking questions about Kira Shanks, Benny. Me."

"Maybe I missed my hometown?"

"After not responding to my phone calls or emails?"

"Is that what's bothering you? Feeling jilted? What happened to the loyal, doting husband?"

"I wrote you as a friend. I care about you."

"Sure you do."

"Whatever you've got going on in there." Riley gestured at her body, head to toe and then back again, like the entire vessel were infected. "It is going to kill you. Feeling like everyone abandoned you."

"Not everyone, Sean."

"I wasn't the one who left."

Alex stepped to him. He didn't back down. Strange, to have this moment play out here, in the state looney bin, in front of a fat psycho killer melting in his chair, but she didn't care; she'd waited too long.

She stared into his eyes. "Tell me it didn't mean anything."

"It didn't mean anything."

For the first time, there was a crack in the hard veneer, and she felt him soften, his resistance begin to melt. She wanted him to kiss her. Alex moved closer. "Your wife feel the same way?"

"I confessed everything to Meg a long time ago. And she's forgiven me."

She reached for him. He caught her hands.

"I'm not seventeen anymore."

Riley let go, backing away, watching her like she were unpredictable, untrustworthy, adversarial. Unbelievable. Her. Inside this killing field.

"Come on," he said, "I'll take you back to your hotel."

"I'm not going anywhere with you."

"Do you know where we are? How far we drove while you daydreamed?"

"I don't care."

"You can't stay here. This isn't a place you visit. Understand? You're only here because you're with me, and now I'm leaving. Let's go."

Alex jammed her hands in her bomber jacket.

"Real mature, Alex."

She jutted her chin forward, flashing a phony grin.

"You still can't stay here."

"Fine. I'll walk."

When Alex passed Benny Brudzienski, she leaned down low, so close to his ear she could smell the sick on him. "You might have everyone else fooled," she whispered, "but I know what you are. And you're going to burn in a hell."

Riley reached over to hurry her along.

"Don't fucking touch me!"

The orderly twitched at his desk. Riley showed his hands.

Alex smoothed her bomber, regained her cool, then patted Benny Brudzienski on his meaty shoulder. "Enjoy the view, sicko."

That's when she made her mistake.

She looked into his eyes.

BENNY BRUDZIENSKI

I will always remember her this way. Beneath the big oak trees. She looks down on me and smiles. No one ever smiles at me. Not like that, not anymore. When I was little they used to. But then I turned into the thing I am now, a thing that people pity or fear. She is new in town and does not know better. I have never seen anything so beautiful in my life. I want to protect her, wrap her up in a box, keep her safe forever.

I am not stupid. Dad thinks I am stupid. My brothers, Dan and Wren. Teachers, classmates, cops, the bakery shop owner, Mr. Miano. They do not use that word. Not around me, at least. They say I am slow, challenged. They say I am special. But they think I am stupid. I can see it in their pitiful expressions when I slog past, in the way they pat my head and say, "Good boy, Benny." Like I am a big, dumb dog. But when I close my eyes I dream too. I cannot write the things I feel or say the words I think. Ideas come out as grumbles, grunts, groans. The harder I try, the more frustrated I get. I do not try to speak much anymore. My dreams stay trapped deep down inside me. But I feel.

And I watch. I listen. No one notices me so I am invisible. I can be everywhere, at all times. I can see and hear everything.

Her name is Kira. She moved here with her family from Buffalo. She is my brother Dan's age, in his grade. I hear my brother talking about her to his friends every night on the telephone, and I can hear the excitement in his voice when he mentions her name. He says he is in love. I have never heard my brother talk about other girls like this. He talks about girls all the time because he plays football and is very popular. Wren is a couple years older and plays football too. But for the college team. Both my brothers are many years younger than me, each with strong shoulders and chins like our father, arms roped with muscle and sturdy hands. They are the sons Dad and Mom wanted. I think Dad and Mom were scared to have another child after the way I came out, which is why they waited so long to try again. I do not blame them for the way they look at me. I once heard Dad tell some men that they left me in the oven too long. He meant the place they keep babies at the hospital, the incubator. Said the heat got turned to high. The other men laughed but I do not think he was trying to be funny. He looked sad when he said it. There is something broken inside me. I am different. But I have good in me, too. For instance, I am strong. Really strong. Before Dad gave up on me being a regular boy, he used to call Mom out to watch me lift firewood in the yard. This was when I was very young, before my brothers were born.

Dad would say, "Mom, watch Ben! Watch how much he can lift!" Then he would turn to me, say, "Go ahead, son. Show your mother how much firewood you can lift."

I would bend down and scoop up seven, eight hunks of wood, logs thick as tree trunks, and Dad would say, "Hold on," as he piled on four, five, six more. My legs did not buckle under the weight. Mom would stand on the porch and clap. My hands would get bloody and raw from the snow and cold, but I would cart the whole haul, heave it on the pile by the woodshed, and go back for more. I did not care about the pain. I would have done it all day to see them proud of me. I liked being good at something. Dad used to say I could crush the life out of a cow if I wanted to. I do not know if that is true. I never tried. I never wanted to.

Kira is the belle of the ball. I am not sure what that means. I hear Mom say that at the dinner table one night when Dan is talking about her. Dad and Wren laugh. I do too. Mom pets my head. I like the way that sounds. Belle of the ball.

She sits on the wood fence, Kira does, and all the boys gather around. I am sweeping the parking lot with the big push broom, picking trash from the weeds, raking the leaves that have started to change color. I need to get the field ready for tonight's game. I like when the seasons turn over, even though it means some things have to die. It is an important job, Mr. Supinski says. Mr. Supinski is my boss. I have a lot of jobs.

I work for the school and the town, prepping the fields, cleaning up the garbage people dump in the woods outside the stadium. My other job is at the Idlewild Motel. I am a handyman. That is what Mrs. Shuman calls me. She owns the motel. I change light bulbs, empty the trash receptacles, and haul away old mattresses. I also work at the rail yard, clearing out produce freighters. Bums like to sleep in them sometimes. When I find one, I clear them out too. People like Mr. Supinski and Mrs. Shuman hire me because they do not have to pay me. I can do simple, repetitive tasks if someone shows me how to do them first. I am good at imitating. They give me treats and sweets, or reward me with apples when it is harvest season, like I am a horse, then they settle up with Dad later. I do not mind. I like knowing I am contributing to the family.

The boys huddle around Kira to show off their skills, preening like fancy birds. The girls want to be near her too, because if they stand close enough maybe the boys will love them too. Being popular in school is important. I once went to a regular school but not for long. After the first few grades they switched me over to a special school. After a couple years, they stopped sending me there too. I liked going even if I could not learn as fast as they wanted me to. I liked being around other kids like me. I overheard Dad say it was a waste of money. "Like putting perfume on a pig," he said. I know he loves me. No one would want a son like me. He meant that the special school was expensive and they could never fix me. So why bother?

Kira is already very popular, even though she just got here. She is new, a present just unwrapped. None of the shine has dulled on her. I have been out of the box for a long time. My parts are janky, and I am not nice to look at. I can see the difference between me and other people. When Mom catches me staring at myself in the mirror, she thinks I am accepting simple truths, like I too am a person. I know I am a person. I am not stupid. I recognize I have a heart and brain. Blood runs through my veins. I learned about the parts of a body that keep a person alive. They taught us that at the special school, too. When I stare at myself in the mirror, I am noting the way my forehead is much bigger than other people's. I want to believe this is because I am actually smart with a big brain and not because I was left in the oven too long. But this is not true. My eyes, so close together, appear crossed, and my forehead is uneven and lumpy. My nose is plump and piggish, and my chin is soft. When I try to speak, my mouth opens and I make sounds. But the words do not make sense. My dead eyes and rolling jaw makes me look like a cow chewing cud in the field. I do not get angry. There is no point getting angry over things I cannot change. I still see beauty too. Even if my face is ugly and my tongue cannot form the words I hear inside my head, there are good things in my heart.

The old oak trees stand tall on the hill behind the field. The autumn winds blow from the west, shedding husks. Leaves swirl in the current, lifted high in the storm. They scatter across the park and pavement. Even though it makes more work for me, I do not mind. The cold air rushing against my skin feels good. Kira waves at me. No one else notices because no one else notices me.

The cold sun shines bright, and the air hurts to breathe in. Winter will be here soon. I do not move. I let the swooping streams carry me away. I close my eyes and leave my body, fly away like a big bird in the sky, soaring above the clouds.

Mr. Supinski hollers at me to stop staring at the girls and get back to work. The girls on the hill laugh. But not Kira. When I do not move fast enough, Mr. Supinski comes up behind me and tugs my earlobe, says it again louder, right in my face, as if my ears do not work. My ears work fine. He flicks one with his dirty, stubby finger. I can smell the hot booze on his breath. I know why he goes back to the storage shed so many times during the day. The girls laugh louder. But not Kira. She looks sad, so I wave back and let her know I am okay.

Standing on the hill behind the football field, her yellow hair shining like straw in the autumn sun, she smiles at me. I do not ever want to forget this day. I want to live it over and over and over again.

CHAPTER SIX

When they got out to the hospital parking lot, Alex, true to her word, refused to get in the car with Riley, no matter what he said, until he finally grew exasperated of pleading with her to just get in the goddamn car and threw up his hands in frustration, and, eventual surrender. No one could make Alex Salerno do anything once she'd made up her mind.

Of course now Alex was stranded. She'd learned what town they were in, Galloway, sixty miles outside of Reine, at least a hundred-dollar cab ride, money she did not have. That's if she could even get a cab to come out here, which was doubtful. Riley had tried to give her the cash for a taxi, but Alex's glaring, silent response prompted him to put the bills back in his wallet and get in his car without another word.

Alex stopped an arriving nurse, asking if there was a bus station nearby. There was not. There was only one person left to call.

She didn't have Tommy's cell, and after last night, she wasn't calling her cousin to get it. Alex had to hunt him down at the plant, a process that involved three transfers, two supervisors, and a ten-minute hold. When she got Tommy on the phone, he said he was happy to pick her up but that his shift ended at three, over an hour away, and he'd still have to navigate rush-hour traffic on the 87. Alex could be stuck up there till dark. What choice did she have?

Ashen gray skies stalked the countryside and skeletal trees

staked the mangled ridge, hayfields trampled, untended and un-ruly. Alex hadn't been paying attention on the way in, trapped in her head. She didn't recall seeing a single store, and she wasn't braving a search now, the ravaged landscape offering scant hope. At least she still had cigarettes.

Alex sat on the edge of the loading dock by the big brown dumpster, cracked pallets stacked haphazard beside her. She closed her eyes, feeling herself slip away. Her life was the exact opposite of everyone else's: awake while everyone slept, sleep-walking while the rest of the world lived.

By the time Tommy pulled up in his battered pickup, the sun had gone down and it was dark, cold; though Alex couldn't re-call exactly when that happened. She only knew at some point the world had turned black, and that when she regained con-sciousness, she was shivering. She hadn't moved from that spot on the docks, hiding in plain sight, had anyone bothered look-ing. All her cigarettes were gone.

"Thanks," Alex said climbing in his cab, which, like Tommy himself, reeked of grease and gaskets. She kicked aside the pa-per cups and empty Gatorade jugs, clearing enough space to plant her feet.

Tommy blasted the heat, returning his cracked, stained hands to the wheel.

"You have any cigarettes?"

He plucked the Marlboros Reds from the breast pocket of his gray coveralls. The towering menace of the looney bin loomed behind them like Arkham.

"What was that place?" Tommy's eyes remained locked on the dark, twisting road. No streetlamps, no moon, no stars. The hospital didn't invite a lot of visitors.

"State mental ward."

"What the hell you doing up there?"

Alex waited for the dashboard lighter. "Visiting Benny Bru-dzienski."

"Retard killed that girl? What for?"

"That's where they put him."

Tommy cast a sideways glance. "What happened to your car?"

"It's back at the motel." She didn't feel like explaining more than that, which was okay with Tommy, who'd never been much of a talker.

Alex saw she'd been right not to venture off hospital grounds. Nothing but scrub brush and untamed wilderness for miles.

Farmland flipped past. Tractors and front loaders abandoned in the middle of wilted crops. Occasionally, far out, a porch lantern, buried among the wreckage of the heartland, flickered.

"You should've seen this hospital," Alex said, placing her palm against the glass, feeling the cold on the other side. "I'm not saying the place is the Waldorf. But it is *not* a prison."

"What else they gonna do? Throw him in gen pop at Riker's? From what I hear, guy can't wipe his own ass after that crew got hold of him."

The way Tommy said "that crew" gave Alex pause. "You know who it was?"

"Who what was?" Tommy thought a second, catching her meaning. "Who ran Benny Brudzienski off the road and took a baseball bat to him?"

"Who said anything about a baseball bat?"

Tommy reached for his own cigarettes. "Why you so interested in Benny Brudzienski?" He pulled out a smoke with his teeth and punched the dashboard lighter. "This because of that cop ex-boyfriend of yours?"

"He was never my boyfriend." When Alex said it aloud, she almost believed it, which was what her therapist had encouraged all along. What really happened. Reality versus fantasy. A couple months before her eighteenth birthday, Alex argued she'd practically been an adult. "Practically," Dr. Amy said, "is not the same as 'is.'"

"Be careful," Tommy said. "You weren't around after Benny.

Things changed after that."

"I was living up here then."

"You might've been in town. But you weren't living here."

"Reine will always be Reine."

"I'm not talking about ugly apartments and shit weather. Something horrible happened at the motel."

"You sound like that reporter, Noah Lee, rambling about plagues and locusts."

This might've been the longest conversation Alex ever had with Tommy, who usually communicated in clipped, one-word sentences.

A pair of headlights flashed in the side-view, a blinding glare. "You didn't answer me," she said, watching the car, now behind them, mirroring their moves.

"About what?"

"You know who beat the shit out of Benny?"

The lighter popped out the dash. Tommy shook his head and inhaled the hot metal coils. "I know what everyone else in Reine knows."

"Which is?"

"Someone put Brudzienski up to it."

They'd entered the town proper, blue signs marking the interstate ahead. All the businesses closed, residents inside for the night, doors locked and dead bolted. The same headlights were still behind them. Alex tried to shake the ludicrous notion they were being followed. Tommy caught her staring out the window.

"You okay, Alex?"

"Fine. How do you know someone put Benny up to it?"

"You know Reine. Only way to keep a secret up here is if one of you is dead." He watched the road but sensed her wanting more. "I don't know who hunted down Benny but I know they were trying to kill him. Got a buddy works as an EMT. Said half Brudzienski's head was caved in."

Tommy hit freeway speed. The other car zipped by, zooming in the fast lane, blending with the rest of the blurring lights, and

Alex felt relieved, followed immediately by a sense of wonder, all these lives that had nothing to do with her or her little world.

"You see him?" Tommy said.

"Who?"

"Brudzienski."

"Yeah. Looked messed up. Then again, he was pretty messed up to begin with."

"He's worse now. My buddy said they scooped part of his brain off the road. Carried it to the ER in a Ziploc. Had to reconstruct his skull."

"But you don't know who attacked him?"

Tommy shook his head. "You hear things."

"Like what?"

"Like Kira Shanks was a slut. Fucked a bunch of different guys. Pissed people off."

"I thought she was little miss popular?"

"She was. I'm not telling you anything that isn't common knowledge. Girl got around. Everyone up here knows the story. Including your cop pal."

"Riley's trying to get Benny released, I think. Or clear his name." Alex stopped. She wasn't sure what Riley was trying to do. She'd gotten so caught up in their personal drama this afternoon she hadn't gotten around to asking about his interests in the case. "How come Linda never told me any this?"

"Why would she?"

Tommy was right. Alex and her cousin didn't talk much. There'd be no reason for Linda to ring down to NYC with periodic Kira Shanks updates.

"I wouldn't waste your time worrying about it."

"But you're certain it wasn't an accident?"

"Benny Brudzienski getting run over? No, wasn't no accident. And, no, I don't have a name. Like I said—"

"Rumors."

"Rumors."

* * *

Linda acted surprised to see Alex, but she didn't ask Tommy where he'd been or tear into him for being late, meaning he'd phoned ahead and told her she was coming. Linda asked to speak with her boyfriend, inside, alone. Tommy told Alex not to go anywhere. The front door slammed, leaving Alex out in the cold.

When Alex told Tommy her change of plans—that she'd be in Reine for a few more days—he said she was staying with them, no questions asked.

The apartment was too small to tolerate secrets, and what began as urgent murmuring soon escalated to unhinged screaming. Alex's willful ignorance couldn't blot out her cousin's shouts of "It's not *your* decision!" and "Well, *I* don't want her staying here!" The bulb in the box buzzed overhead, generations of dead bugs coating the bottom, a winged graveyard. That's what happens when you get too close to the flame.

There was a little patio table with two weathered wicker chairs, a ten-pin of empty beer bottles and jar of Folger's instant that was being used as an ashcan. Pairs of sneakers hung from telephone wires. Alex recalled the urban myth about shoes dangling from power lines, how it meant drugs were sold in that neighborhood, a story whose origins no doubt rooted in PTA potlucks and homogenous book clubs. Sheltered white people will believe anything.

Sick of waiting, Alex opened the door. Linda stopped squawking. Tommy plunked down on the couch and grabbed his can of Bud off the armrest, switching on the TV. In the brighter apartment light, Alex saw his knuckles weren't stained from the job; they were red from the fight last night at the Fireside, the blood too deep in the cracks to scrub clean.

"What's up?" Alex asked. "Not happy to see me?"

"Wasn't expecting company, is all." Linda attempted a grin. "Thought you'd be back in the city by now?"

"I changed my mind."

"About what?"

"A lot of things." Alex nodded at Tommy, whose meaty fist wrapped around the beer. "Offer to stay with you still stand?"

"Yup." Tommy stared straight ahead, watching the talking heads on the evening news.

"Well," Linda said, drawing out the word, letting her eyes wander over the cramped space of their apartment. "This place is pretty small—"

"Couch is fine."

"We got a spare room in the back," Tommy said, switching off the television and prying himself out of the cushions. "You'll have to clear junk off to make the bed. Been using it as storage. Stay as long as you want." He headed into the kitchen.

Linda swiped her purse and car keys off the end table, knocking over a baseball bat tucked behind the lamp. She stormed past Alex but didn't glance over, slapping the screen door with the butt of her palm and stomping down the porch steps to her car. The Louisville Slugger rolled across the hardwood floor.

Alex joined Tommy in the kitchen. "You in a softball league or something?"

"Huh?" He was bent in the fridge, backside sticking out of the box, a bear raiding the pantry, plumber crack on full display.

"You have a baseball bat by the front door."

"Rough neighborhood. Had a couple break-ins. You want a beer?"

"Sure."

He brought back the last two cans of Bud Light choked in plastic rings and a plate of leftovers that he stuck in the microwave. The kitchen sink overflowed with a week's worth of dirty dishes. Black-ringed coffee mugs and crusted pasta bowls stacked in a tottering pyramid.

Alex pointed to the path Linda cleared, footprints burned into the carpet, smoke all but rising. "Did I do something?" Alex snatched her beer.

He shrugged.

"I'm serious, Tommy. What have I done to her? Why does she hate me so much?"

"Linda doesn't hate you." The bell dinged. Tommy scarfed his dinner standing up at the sink, polishing half the plate in three large bites.

"Could've fooled me."

"She's jealous of you."

Alex rolled her eyes even though she knew it was true. Her cousin had always had an inferiority complex around her, ever since they were kids, which was strange, given that Alex had grown up in the same dank conditions and squalid bars Linda did. And it's not like Alex's adult life turned out any better. At least Linda had a long-term boyfriend, an actual apartment instead of renting a glorified closet in someone else's house. Linda and Tommy weren't rich by any stretch, but they had enough income to cover insurance on two cars. They owned cell phones. Tommy was the day shift foreman at the paper cup plant. Steady work, decent pay, health care. Which was more than she had.

"Yeah," Alex said. "I'm knocking it out of the park."

"It's not that." Tommy halted, scratching the back of his longshoreman's neck.

"What?"

"I love your cousin but she's not a runway model."

"And I am?"

"Come on, Alex. You know you're the pretty one. And, fuck, it ain't been easy for Linda living in your shadow."

"My shadow?"

"Your star has always shone brighter."

"Brighter? You mean because I was kidnapped when I was a teenager and chained up in a basement?"

He slid his empty plate into the sink, looming above her,

paw on shoulder. "I got to go to bed. I pay the rent here. You can stay as long as you want."

"What was that business about a PO?"

"Got into a fight. Long time ago. Long story."

"I don't remember you fighting so much."

"I fight. If I have to."

"You had to last night?"

Tommy didn't answer.

"Don't want to tell me what happened?"

Tommy squeezed harder till Alex let it go.

He motioned toward a rear door. "That's the spare room. Ain't much. But the couch pulls out." Tommy pointed at the closet. "Pillows and blankets are in there. I expect to see you when I leave for work in the morning, understand?"

Alex nodded.

"Linda went out for more beer. She'll be back in a few."

"I don't have the energy to fight right now."

"Won't be a fight."

Alex took her beer to the porch. Pulling the hoodie and zipping the bomber, Alex felt for her cigarettes, remembering she'd smoked the last one at the hospital. She hadn't thought to ask Tommy to stop at Cumberland Farms. Even after he dropped her at the Royal Motel to grab her car, she'd neglected to pick up another pack on the way over. Her thoughts zoomed in other directions, most circling back to Riley. She glanced at the bedroom door, wondering how fast Tommy fell asleep.

A few minutes later, her cousin hoofed up the steps with a brown paper sack, which she set on the porch between them. Linda reached in her bulky coat, pulling a new pack of Parliaments and tossing them to Alex. Then she reached in the bag and extracted a case of Bud Light and fifth of Jim Beam. She plucked a pair of paper cups from the floor, peering inside to make sure they weren't too dirty, blowing to remove any dust and debris, and filled a few fingers in each, handing one to Alex and hoisting hers in a cheers.

Linda downed the shot, poured another, and stared at the brownstone and brick.

Alex held the burning Parliament. "You remembered?"

"Sorry about before." Her cousin plucked the burning cigarette from her fingers. "What's the deal with this reporter?"

"He's not a reporter. Just some college kid working on a class project. He wanted to talk about Kira Shanks."

"Kira Skanks?"

"Shanks."

"Yeah, I know. That's what they called her."

"Who?"

"Everyone. She had a reputation. You were gone by then."

"I was still living here when she went missing."

"No. You weren't."

"Reputation?"

"She was the town bike."

"Town bike?"

"Everyone got a ride." Linda drained her second shot, sucked her beer dry, and stood with a stagger. She leaned her stocky frame against the wall, bending down for a clumsy kiss on the top of Alex's head. "I'mma hit the head. Then turn in. Sorry about before."

"Don't worry about it."

"You know I love you, right?" She didn't look at Alex when she said this.

Alex clasped a hand over hers, until Linda peeled away and stumbled inside, toward the bedroom.

Alex sat on the porch late into the night, smoking cigarettes, drinking alone, and watching sneakers sway on the telephone line.

CHAPTER SEVEN

Even though Tommy had told her the couch pulled out into a bed, Alex hadn't bothered making the effort. She grabbed the afghan shawl from the backrest, curling up in her jeans and tee. The long day had stumbled without grace into night; she was beat, drained, and didn't have the heart for commitment. And right then converting a sofa into a pullout constituted a commitment. As usual sleep didn't knock her out all the way. Alex spent listless hours tumbling, turning, tossing, listening to cars cruise the block through a haze, shadows transmogrifying into monsters behind her eyelids.

Sharp shafts of sunlight sliced through bent plastic blinds, dust mite constellations clogging the beams. Alex sat up and cradled her head, which like yesterday morning throbbed with a vicious hangover. Except Alex hadn't drunk enough to be hungover. These last couple days felt like straight edge compared to her usual intake. Maybe that was the problem and she was suffering withdrawal. Except Alex Salerno had never been strung out on anything. She made sure of that. After witnessing Denise dragged down by drugs, drink, men, the desperate depths to which her mother sank in pursuit of a fix, Alex swore she'd never let herself get addicted to anything. Maybe it was a caffeine headache.

Alex knew Linda and Tommy were gone. She felt the emptiness inside the apartment, the vacant sound of empty rooms. She checked the time on her cell to be sure. She wasn't up for company or conversation. Her head wouldn't stop thrumming. She made for the kitchen to rehydrate and find coffee. Defective paper cups that failed to pass inspection stacked along the counter, tottering in towers, Have a Nice Day slightly off center. She filled one with tap water and downed it in a single swallow. Empty pints and handles, flattened beer boxes stomped like accordions were stacked up in corners, waiting to be carried to recycling.

She made a couple calls to get her upcoming shifts at the bar covered. She'd worry about the dogs later. Rifling cupboards, Alex found a bag of coffee grounds but no maker. There was a jar of Folger's instant on the counter. Maybe city living had turned her into another hipster snob when it came to her coffee. Back home, there was an artisan shop on every corner, barista a legitimate career choice, good macchiato an art form. Headache or not, she wasn't drinking Folger's.

Alex shut the cupboard doors, squeezing her skull, jamming thumbs into eye sockets to block out that final image from the hospital, the one that didn't gel with the rest of what she thought she knew.

When she'd left the hospital yesterday afternoon, Alex had stolen a last look at Benny Brudzienski, slumped in his chair, melting like a dirty snowman in the sun. She'd hoped to impart one final, searing condemnation, let him know, hard luck or not, she had no sympathy for his kind. What he'd done was unforgivable; he deserved no mercy, death too good a fate. But when their eyes met that last time, Alex saw something she didn't expect: life stirring within. Which on the heels of Noah Lee's claims should've been enough to make her scream, "Faker!" Except the transitory glance conveyed something else, wrenching emotion Alex couldn't qualify at the time, so she stuffed it away with the rest of the inconsequential information she had no use for, kind words from ugly boys, career trajectory, algebra. Overnight that expression had burbled back to the surface, crawling, scratching, clawing at the light. Until she couldn't ignore it any longer. Standing in her cousin's kitchen, she understood what that look had been: a person trapped under the ice, very much alive, desperate for release.

Alex shouldn't be here. She needed to get back to the city. She had to start looking for another job, find a better roommate situation, maybe get a place of her own, a means to improve her lot, because at this rate she might as well be stuck in Reine, where it cost a helluva lot less to be going nowhere.

Someone banged on the door, the hard, bottom-of-the-fist kind used by cops. Alex had been tossed out of enough late-night parties to recognize the calling card. She didn't move right away, instinctual guilt taking hold.

"It's me, Nick. From the Fireside." A mop-top of bedhead poked above the archway window, eyes peeping through the glazing. "Nick Graves?"

Alex crossed the floor and let him in. "What are you doing here?"

"I need to talk to you."

"How did you know I was here?"

"Tommy."

Alex waited, but Nick didn't say anything, so she wound her hand to hurry up. She didn't want to be rude but the caffeine headache—and by now that's what she'd convinced herself it was—made getting coffee inside her bloodstream priority number one.

"I wanted to apologize for what I said. I was drunk. Shooting my mouth off. I didn't mean that stuff about you."

The guy had been staring all night, fluctuating between mean-mugging and moon-eyed. He'd been impossible to get a read on. Either way, he'd offered little more than his name. He certainly hadn't said anything inappropriate. Then she began to understand.

"That's why Tommy kicked your ass." She had a tough time fighting back the grin.

"I wouldn't say he kicked—"

"Oh, he kicked your ass." Alex smiled, pointing at the black eye and Band-Aid slapped over the bridge of his nose. "You said something bad about me and Tommy beat the shit out of you." Good ol' Tommy defending her honor. She lifted her chin. "What did you say?"

"Does it matter?"

"Um, yeah. You came all this way to beg forgiveness, 'fess up."

Nick shuffled his feet, staring at his shoes. "I called you an attention whore."

"You called me a...whore?"

"*Attention* whore. I was drunk. That's why I came here. To say I'm sorry!"

"Okay, Nick Graves. You said you said were sorry. Apology accepted." She didn't mean it but she didn't care either; she'd been called worse. Let him ease his conscience and move on. She had places to go, the first being somewhere with a decent cup of coffee.

She went to close the door.

"You don't remember me, do you?"

"What are you talking about? I saw you two nights ago."

"I mean before that. Tenth grade? Reine High? I sat behind you in Mrs. Hallback's homeroom class all year. The spring before, you know."

"What about it?"

"Do you remember me?"

"Sure. I remember you."

"It's not a trick question."

"No, Nick, I don't. Okay? Sorry. Nothing personal. I don't remember a lot from that time. I try to forget it."

"We were back to back. Our names. Saldana, Salerno. I was only there the year. My stepdad was in the military. I had his last name while he was married to my mom before switching back to my real dad's name, Graves. We're from here but bounced around a lot. My stepdad, Joe, was in the military.

Army. Actually finished high school in Virginia, before moving—"

"Great. I feel like I know you so much better. Why are you telling me this?"

"Because," Nick said, face flushing, "I had a crush on you back then but you didn't know I existed. And then you show up the other night, and I was piss drunk, and in a bad mood, and I don't know. Suddenly I'm sixteen again. Trying to get you to notice me, which was pointless since you don't even remember me. So I acted like a dick. I'm sorry." He waited, like he wanted to shake her hand, pulling up short, averting his eyes.

It was adorable how flustered he was getting.

"We cool?"

"Yeah," Alex said. "We're cool."

Nick nodded over his shoulder toward a flatbed pulled on the curb. "You want to get breakfast? I have the day off. I move furniture for my Uncle Jimmy, but today—"

"I have a boyfriend."

"And I have a girlfriend. Fuck, I'm just trying to be nice. There's a great roadside café on the way to Rensselaer. They make the *best* coffee. I'm serious, freshly ground, like one cup at a time. It's the shit. Homemade pastries delivered too. Thought I could buy you a bear claw, make up for being an asshole the other night. But I mean if you're too busy—"

"Good coffee?"

Nick Graves wasn't lying. In a town fueled by watered-down Dunkin' Donuts swill and burnt gas station brew, good coffee had finally found its way to Reine. Alex cupped her hands around the piping hot cup, savoring each sip. She tapped her Chuck Taylors in the squishy mud underfoot, downright giddy with the charged rush of quality caffeine.

The two sat outside Java the Hutt on railroad ties, the only seats provided. The pop-up mobile shop was designed to gas and go but couldn't meet the demand fast enough. A line stretched around the edge of the truck, overflowing into the trampled weeds that served as a makeshift lot, which showcased two types of vehicles: old pickups and puke-green Priuses. Place was packed for a weekday morning, and the crowd was younger than Alex would've guessed, a trendy new hot spot, tech kids fueling up before zipping off to the jobs where important things got done. Even Reine was getting in on the hipster action. Alex dug out her cigarettes, absentmindedly offering Nick the pack.

He shook her off. "That shit will kill you."

"What won't?"

"So," Nick asked, "what have you been up to since I saw you last?"

"Well, there was that whole abduction thing."

"I mean, after that."

"Like what have I been doing for the last twelve years?"

"Sure. We can start there. How about work? What do you do?"

Alex could see where this was headed. She wasn't up for being the answer to anyone's problems, revisiting high school what-ifs. "Thanks for the coffee and bear claw, but this isn't a date."

"I'm just trying to have a conversation."

"I'm sure you are doing your best."

Nick laughed uneasy, unsure how offended he should be. He turned away and pretended to be interested in a particular license plate.

The morning commute limped along the one lane, either headed for downtown Rensselaer or making wide, looping arcs for Interstate 787 or the 90, en route to Albany or Rye. Even the way the traffic here flowed was depressing, everything mismatched and unappealing, like poor people picking out glued-together ribeyes at the dollar store.

Nick stood, zipping the sleeveless vest over his thermal. "I'll drop you back at Linda and Tommy's."

Alex panned around the borders of her old hometown, skyline plugged with ash and soot from nearby factories along the river. Strange something so hostile and ugly could invite such nostalgia. She wasn't ready to go just yet.

"What are you doing today?" she asked.

"Sorry?"

"You don't have to apologize. It's a simple question. What are you doing today?"

"Nothing. I have the day off."

"Want to take a ride with me?"

The Idlewild Motel where Benny Brudzienski killed Kira Shanks sat kitty corner to the IHOP. Long-haul truckers and families on their way to Niagara Falls often stopped at the restaurant because of its close proximity to the interstate and easy on-and-off access. Tourists never stayed at the motel, which featured a dozen rundown ranch-style rooms at rock-bottom prices. Back in the day, the motel remained in business because college kids rented these rooms to high schoolers looking to party. The kids had a place to get loaded, the richies from Uniondale made an extra buck, and no one in Reine seemed to care. But when Benny Brudzienski killed Kira Shanks, that all changed. No more underage alcohol sales, no more raiding Mom's pill stash. No more turning a blind eye. The party was over. The Idlewild had the misfortune of being the last place anyone had seen Kira alive, transforming the old motel into a ghost town.

As Nick steered into the unpaved lot, Alex saw half the windows were covered with plywood but the other half of the motel was still operational. A dingy sandwich board boasted rooms for twenty-nine ninety-nine with free HBO. A man carrying a ladder—bushy yellow mustache, oversized glasses—squinted in their general direction before slinking around the corner.

After Kira went missing, authorities called in the dogs and sent out search parties into the dense forest behind the motel. The woods back there were enormous, thick with vegetation, rife with hidden alcoves and underground caves, countless streams and creeks. Hundreds of places to hide a body. The tall trees and uncultivated bramble obscured views of the river but if you listened hard enough you could hear its rushing waters. The tributaries met up with the Mohawk, which fed the Hudson, sweeping all trash out to sea. Alex didn't know if they'd dragged the river. No body ever floated to the surface.

Standing beside the truck, Alex studied the crime scene. Where was the room where it happened? How could a man with Benny's diminished IQ cover up the crime so well? And, most importantly, how had no one found the body after all this time?

"I like mysteries as much as the next guy," Nick said, "but you want to tell me what we're doing here?"

"You know what this place is?"

"Yeah. It's where Benny Brudzienski murdered that girl."

"I saw him."

"Who?"

"Benny Brudzienski."

"When? Where?"

"At the hospital. Yesterday."

Nick had to think about that one. "He's not in prison?"

"No. He's in a psychiatric facility up in Galloway."

"They just let you in? Why would you want to go there?" Nick grew excited. "Did they have him all restrained, like with a mask so he couldn't attack people?"

"This isn't *Silence of the Lambs.* Besides, he's catatonic." Alex counted the operational motel rooms, wondering if they were still renting out that particular one. Simple math, basic overhead and budget pricing, didn't leave a lot of wiggle room for electric bills, let alone turning a profit. "You familiar with the story?"

A brisk, pre-storm wind swept across the gravel as the thunderheads rolled in, slapping dead leaves against the hulls of big-barreled garbage cans.

"I know that fat freak killed her," Nick said. "They found his blood in one of these rooms. Probably raped her first."

"Why do you say that?"

"Because I doubt it was consensual. I remember reading they found..." Nick glanced around uneasy.

"You can say cum."

"I'd probably go with semen. But, yeah, they found that, too."

"Benny's?"

"How the fuck should I know? Ask your cop boyfriend."

"Excuse me?"

"Sorry. I don't understand why we're standing outside the Idlewild Motel at eleven a.m. on a Thursday. Are you, like, writing a book about this?"

"Why would I be writing a book?"

"Because of what happened to you."

"No. I'm not writing a book. I work at a bar and walk dogs a couple times a week." She didn't feel like adding dealing painkillers to her resume. Though she wouldn't mind a couple oxys right now. This might be her best chance at a decent payday.

"Were you here when she went missing?" Alex said.

"Kira? Yeah. I was back from Virginia by then. Couldn't go online without reading about it. It was like our Summer of Sam." Nick turned toward her. "Were you still here? Or had you already left?"

"Something like that." Alex couldn't explain that, like that cat in the box, she'd been both, alive and dead, here and somewhere far away. "Did you know her?"

"Not really. I remember when she moved to town, how big a deal it was. She was—I mean, she was in high school and I was older, but she was pretty. And wild. I don't want to talk bad about her because she's dead, but she got around."

"You know any of her friends?"

"You know Reine. Everyone knows everyone."

"You remember any names?"

Nick thought a moment. "Meaghan Crouse. Trista White."

Nick struggled to dig deeper. "I think Benny's younger brother, Dan, was part of that scene. Not sure. It's not like I partied with them. Oh, and Sharn DiDonna. Dude was a fucking asshole. There was one other guy too. A lot older than us. Always hanging around. Shit. What was his name? Cole something."

"Are any of these friends still around?"

"I know Meaghan is. She works at the CVS by my place. Photo department. I see her a lot. But we don't, like, talk or anything."

"Go grab a coffee," Alex said, nodding toward the IHOP.

"We just had coffee."

"Then order pancakes. I don't care. Just don't stand near me."

Nick looked confused.

Alex brought out her phone, held it up, spoke slowly. "I am going to make a phone call. Private. I don't care where you go, but move far enough away from me so you can't hear what I am saying."

"You are a very strange girl, anyone tell you that?"

"I'm twenty-nine. Which makes me a woman. And, yes. Now..." Alex flicked her fingers until Nick started moving.

When he was out of earshot, Alex dug around her email, punching in the digits, watching fat raindrops plop in puddles, concentric circles expanding and pushing boundaries. The phone rang a while before anyone picked up.

"Offer still stand?" she said. "Yeah, well, the price has gone up."

CHAPTER EIGHT

Any time there was a storm at the Galloway Institute of Living the inmates grew restless, thrashing like spooked farm animals. Some would bite their own hands, chomping down hard enough to draw blood. The staff had to cover fingers in mittens, wrap wrists with twine, secure them to armrests, bedposts. At least for the ones who still possessed ability to move limbs. Some were too far gone by this point; they just sat and stared. All. Day. Long. Can you imagine living life like that? Staring out a window at nothing at all. Used to wig Dontrelle out. But he'd gotten used to it.

Being an orderly at the funny farm was the last job Dontrelle ever saw himself taking out of college. But he had to support himself somehow. And it wasn't gonna be on his knew, not after his ACL joint gave out. All it takes is one ill-timed jump shot, and your whole life can change. Soon as Dontrelle heard the knee pop, the free ride was over. The job market's tough, beggars can't be choosers, and girls get sick of deadbeat boyfriends real quick.

Dontrelle wasn't naïve. He knew what these men had done. When he first signed on, he'd read the files. Scared the bejesus out of him, the evil some men were capable of. One man, Lewis Brewster, had kept his neighbor's heart in his refrigerator for a month. He lived across the hall from her. According to the other tenants, Brewster never said a word to anyone. Then one day he walks over, maybe asks to borrow a cup of sugar, a stick of butter, whatever, then slices her up, cuts out her heart. The cops found it in a Tupperware container in the freezer. Another man, Silas Freeport, had murdered twenty young male prostitutes. What he'd do, he'd pick them up at truck stops and bring them back to his parents' house, butcher them right there in the garage. Twenty had been the figure the prosecution agreed upon to make trial. Although, given the transient nature of his victims, most speculated the real number was much higher. Even creepier, authorities maintained Silas' parents had known what their son was up to all along and had chosen to do nothing about it. But it's hard to prove that kind of stuff.

Men like Brewster and Freeport had been deemed unable to stand trial by reason of mental defect. Dontrelle didn't get hung up on legalities. He was *supposed* to be playing point guard for the Knicks. The worst of the worst were kept in the bowels of the facility, in padded cells, chained up like the dogs they were. Dontrelle liked the third floor better.

Not that the crimes here were any less heinous. You still got rapists and murderers. But by this point most of the men were pumped full of drugs—chemically castrated, electroshocked into submission, brains scrambled—they were harmless. Like pillows with arms, heads on a stick. The only time they caused trouble was on evenings like this when the rains slashed against the glass. Lightning crackling, thunder rolling. Then, like feral beasts, the crazies freaked the fuck out, flapping arms, squawking, howling. A goddamn zoo.

Except Benny.

Dontrelle didn't have sympathy for any of the psychos in the basement, and he didn't give a shit about most of the men on the third floor either, but goddamn it if he didn't have a soft spot for Benny Brudzienski.

He knew what Benny had been accused of doing to that girl. But being accused ain't the same as being found guilty. And Benny had never been convicted. Never tried. Never even formally arrested. Who knew what would've happened if Benny had his day in court? Maybe new evidence comes to light. Maybe a body turns up, an eyewitness steps forward. Didn't matter because some good ol' boys got hold of Benny Brudzienski and fucked his shit up. Vigilante justice. Having grown up down South, Dontrelle remembered when they called it something else. What got to him most were those fucking eyes.

Some of the orderlies didn't bother getting Benny out of bed, would let him lie there in his own filth. But Dontrelle thought the man ought to at least be able to look out the window in clean underpants. Usually when Dontrelle attended to Benny, changed his linens, diaper, applied ointment to the bedsores, rolled him out to the plate glass window, nothing. Blank slate, dead eyes. Like staring into the face of a tuber. But every once in a while...

Happened again tonight. Dontrelle was about to eat dinner in the break room. He walked past Benny, who never even blinked, and somehow he was in a different position. Not an arm at a different angle, or fingers resting higher on the thigh. His whole chair had been scooted over, like three, four feet, which wasn't possible. No one else was working, and Benny was all but brain dead; he hadn't moved a muscle on his own in years. Doubted he even could, atrophy so bad.

Dontrelle should've continued on to the break room, warmed up his dinner, let it go. But he had to know—was he going nuts? Because that chair had definitely moved. Stooped over, Dontrelle searched for scuffmarks on the floor, but it was too dark to see anything, even with the sporadic flashes of lightning illumining the fields. Another orderly must've moved him; someone from another floor stopped by while Dontrelle went to the can to take a leak. Unless Dontrelle did it himself and forgot? He *did* smoke a fatty before punching in.

He was ready to let it go, chalk it up to chronic paranoia. Then he looked in Benny's eyes. Normally black, soulless pits, this time his eyes shone vibrant and alive. The big man still slumped in his chair, head drooping halfway down his chest like it might slide off his body, but his eyes told a different story. Dontrelle almost asked how he was doing before he caught himself. The man couldn't talk, couldn't comprehend a damn thing. The best doctors and head-shrinkers, prosecutors and the courts—some of the smartest men in the state of New York— had examined Benny Brudzienski and concluded he was toast. If it were that easy to beat a murder rap, there wouldn't be a man doing time in Riker's. But that look...as if he yearned to say something. So Dontrelle waited, stood in place, actually leaned in to give the impossible a chance.

Until Dontrelle started laughing. This is what happens when you work too long in the looney bin. You start goin' looney too.

Dontrelle straightened up. "Gonna miss you, my man," he said shaking his head, walking away.

BENNY BRUDZIENSKI

"Hey, dumb dumb. Get over here!"

Mrs. Shuman is standing outside one of the rooms with the door wide open. As I shuffle up I see the mess inside. Every weekend, they have another party here and each time they do more damage. I do not know why Mrs. Shuman lets Cole do this to her motel. It is not very respectful.

"One of those high school fuckers threw up all over the room. It's on the walls and everything. Where's your bucket and mop?"

If I could talk like regular people, I would say it is back where I left it, where I had been doing my job like I am supposed to. She called me over and said to hurry so I did not bring it. If she wants me to bring my bucket and mop, next time she should tell me to bring my bucket and mop. But I cannot talk like regular people, and I know if I try, the words would not come fast enough, or they would not be in the right order, and Mrs. Shuman would tell me to stop stuttering like a fool. So I do not say anything. Instead I nod like I am sorry, even though I am not sorry at all.

"Clean this puke up," she says. "Then head over to number eight and clear them out of there." She looks at her watch. "It's almost noon."

I do what Mrs. Shuman says. It takes a long time. I start with the biggest chunks first, picking them up with a rag, then I gather the smaller ones. I wipe and spray with bleach. I mop and wring out the sick. When I am done, I head over to room eight.

It is very cold walking across the lot to number eight, which is on the other side. The motel is in an L-shape. That room is at the far end. The air smells like it will snow soon. Clean, cutting, chemical, like the bleach I used to sanitize the vomit. It hurts my lungs to breathe all the way in. I like the snow. Even though the snow makes more work for me. Mrs. Shuman will not pay for a plow. It is up to me to shovel and clear a path for guests. But I like being out in the snow. It reminds me of when I was little, before Dad and Mom gave up on me, back when we would build snowmen and throw snowballs and I would carry the wood.

The curtains are open. I see her sitting inside the room on the unmade bed. The curtains are not open all the way, just enough that I can see her. She is sitting on the bed, naked, arms wrapped around her knees. I know I should look away. I know I am spying and that is wrong. It is important to respect personal space. Mrs. Collins, my last teacher, told me that. There were a bunch of rules at the special school, like Be Kind, Be Considerate, and Respect Personal Space. They hung these rules on the wall and told me what they meant. When I first went there, I liked to hug everyone. I did not mean anything bad by it, but I got in trouble. Mrs. Collins told Dad and Mom that I needed to respect personal space. I am not respecting personal space now. But she looks so beautiful and sad, and I want to hug her and make her feel better.

I step away from the window and knock on the door. I knock softly so I do not scare her. Kira comes to the door. She cracks it open and pokes her head out. She looks like she has been crying.

"Sorry, Benny," she says. "It's past checkout time, isn't it?"

I nod and turn my head away. I wonder if she is still naked.

Kira turns over her shoulder. With a bob, she gestures behind her. "Give me a minute, okay?"

"Take. Your. Time." I am surprised by the sound of my own

voice. I have not heard it outside my head in so long. I did not stumble over my words or anything. They did not come out fast but they sounded normal. I did not stutter or stammer. They were normal, regular words. I wished I could have saved it for Dad and Mom, Wren and Dan because I know I will not get it right again anytime soon. I was not thinking of talking this time. I was thinking about what she looked like behind the door, and my brain clicked. It is gone now, I can feel it going away, sinking into the muddy waters of my mind. My cheeks burn hot.

Kira wrinkles her nose, like a bunny. "Look at you," she says. "I knew you could talk. Everyone tried to tell me you couldn't, but I could see you were a smart boy, Benny."

This is not the first time I have seen her in a room at the motel. I can smell she did not spend the night alone. Maybe my brother was here with her. Dan is in love with her. He talks about her on the telephone every night. It makes me happy to think that. Dan is a good person. He is not mean like Wren. I am not stupid. I know what men and women do together in the dark.

She does not close the door and she does not cover up. She walks around naked. She looks at me as she puts on her underpants first, one long leg at a time. I see the faint white crosses on her arms. I try to turn away. But it is hard.

"It's okay, sweetie," she says. "You can look."

When she is done, she comes outside. She is wearing jeans and a sweatshirt, and she has dried the tears.

"Walk with me a little while?"

We walk to the front of the driveway. It is not far. I do not know if she is waiting for someone to pick her up. I do not see any car.

"Thanks for walking with me, Benny." Kira points down the road. "I live down there." She bites her lip. "You probably have to get back to work, huh?"

I shake my head.

"You're done for the day?" she says, eyes bright and happy.
I nod.

She thumbs down the road. "Want to walk me home?"

I do not go back and get my bicycle or tell Mrs. Shuman I am leaving. I am afraid if I turn from Kira, she will vanish like snow in the spring, and I will never see her again.

We walk together. Kira starts talking. She tells me things. She tells me a lot of things.

I listen.

CHAPTER NINE

"Thanks for meeting me."

Applebee's, Reine's latest chain jewel, frenzied with the dinner crowd—Mom, Dad, screaming baby, grandpa about a week from dying trying to cram in one last two-for-twenty-dollar special.

"No problem," Riley said, sounding as though it was very much a problem.

Alex knew she'd acted childish the other day. She wanted to accept responsibility, apologize, move on.

"I haven't been fair to you," she said. "Coming back here hasn't been easy."

Riley's tense shoulders relaxed a bit, but he was far from at ease.

"It's more than Parsons. This place..." Alex paused, trying to get the inflection right. "I've held the entire town to blame. Reine became this convenient, I don't know? Excuse? For every wrong committed against me. Which isn't fair to this place."

The server interrupted her pitch, running down the list of "specials," slabs of mid-grade meat slathered in sweet sauce, wrapped in plastic, and reheated in a microwave.

"Diet Coke," Alex said. No alcohol tonight. Be responsible, act grown-up. Before meeting Riley for dinner, she'd stopped at Marshall's, picking out a white top and pair of flats. Couldn't go too crazy, even if Noah Lee had agreed to mail the first installment.

"Coffee's fine," Riley said, not yet ready to forgive.

The waiter left to get their drinks, leaving Alex and Riley to defend their moral ground. She knew it wouldn't be easy. But why did it have to be this hard? They once were lovers sharing a bed. Now they negotiated like strangers. She hadn't held up her end of maintaining the friendship, it was true, but she also hadn't committed some egregious offense, the other day's outburst notwithstanding. Alex didn't expect them to pick up where they'd left off, but she deserved more than this cold shoulder routine.

"How is Meg?"

"You want to talk about my wife?"

"Just trying to make conversation."

"Please. Alex. Cut the shit. I agreed to meet you because you asked and said it was important. We're past playing catch-up. I have to get back to the precinct."

Alex tried to act surprised, hurt, offended, but couldn't pick any one emotion fast enough, which left her stuck in an awkward in-between state, like permanent pre-pubescence.

She balled the napkin she'd taken the time to smooth over her lap, dropping it on the plate. If this was the way he wanted to play it, what choice did she have? He was the link to the information she needed. "Benny Brudzienski."

"Didn't we cover that particular topic the other day when you threw your hissy fit at the hospital?"

"I apologized for that."

"I tried to be square with you. I brought you up to Galloway, on my own time, to show you what's what."

"The hell you did. You brought me up there to scare me straight, like some eighties' afterschool special bullshit."

The waiter returned with the Diet Coke and coffee. What was the point? "Beer and a shot," she said.

"Which kind would—"

"Whatever IPA you got on tap. Tequila, whiskey, whatever." Alex didn't take her eyes off Riley, nor his off hers.

"What do you want from me, Alex?"

"I want to know why you suddenly care so much about Benny Brudzienski."

"I could ask you the same thing."

"That could've been me."

"Until two days ago, you didn't even know who that girl was. Spare me the same suffering sisterhood crap."

"I knew who Kira Shanks was. And she deserves better."

"I tried to tell you the other afternoon—you can't believe everything you read in the papers or online. You don't know what happened."

"Enlighten me."

Riley folded his arms. "I am not discussing private police matters."

"Why? Worried about the review board? Internal Affairs? This isn't New York City."

"No, it's not. This isn't your home anymore. Go back to the city. This has nothing to do with you."

"I think it does."

"Why? Because of what happened when you were seventeen?"

"Don't trivialize what happened to me."

"I'm not trivializing anything. I am the one who found you, remember?"

"And I've thanked you for that."

"I don't want your thanks. I want you to get on with your life. Make yourself better."

"You don't know shit about my life."

"This might not be the big city, but I can tell when someone is fucking up."

"Fucking up?"

"You look like you don't sleep."

"I don't sleep. I haven't slept in twelve years!"

Several families stared, hugging their kids close as her voice escalated.

The waiter returned. Alex grabbed her shot and beer from the tray. Downed the shot, pounded the chaser.

Riley shook his head, a pitiful response to her pathetic gesture.

Alex snagged her bomber and hoodie, feeling eyes burn holes in her back, unable to flee the restaurant and Riley fast enough. On the sidewalk, she stared down at the new shoes she'd bought, feeling stupid for taking the time to make herself look pretty.

Riley slapped open restaurant doors, chasing after her. "What the hell was all that about?"

Alex spun around. "My attempt to be friends?"

"We *are* friends." He reached for her, speaking softer. "You know you will always have a special place in my heart—"

She stepped back. "I made a deal with that reporter."

"That college kid, Noah?"

"He's writing a story for the school paper about how Benny is faking it."

"Faking it? You saw the guy. Does it look like he's faking it?"

"I don't know. I don't care. But I told Noah I'd get some quotes from you, find out the real reason behind your big rush to spring Benny. If I do that, I make a few bucks. Is that so wrong?"

"I don't know if it's wrong. But telling me about it is pretty shortsighted."

"Why's that?"

"Because tomorrow morning, I'm going to call Noah Lee back myself. The only reason I haven't before now is I've been busy. I'll give him a direct quote. As a member of the press, he'll be invited to see everything we're allowed to share."

"I just told you I could make a few bucks doing this. You're going to screw me over?"

"No one is screwing anyone over. But you're not a cop. You're not even a reporter. I am not going to have you poking around *my* town, upsetting residents because you want to play dress up."

"What happened to not sharing official police business?"

"With you, Alex. With you."

"Why would you do that to me?"

"For one? I don't need you supplying my wife with any more ammunition. You know how small this town is. Meg knew the second you got back. You've been gone. I've been here. You think you're the only one whose life hasn't turned out the way you wanted it to? The world keeps spinning with or without Alex Salerno's permission. And as for *why* the urgency to get the charges against Benny dismissed? Not that it's any of your business—but you can read about it online if you'd taken two minutes to do any investigative legwork. Politicians up here want to appear tough on crime. Election year. A conviction on the books ships Benny down to Jacob's Island. They call it a mental facility, but it's nothing like Galloway. Jacob's Island is a prison, pure and simple. Vicious, violent. Benny wouldn't receive the treatment he needs."

"I don't give a shit about what Benny Brudzienski needs."

"I do. It's my job to give a shit. He won't last a night down there. Jacob's Island is understaffed and underfunded. There is no segregation between men like Benny and the real sociopaths. It's a shithole. If he's not shivved by sunset, he'll be gnawed to death by rats in the tomb. He doesn't deserve that."

Alex studied Riley's expression. There was more than anger and compassion brewing behind those eyes. "You don't think he had anything to do with Kira Shanks' disappearance."

"I didn't say that."

"Why else would you be fighting so hard to keep him in Galloway?"

"Galloway is hardly a four-star resort. But to answer your question, because political grandstanding has nothing to do with justice, neither for Benny nor Kira."

"I'm sure." Alex turned her back to him and walked away.

"Where are you going?"

"Not your problem."

"Go back to the city, Alex. Don't make me—don't put me in that position. I have a job to do—"

"So do I," she shouted over her shoulder, weaving through the cluttered Applebee's parking lot as more minivans arrived by the second.

Back on the road, Alex fished a scrap of paper from her glove compartment and plucked the pen rolling around the cup holder. She scrolled through the contacts on her phone until she found Nick Graves' number.

"Give me those names again."

"What names?"

"Kira's friends. The ones you mentioned at the Idlewild this morning."

She could hear Nick drop in a chair making exaggerated breathing sounds. "Why do you need them?"

"You already told me. What's the big deal? Shane something?"

"Where are you?"

Alex tried to find the name of whatever street she was on, new strip outlets and indiscernible chain restaurants blurring past. "I don't know."

"What's around?"

"I just left Applebee's. There's an Arby's up ahead. A little shopping plaza…Country Farms sandwiches?"

"I'm less than a mile away. Why don't you stop by? There's a bridge coming up on your right. Crosses a creek. Number Four, Cherry Hinton Lane."

"You're not getting anywhere with me, Nick." Alex passed a CVS Pharmacy.

"I'm not trying to get anywhere with you. Come over. You sound a little…"

Alex hit the brakes, making an abrupt U-turn. "Meaghan, right? That was one of their names. Meaghan Crouse. Works at CVS?"

"Come over. Let's talk, okay?"

"You're a nice guy, Nick. But no offense, if you can't help me, I don't have any use for you."

CHAPTER TEN

Alex headed inside the pharmacy, making for the photo department, wondering who even bought film like this anymore. Didn't everyone snap pictures with their iPhones? And professionals aren't buying supplies from CVS.

A heavyset girl crouched in front of a display stocking trays. Dyed black hair, acrylic nails like talons. Alex coughed. Even before the girl turned around, Alex knew what the nametag would read.

"You need something?" Meaghan Crouse was only seven years removed from high school but apparently they'd been seven long, hard ones. Thick foundation colored her skin an unnatural orange. Her hair was dyed so black it appeared almost blue under the store's overhead lights.

"I need some film."

"What kind?"

Alex scanned the racks and spotted a cheap disposable camera. She reached around Meaghan to pick it up. "This one."

"Great," Meaghan said. "Film's built in. Have a nice night."

"I want to buy it."

Meaghan pointed toward the automatic doors where an elderly cashier waved, eager for the company. "She can take care of you." There was no one else in line.

"I'm a reporter," Alex said, straining to remember the name of the paper Noah Lee mentioned. The whiskey, beer, and Riley were making it difficult to think. "The *Codornices*."

"Cool."

Alex glanced up pharmacy aisles, unsure what she was looking for among the knee braces, heating pads, and old man canes.

Meaghan squatted back down.

"I'm doing a story on the Kira Shanks' disappearance. The anniversary is coming up. Did you know her?"

"Kira?" Meaghan rearranged her inventory without looking up. "A little."

"I heard you were good friends?"

"I wouldn't say 'good friends.' But, yeah, like I said. I knew her." She swapped out a roll of film for another of the same kind.

"Anything you can tell me? Might get your name in the paper if you give me a quote I can use?"

"I don't care about my name in the paper, but you want to know what happened to Kira Shanks, go talk to Benny Brudzienski. He's the one that killed her."

"What makes you think she's dead? I mean, for sure?"

Meaghan let out a long, bored sigh. "Because no one has seen her in seven years? They found that retard's blood all over the room?"

"Benny isn't talking."

"No shit." Meaghan pushed herself up.

"I heard Benny was put up to it."

"Who told you that?"

"A source."

"Same source who told you I was 'good friends' with Kira Shanks? Your source is an idiot." Meaghan turned toward a man in a pharmacist's white smock standing at the other end of the store, glowering in their direction. "I have to get back to work. I'll tell you this, though. You *really* believe someone put Benny up to it? Try his brother, Dan. He was in love with her. Like, psycho stalker shit. Obsessed."

The man at the end of the aisle cleared his throat. "Meaghan, can you come back here?"

"Yeah, Carl. Be right there."

Alex put the film down on the counter.

"Thought you wanted to buy that?"

"Changed my mind."

Nick's place was on the second floor of a small complex, six cramped units, three up top, three on the bottom. Whole building could use a good power wash. The white exterior had turned gray, stained with age and crud, decayed leaves and abandoned caterpillar cocoons. Junky trikes and abandoned sneakers littered the landing. Beneath the stairs withered plants no one bothered to water died slow deaths on the vine.

The inside looked like she expected. Low ceilings, bad lighting, cheap furniture. A narrow kitchen, with barely enough room to slip through, cut off the living room, which doubled down as a place to eat. Small couch, smaller table. The apartment reminded Alex of the shitholes she'd shared with Denise growing up. The first thing they did when her mother found a new apartment was hit up the tag sales, buy all the twenty-five-cent paintings they could find to hide the holes punched in the wall.

Nick had answered the door in pajama pants, shirtless. The guy kept himself in good shape but his skin was so bare. Alex couldn't remember the last time she saw a naked man without any tattoos, even a tiny tribal bullshit one. He'd clearly been in bed. It wasn't nine-thirty. When he closed the door he slid the deadbolt. Reine had its rough-and-tumble parts but this wasn't the projects.

"You want something to drink?" he asked.

"What do you got?"

"Water. Muscle Milk. Beer."

"Harder."

Alex ground her back teeth. Last time she saw the dentist he recommended a mouth guard because she clamped down so hard when she slept her molars were riddled with fissures. Right now, it wasn't the nightmares that had her so wrenched up.

Two days ago, she would've sworn she had no place in her heart left for Riley. Now she realized that was the only reason she'd said yes to Noah Lee's interview. She hadn't made the connection at the time, despite how obvious it should've been. Alex felt like she'd walked into a trap she set for herself, which echoed phrases like "self-sabotage" from those sessions with Dr. Amy.

Nick reached above the sink, fishing deep inside a cupboard. He returned with a sealed, dust-covered fifth of gin.

"Was supposed to bring this to a party." Nick handed her the unopened bottle. "Never made it."

"Can you get anything?"

"Like what?"

"Something to bring me down."

"You're up?"

"Don't be a smartass. Can you help me or not?"

"Thought you wanted Kira Shanks' friends' names?"

"I do. And I want something to take the edge off. Fuck, can you get something or not?"

"I think I got a couple Percs left over from when I broke my ankle." Nick turned toward the darkness. "Don't know if they're still good. There're like from two years ago."

"It's a start."

Nick headed to the bathroom. Her nerves were fried, anxiety tearing her up. A little something to spell the worst of it, get her to relax, think straight. Alex walked to the fridge, searching shelves for a mixer. Juice, soda, anything. All the guy had was milk and pre-made protein shakes. At least there was some beer. Miller Lite. Fuck it. She'd drink the gin with a beer back. She grabbed a can, popped the tab, and kicked closed the fridge. There were photographs of a couple kids on the door. Young. Boy and a girl. Playing in a park. Laughing on a jungle gym. Baptism in a church.

"Didn't picture you as such a family man."

"My niece and nephew," Nick said walking back in the room, holding out a prescription bottle. "The label says they're expired—"

Alex snatched the 'script, uncapped the childproof top, and slid two Percocet into her waiting palm. She washed the pills down with a swish and swallow of piss water. Alex searched the dish drainer for a mug, squinting to peer inside.

"It's clean."

She ran her finger along the rim to be sure, before pouring a glass of room temperature gin, savoring the burn, like she were bleaching her insides clean. Feeling her mind clear, she held up the bottle. Nick shook her off.

He dug out a square of paper from his pajama pants' pocket.

"What's that?"

"The names you wanted? Wrote them down for you. I'm not sure who's still in town. I know Meaghan and Jody are. Or were a couple months ago." He pointed over her shoulder, at the windowless wall. "I saw Jody at the new Applebee's. Meaghan works at the pharmacy down the road—"

"I think you're right. Those Percs aren't good any more. Got anything else?"

"You're lucky I still had those."

"What if I wanted to get something harder—do you know anyone?"

"Like a drug dealer? No."

"The whole town is straight-edge these days?"

"I don't know. Not my scene. Probably get some weed or coke down at the Fireside. Ask your cousin or Tommy."

"Oxys, Dilaudid, fucking Vicodin."

"I don't know. You can try one of the bars past Rutledge."

"Names?"

"There's a few of them. Sweetwater? Jackal's Den. There's like three or four by the rail yard, right on the river. Sketchy as fuck. I wouldn't go down there—"

"Thanks." She popped up, grabbing her jacket.

"Wait. Where are you going?"

"Why?" Alex had started to slide her coat on but stopped, affecting a pout. "You going to miss me?"

"Are you okay? You seem—"

"What?"

"On a mission."

Alex pulled the paper out of her pocket, waving it in the air.

"Not that kind of mission." His expression conveyed genuine concern for her safety. It was cute.

She smiled, put the bomber down, and poured another mugful of gin.

"What are you planning on doing? With those names?"

"Can I smoke in here?" Alex blew the hair out of her eyes.

Nick squeezed past, between the fridge and counter. She could've moved and made it easier for him but didn't. He opened the window, leaning over with one arm to pop the latch and slide it open, trying not to rub against her, which Alex found endlessly amusing.

"Where's your buddy, Mikey? From the other night at the Fireside."

"How would I know?"

"Figured you two were roommates."

"Why would you think that?" Nick squeezed back out, motioning over his tiny apartment. "You think another human could fit inside here? I live alone."

"Thought you two had a Batman and Robin thing going on."

"We don't. I hadn't seen that dude in years before I ran into him that night."

Nick retreated to the living room, Alex following close behind, so close he could feel her breath on his neck. He twitched, uncomfortable, swatting at the back of his hair, trying to get separation, which made her laugh. She loved this part, being in charge, creating unease, able to make them do anything. The old radiator kicked on, hissing pipes clanking to life, rumbling and knocking, spitting steam. He flinched. She stepped toward him, backing him against the wall.

"How high you got the heat jacked in here?" She undid the top button of her new white blouse, sliding closer. She was practically on top of him, pinning him.

"I have bad circulation," he said, squirming. "You didn't answer me? What are you going to do? Go around talking to all Kira Shanks' old friends? You think that is going to accomplish anything? Besides piss people off."

Alex set her gin down on a bookcase, then draped both arms around his neck, lightly brushing his skin with her fingertips. "You worried about me?"

"What are you doing?"

"Tell the truth. You don't really have a girlfriend, do you?" She pulled on her cigarette, cocking her head to blow smoke out the other side without letting him escape.

"And you don't have a boyfriend."

"No," Alex said, shaking her head slow, "I don't."

She leaned in and kissed him on the mouth, soft, sweet, warm. He started to kiss her back but stopped, halfheartedly trying to turn his head. She gently guided his face to the center, kissing him slower, biting his lip, scraping nails on his back, lightly tracing his stomach, slipping a hand down the front of his pajamas, under the elastic. She felt him get hard, and waited for him to make the next move, the one they always make, the one to the bedroom. But he didn't. He lost interest. She tried stirring him back to life, pulling his hands down to her ass, pushing her hips in, but he eluded her grasp.

Alex kept her back to him. This was turning into quite the night. Rejected by Riley. A two-thousand-dollar payday gone. Now she couldn't even score a pity fuck. And the worst part? She wasn't sure who was supposed to be on the receiving end of the sympathy.

"Listen, Alex. I like you. And I want to. But not like this. Not with you like this."

Alex finished her gin, smacking her lips. She brought her

mug to the edge of the sink, tipping it over with one finger, ceramic echoing off stainless steel. She slid her jacket on.

"You seem so pissed off, angry. Fucked up. I don't want it to be like that."

"This isn't prom, Nick." She fanned her hair over the collar. "Every lay doesn't have to be a special moment to cherish forever. I wanted to feel something other than what I'm feeling right now. It was a one-time offer." Alex zipped her coat, holding up the square of paper before tucking it away. "Thanks for the names."

"Where are you going? What do you plan to do?"

"Don't worry about it. Go back to bed."

Alex headed down the rickety old steps to her car. She could feel Nick standing on the stairs, watching her, but she didn't turn around.

CHAPTER ELEVEN

Sometimes when prescriptions expire, the drug gets stronger, not weaker. That's what was happening now. Or maybe the gin was making a fiercer impression than she'd anticipated. More than likely it was a combination of things. The pills, the liquor, the seething indignation for having been wronged. Alex had the windows rolled down, the night bitter, crisp, frigid. The harsh winds by the river made her eyes water the faster she went, so she went faster, harder.

Even at her worse, Denise seldom ventured down to these bars along the waterfront. Less because of their rowdy reputation and more because you couldn't get blood from stones. The wharf was home to welfare cases and lowlifes living on the dole. Then again, her mother couldn't offer what Alex could. Denise wasn't smart, wasn't savvy. Alex passed her mother's limited intelligence by the time she reached middle school. Worn out and used up, Denise wasn't as pretty.

Outside the Sweetwater Tavern, Alex had to park in the street, place so crowded, or rather the parking situation so screwy. Walking up to the bar, she saw there was a second, more secluded lot by the water, concealed from the road by a pair of weeping willows. This lot was less congested with only a few vehicles, a pickup truck, a couple bikes, the crotch-rocket kind, secondhand and mickey-moused, but by then she was almost through the door. No point moving her car now.

Unlike the Fireside, Sweetwater wasn't trying to be something it wasn't. There were no big-screen TVs or dartboards, no suburban sports bar vibe. Just billiards and booze, low lighting, the way a bar should be. There were still some college kids traveling in small packs, hoarding a pool table. Frat boys never slum it alone. She didn't see many women. At least none Alex's age. Sweetwater comprised serious drinkers, career alcoholics, seasoned locals with that etched-in, hardened look and whittled, uneven eyes, leathery crevices approximating laugh lines.

As soon as Alex stepped inside, she knew she'd be able to find whatever she wanted here. If Alex hadn't spent the last five years in some of the toughest parts of New York City, she might've been intimidated, but the roughest parts of Reine were a block party compared to the mean streets of NYC.

Still, Alex didn't like flying blind. New place meant she'd need to poke and pry to find out who was holding what, which involved a lot of small talk, flirting and playing the part. Some idiot asking if you're a cop because he's seen too many TV shows and believes that cops are obligated to tell the truth.

Getting high tonight started to feel like a chore, requiring more effort than she had to spare. She was about to say forget it, turn around, grab a six-pack and watch sneakers sway from telephone lines, when someone called her name.

"Alex? Alex Salerno! Oh my God! Is that really you?"

Alex forced a smile as the woman rushed over, leaning in for a hug, which Alex returned because she didn't know what else to do. She had no idea who this woman was.

"I thought you were living in the city."

"I was. I mean, I am. I'm up visiting."

The woman pointed at a back table clustered with haggard drinkers. "Come have a drink with us. Cooper is supposed to be stopping by."

"I can't," Alex said, turning over her shoulder, gesturing at the door as if that would explain everything. Alex didn't know this woman, and she didn't know anyone named Cooper either. If the woman hadn't used her full name, Alex would've assumed she'd gotten her confused with somebody else.

"Next time, honey, okay?"

"Okay."

"Promise?"

"Promise."

The woman squeezed her hand and began to walk away.

"Hey," Alex called after her. "Is anyone holding?" It was worth a shot. Like getting a tattoo or eating sushi, a referral is always best.

The woman pointed past the bar, to an adjacent room.

Maybe she was slipping. Alex should've been able to sniff this out. She'd forgotten to let instincts kick in. Because the moment Alex stepped in the other room, she couldn't believe she'd considered bailing. It was obvious whom she needed to talk to.

He sat in a booth by himself, Yankee baseball hat, older but not creepy old. He spotted her, too. A head bob granted permission to approach. Drawing nearer, she saw he wasn't bad looking. Considering the slim pickings of this town, might as well have been Hugh Fucking Jackman.

Alex stopped at his table, hands in back pockets, rocking on her heels, surveying surroundings.

"What's up?" he said, keeping it casual. "Rick."

Alex had been expecting "Gluehead" or "Hitch," something more exotic than "Rick." Rick was the name of the guy who fixed your car, not your neighborhood drug dealer.

"Have a seat," he said, sliding over, patting the cushion next to him. "I don't bite." She didn't take him up on the offer. Exchanges like this were all about maintaining the power dynamic, the control. "I'm good."

"I hear you. What are you up to tonight?"

"This and that."

"This and that?"

"More this. Not enough that."

Rick grinned. "I might be able to help you out with...that."

Alex tried not to laugh, how cool he was playing it, King Shit in a shit-kicker town. He had a nice smile, though. Some college boys milled beyond the separation, playing pool, glancing back, checking out her ass.

"Fucking Uniondale, eh?" Rick said. "Hate that fucking college."

She was starting to like this guy.

"You going to tell me your name?"

"Sorry. Alex."

"Nice to meet you, Sorry Alex. You live around here?"

"The city."

"Visiting?"

She nodded.

"Not much of a talker, eh, Sorry Alex visiting from the city?"

The line made her laugh, even if it wasn't funny or terribly original. "Been a weird day."

"Yeah, most of them are weird, aren't they? We just don't take the time to notice *how* weird." He slipped out of the booth. "What are you drinking?"

"Scotch and soda?"

He slapped the tabletop, pointing a finger. "Scotch and soda, it is."

Rick headed off to the bar. Alex felt calmer. Relief was moments away, and it was nice to have a normal guy to talk to. Okay. Not normal. But her speed at least, one of her own, water seeking its own level and all that. Since she'd been back, Alex had been struck by persistent reminders of how much she didn't belong here anymore, like returning to your old high school, walking down miniature hallways and seeing all those tiny lockers. Nothing fit right. What did it say about her life that the first person she felt comfortable around was a drug dealer at a sleazy dive? Then again, she didn't know for sure he dealt. Except, yeah, she did. And as soon as he sat down with her drink, he dropped any pretense.

"What are you looking for? Up? Down? Sideways?"

For whatever reason, the first thing that came out of her mouth wasn't "weed" or "Vicodin" but "Kira Shanks."

Rick didn't miss a beat. "Girl who went missing way back?"

"Yeah."

"I was talking about something else."

"I know."

Rick looked her over, trying to peg her angle. "Friend of yours?"

"No."

That made Rick suspicious. She didn't need that. Should've kept her mouth shut. Maybe she'd mistaken his expression, or else dude really was as chill as he projected. Because all he said was, "Cool." Rick took a sip of his whiskey. "They caught the guy who did her, right? Fat fucking lunatic. What's his name?"

"Benny. Benny Brudzienski."

"That's right. I remember seeing that mongoloid freak walking all over town, picking up plastic bottles from the weeds, eye-fucking crows. People like that—I know it's not politically correct—but they're like a mad cow in the slaughterhouse." Rick mimed firing a shotgun, blowing out make-believe bovine brains.

Alex pulled the paper Nick had given her. "Do you know any of these people?"

Rick read the names, wrinkling his brow, finger to lips, giving it real consideration. "I do. Cole Denning comes in here a lot. If he's not in this bar, he's in another one. Don't see much of Meaghan and Jody these days. Used to. I know they live in Reine. Trista and Patty? Maybe." He pushed the sheet back, squinting. "Why you so interested?"

Alex shook her head, trying not to crack up. "I don't know."

"Come on," he said, sliding out of the booth.

"Where we going?"

"I think I can help you out with those names. Get you some numbers. I have to make a few calls." He winked. "I know everyone in this town. And in the meantime..." He let the words hang there.

When she didn't move, Rick pulled a crystalline baggie from his breast pocket, dangling the prize between forefinger and thumb. "You look wound tighter'n a drum. Trust me. This will take the edge off."

Alex usually stayed away from powders. It was a line she'd drawn. Pot, alcohol, pills. That's it. Right now, though, her head was rumbling like a late-night freighter. She'd only snorted heroin—she assumed that's what Rick was holding—once. She didn't get all the fuss. Didn't do much but make her sleepy. But if that's what it took tonight, a small line to smooth the rough and jagged parts, she'd go with it.

As she walked out, the college kids eyed her, no doubt wondering how a guy like Rick got to leave with a woman like Alex. Let them wonder all they wanted. They'd never understand.

Passing through the cluttered parking lot, Alex spotted what she'd missed coming in, the telltale signs that Uniondale University had, indeed, infiltrated the lowdown. On the surface, these beat-up junkers resembled Alex's car, except these shitboxes had brand-new ski racks on top, high-end stereos inside, blue security lights blinking to ward off any B&E. That's what Alex hated most about the Noah Lees of this world: they wanted the credit for trenching it without actually getting their hands dirty.

Her cell buzzed with a text. Nick.

You okay?

She'd been expecting this. She fired back a rapid reply, fingers flying in a flurry. Her first response was clear-cut and snarky, but she erased that one, opting for casual, cryptic, cool, and detached. Then she decided he didn't deserve a response. Let him twist in the wind. Who was he to turn her down?

She'd been so busy raging in her texts she hadn't realized they were almost to the river, standing in the second, more secluded lot, far from the bar. Weeping willow trees canopied ink-black waters.

"Where are you taking me?"

"That's my truck." Rick nodded at the four-wheeler parked river's edge, mud-splattered undercarriage, jacked-up suspension. "Reine ain't the wild west anymore. Can't rip lines on the table." He wound a reassuring arm to follow.

"That's okay. I think I changed my mind."

Alex turned to go and bumped into the other man who'd been hiding behind the tree. Older, more ravaged, reeking of low-tide silt like he'd just crawled out of a tent in the ironweeds.

"I hear there's a party." His crooked grin revealed rows of eroded teeth, tiny brown nubs like a kid with a mouthful of Halloween chocolate. He closed in, backing her up to the truck. The door kicked open.

"Come on," Rick said, patting the seat. "Get her in here, Jackie. Don't need the fucking cops drivin' by."

Jackie hurried Alex along. She had nowhere else to move, backing up the runner. Rick yanked her in by the underarms as she kicked her feet. Jackie hoisted in after, and slammed the door shut.

Out the dirty windshield, discarded train parts—rusted wheels, railroad ties, gears—lazed along the shore, floating on the field's currents. Moonlight reflected off old storage units, decrepit boat sheds, decimated walkways and pillars, the wreckage of the pier.

No one bothered with introductions. This wasn't that kind of party. Rick had already taken the liberty of cutting up a couple fat lines. He held out a dollar-bill straw. Sandwiched between the two men, Alex had a line shoved in front of her face.

"I'm good."

"I'd say you're a little better than good—"

When Alex didn't move fast enough, Rick checked her in the ribs to get her attention. "Not a question."

She took the straw, snorted it all. Threw her head back, eyes burning, ears ringing. "Damn," was all she said, eyes clearing but tinnitus lingering. She tasted the nasal drip and her heart started to pump double-time. The tingle made her think Molly.

Rick howled. "Shit's no joke." He hit his line, snorting harder than a horse. "Goddamn! Now *that's* what I'm talking about!" He took off his ball cap, thwapping it against the dash. Up top, he was bald as a cue.

"What about me?" Jackie whined, and Rick dabbed a tiny pile, passing it along, leaning in to nuzzle Alex's neck as he did so. Alex tried pushing him away, but Rick kept burrowing, like a blind, hairless mole. She heard a loud snort, and felt another set of hands start groping, probing her body. She tried to flare out, wriggle free, but crammed so tight together, she had no room to move, left or right.

Rick nodded out the window, addressing his buddy like Alex wasn't there. "I'll go first. You keep watch. Then we switch up."

"Why I get your sloppy seconds?"

Rick passed along the bag, and Jackie snatched the deal. He kicked open the door and Alex tried to jump out with him but Rick grabbed her hair and yanked the handle shut. He slithered to her neck, licking her skin, his breath rank with halitosis. His hand kneaded her stomach, pawing skin under shirt. She swatted, pushed, shoved, but in the restricted space, Alex was pinned, unable to lift an arm without smacking against the dashboard or glass. She started to scream and Rick punched her in the mouth. Out the dirty window, she couldn't make out the moonlight anymore, everything growing dark. Hand between her legs. Alex flailed frantic, fighting back. They wrestled. He won. Hand over mouth, she was flipped over, face down, head pressed into the cracked vinyl, the whole of his weight on her backbone. He tugged at her jeans, pulled them down below her hips. He unbuckled his belt, and when she tried to jerk away this time she took a hard hook to her ribs, to the soft spot underneath, which sapped all air from her.

She drifted far away on pillows of wind in darkening skies...

"Hey! What are you doing in there?" The voice—young,

male, aggressive—came from the direction of the bar.

Now several footsteps ran toward them, swarming the truck. "Get out of there!"

At first Rick didn't stop, kept her head pressed down, hand over mouth. Then more voices surrounded, shadows rising, looming outside the window. Someone reached for the latch. Rick eased his grip and Alex broke free, cracking an elbow against his teeth.

"You fucking bitch!" Rick covered his face as blood gushed from his nose.

Alex scrambled out the truck, bumping into Jackie, who stood silent, horrified eyes wide with stimulants, hands held high in the sky like he was used to being collared. She bounced off him, trying to pull up her pants, stumbling and spilling in the mucky reeds.

A pair of hands reached for her, but she flung them off.

A college kid stood over her as more of his broad-shouldered brothers arrived, flanking both sides of the truck, making sure doors stayed open and nobody moved. They were clad in Uniondale colors, gold and burgundy, lettered jackets with the word Crew emblazoned in the center.

Rick now sat on the edge of his seat, spitting blood.

"We was just having fun," Jackie said.

"Doesn't look like she was having fun." One of the boys bent down to help Alex to her feet. She couldn't see straight, blood rushing between her ears, vision blurry, a tidal wave of panic and self-loathing gripping her. She'd walked out with him, gotten in that truck. Why hadn't she clawed his eyes, fought harder, made a run for it? Screamed bloody murder on the spot? Everything moved too fast. How had she let this happen again?

A member of the team tried to steady her, but she ripped away, shrieking at being touched.

The kid stepped back. "It's okay. No one is going to hurt you."

The college boys circled Jackie, who backed up to the truck, hands still held high. One of the college kids arched over, palming Jackie's head like it were a melon, and smashed it against the truck frame. There was a loud, sickening crack. Jackie bellowed, falling at Alex's feet, whimpering. When he gazed up, a giant purple knot blossomed around his eye, instantly sealing it shut. On the other side of the truck, fists connected to bone. Alex didn't see Rick. But she heard his cries.

Six or seven college kids closed ranks around the two men and began punching, kicking, stomping, beating the ever-living shit out of the two would-be rapists, who writhed and squirmed in the mud like eels snagged on the fishing line. She wanted to speak up, thank them for saving her, say she was sorry for talking so much shit, that she didn't mean it. Don't hurt them too bad, hurt them worse. Instead she turned and ran to her car. Someone shouted something about calling the cops. Alex didn't answer. She kept running.

CHAPTER TWELVE

Alex hovered between worlds, neither in this one nor the next; she was in both places at once, equally discomforting. She experienced fleeting moments of being cognizant, lucidity shattering the dreamscape, at least long enough to answer the calls from the other side, say she was fine, no problem, leave her alone, everything good. But she was unable to get out of bed and face the music, or in this case her cousin, no matter how many times Linda screamed her name.

As Alex lay wrapped in the blanket, part of her recognized someone was outside the spare bedroom door, jiggling the handle, pounding, kicking the base. Or it could've been part of the same bad dream. Maybe she imagined the fight in the next room where her cousin was shouting, "That's why I didn't want her here!" and Tommy saying, "She's family." And if she dreamt that, then maybe she'd made up the other parts too.

Alex could still see the inside of that asshole's truck, feel his hands on her, pressing down, holding her hostage, the numbness from the drugs, the resignation that it was happening again, payback for having escaped the first time, the Universe conspiring to return damages owed. She saw Parsons. Felt another presence looming in the shadows at the lake house, another set of eyes clocking her, tracking movements like a predator in the wild. She saw Benny Brudzienski, slumped in his chair at the hospital, only this time when their eyes met, he smiled, thin lips parting to reveal rows of tiny, razor-sharp teeth.

Alex wasn't sure how long she'd been in Tommy and Linda's spare room, curled up with the door locked. Might've been a few hours or a few days. She must've left the room to pee at some point but didn't remember doing so. She didn't want to turn on her phone and find out how much time she'd lost. Felt like she'd seen the light and the dark trade places more than once. One thing was for sure: that wasn't Molly she'd snorted, not unless it was Molly cut with benzos and Seconal, ketamine. Maybe she should've stuck around to call the cops, file a report about what happened. But what *had* happened? She'd put herself in a stupid situation. Again. She was high on drugs. That's all anyone would care about. She'd gone with him willingly, like the first time.

Dragging herself from bed, Alex pulled up her hoodie and cracked the door. It was dark, cold. Rain pinged off the roof and windowpanes. She peered into the kitchen, having no idea what she'd find. A troupe of mimes on roller skates wouldn't have surprised her at that point. The clock on the microwave read 2:07 a.m. Her insides gnawed with hunger.

On the kitchen table, a newspaper, ringed with coffee stains, read Saturday. She filled a defective paper cup with tap water at the sink and drained it. Then another. And one more. Alex pulled her cell and confirmed the date. Two days and four missed calls from a blocked number.

She felt someone watching her and turned to find Tommy standing in ratty long johns bulging at the gut.

He opened the fridge and extracted a plate of chicken leftovers, carrots, and potatoes, placing it in the microwave. "Sit."

"Can I smoke in here?" Watching raindrops roll down the pane, she could feel the cold penetrating. She needed a cigarette but couldn't fathom stepping outside in that.

Tommy looked over his shoulder, toward the closed bedroom door, then walked around the table, slid up the window, frigid gusts swishing in. He placed a small fan on the sill and switched it on, blowing the cold air back out.

Alex smelled the ends of her hair. They reeked of vomit. Tommy waited for the microwave to finish. Then slid the plate in front of her as he sat, cautious and slow, like he was feeding a junkyard dog.

"Jesus, Tommy. I'm not dangerous." Even after a couple days of recovery, her face still felt swollen, sore, like a few teeth had dislodged up in her cheek. It hurt to talk.

"Your cousin wanted to bust down the door. Almost called fire and rescue." He pointed out front. "You left your car in the middle of the street."

Alex started to get up.

Tommy gestured to stay put. "Already took care of it. You left your keys on the counter." He pointed at the plate. "Eat."

Alex dug in, smoking in between big bites, needing both, the food and nicotine, desperately. Every time her mouth moved, a searing pain, like an electric shock, radiated from the nerves in her jaw.

"Want to tell me what happened to your face?"

Alex didn't answer, consumed by the hard rain pelting glass.

"Finish that and go back to sleep." Tommy placed his big hands on the table.

"Did you know her?"

"Who?"

"Kira."

"Didn't we talk about this coming back from Galloway?"

"I'd like to talk some more."

Tommy rubbed a meaty palm over his bleary eyes and sat back down. He reached for her cigarettes. "Mine are in the other room. More like knew of. Told you. She had a reputation."

"How about her friends?"

"She was younger than us, so, no, I didn't know them. Not really." He stopped. "I mean, I know some of their names. Meaghan Crouse works at the CVS, I think. Patty Hass used to wait tables at the Waffle House. I don't know if she does anymore. I haven't seen her around in a while. I think she dated

Sharn DiDonna."

"I keep hearing that name. Who's he?"

"An asshole. Graduated same year. One of those rich kids who parties poor in between summers in Newport. I know he was doing Kira for a while too. If I remember right, they had a bad break up."

"He still in town?"

Tommy shook his head. "Went back to live with his father in Bethlehem after Kira went missing."

"How about Cole Denning?"

"Handyman at the Idlewild? Got Benny's old job. About the only job a guy like him gets."

"Guy like him?"

"Old drunk. Why do you care about this so much?"

Alex stared out the window. Eyes adjusting to the darkness, she spied a birdhouse. In the trees, next apartment over. The homemade popsicle kind a small kid makes with his dad. It rocked in the boughs as the midnight winds howled.

"Alex?"

"Remember after Parsons, there was that rumor he had a partner? Someone helping him?"

"But that wasn't true. He confessed. Said he acted alone."

"He did. But for a long time I'd look into every stranger's eyes. On the subway. The bus. The supermarket. Study them, wonder, what if it was true? What if someone was coming for me someday? I remember the look in Parsons' eyes. But only after the fact. Years later. At the time I blocked it out. And then, like a heavy curtain lifted, I could see them, clear as day. What was there. Or what wasn't there. Something lacking, a basic...I don't know...humanity."

"I'm not following."

"When I was at the hospital the other day, I looked in Benny's eyes. He looked at me funny."

"Funny?"

"Like he was trying to convey something." Alex caught herself. "I know. It's crazy. Guy can't move. Practically brain dead. He's giving me secret messages. But I can't get that look out of my head, Tommy. Parsons was a killer. He was a bad man. When I looked in Benny's eyes the other day at the hospital, I didn't see a bad man. I didn't see a killer. What if he—"

"What?"

"Is a man like Benny Brudzienski really capable of pulling off a murder and cover-up? You remember him walking through town. Did he seem violent to you? If someone put him up to it—"

"You don't know that's what happened."

"That's what you said."

"Rumors, Alex. People say stuff. Can't prove any of it. Doesn't matter if anyone egged him on. Benny still killed her. They found his blood, his DNA. I'm sorry. The guy's guilty. And I know what you went through was horrible, but what Benny did to Kira Shanks doesn't have anything to do with you. You need to find a way to move on, leave it behind."

"They're trying to send him to Jacob's Island. He'll die there. They'll kill him."

"Benny? He's an invalid, right? They have a special place for guys like that. What do you think they're going to do? Roll him into the prison yard every morning?" Tommy stood and pointed at the plate. "Finish eating and go back to bed. Morning ain't gonna be pretty. You gave your cousin a lot of ammo this time."

Alex ground out her smoke on the plate and poked around the dead bird scrapings.

Tommy stopped, picked up something off the counter. "This came for you yesterday." He handed Alex an envelope.

Then Tommy, never the most affectionate guy, leaned down, wrapping her in a big bear hug, holding her snug and close.

She wished he never let her go.

BENNY BRUDZIENSKI

We have been spending more time together but no one can know. People would not understand because of what I am. It is our secret.

Kira read a book to me today, on the hill under a tree. I do not remember the name of the book, and I do not know who wrote it. I missed a lot of the words. She reads to me often. I have a hard time following the story because my brain does not work in the right order. But I like listening to the sound of her voice.

Mrs. Shuman told my father I could not come back to work at the motel after I left without permission to walk Kira home. When I went back for my bicycle, Mrs. Shuman had already called my father, and he was waiting for me. He was not happy. He asked where I had gone. I did not point or draw my stupid pictures. I did not try to stutter a response. I could not explain that I had to make sure she was safe. You cannot let a girl walk alone in this town. Not long ago, a man started stealing girls, doing bad things to them. When he was done, he buried them in his backyard. I do not understand why a man would want to destroy something beautiful. Kira is the one good thing I have. Besides, Mrs. Shuman has Cole. He can do the same things I do.

Kira meets me at the football field on afternoons before the game. She waits until Mr. Supinski leaves for the day, when she knows he will not come back and we can be alone. She tells me things. I am safe. I do not judge. There is no one to tell.

Before Dad and Mom knew my head could not be fixed, they brought me to church. They are Catholic. I guess I am too. We do not go to St. Paul's anymore. I think they are mad at God for making me this way. I am not mad. God gave me a purpose. God does not make mistakes.

This one time I found Dad's magazines in the closet. There were pictures of women without clothes. Mom found me looking at the pictures. Dad was very angry. They brought me to see Father Mark. You are supposed to go into the booth by yourself but I could not get the words out, and it was too dark to draw pictures, and there was no pencils or paper. Dad came with me. He did not say the magazines were his. I did not understand why everyone was so upset. I did not see anything wrong with the pictures. Everyone seemed happy in them.

When we got home Wren sneaked me in his room and showed me a movie on his computer. It was like the pictures in the magazines but different. No one seemed to be having fun in the movie. They were hurting the woman. Wren thought it was funny. I am not dumb. Movies are not real, but I did not understand why anyone would do those things or laugh at them. They seemed mean and cruel and wrong. Wren said, "What's the matter, Benny? This is what men and women do when they love each other." It did not look like love to me.

We sit under the bleachers, Kira and me. The sun is a tiny yellow dot. It is about to set. Kira tells me to put my head in her lap, and she pets me like I am her dog. I close my eyes, and dream of bigger places far from this one. I imagine shooting stars and lights in the sky, like fireworks on the Fourth of July.

Kira tells me about her old school and how much she misses her old friends. She shows me photographs. She says new schools are scary. "You wouldn't understand, Benny." But I do understand. I know what it is like to feel alone and be an outsider. I open my mouth to try and get the words out but they do not come like last time. Kira says, "It's okay, Benny, you don't have to say anything." She looks in my eyes, and I stare back.

Even if I cannot say the words I feel in my brain, I want her to see there is a man inside this busted body, and he has a heart and a soul, he has feelings and believes in things, too. I ache for one person to see it, for her to see it, because if Kira cannot see it, what chance do I stand? And then she pets my head and strokes my hair. The wind rips through the valley and we both disappear for a while.

I know I do not mean the same thing to her that she means to me. I am not Dan or Wren or any other whole person. Kira is never running away with me. We are not living in a house with a white fence and babies of our own. I understand that it takes money to buy a house and pay for food. I am not stupid.

She tells me about the men she loves but who do not love her back, who take what they need from her but do not give back. I get so angry thinking of the way people hurt each other. When she tells me these stories, of the things she lets men do to her, I want to tell her she is worth so much more. I do not understand why she cannot see that.

I wish we could stay this way forever. I can protect her, keep her safe. If she will let me. No matter how fast winter comes. We can stay warm under these bleachers together. I close my eyes and drift off to sleep...

When I awake, it is later, and I am alone. I do not know how I got here, why it is so cold, why I cannot move. I do not know these men who squawk like chickens when it rains. I do not know these people in white coats who feed me pills and mashed bland meals. I stare out of the window at the big black birds. I do not know why those big black birds do not fly away. The whole sky is open. They can go anywhere they want. But they just sit on those power lines. They do not even try.

CHAPTER THIRTEEN

"Get the fuck out of my house!"

Her cousin came at her from across the kitchen floor, a battering ram two-fisting empty bourbon bottles. Alex closed the door and turned the tumbler. Let Linda rain down blows and tire herself out.

Alex didn't recall going to bed after Tommy gave her a much-needed hug and Noah Lee's check, one thousand dollars that would be worth less than the paper it was printed on if Riley made good on his threat. Having stumbled out in the middle of the night like she had, Alex couldn't be sure if what followed had been another dream. She knew she'd taken a shower, washing her hair in the dark, ringing her damp tee and panties, draping them over the radiator, because she'd found the shirt and panties overcooking when she went to the bathroom this morning. Her face looked better, the swelling down. The discolored, yellowed bruises were easy to cover with concealer. Not that she had much time for makeup. She'd barely been able to arrange thoughts and put them in a cogent order when her cousin's shrill voice cut through the stillness, along with the heavy foot kicking the bottom of the door, ordering her out.

Alex got dressed in the same dirty jeans she'd been wearing since she got to town, sliding the hot crinkly tee over her head. She'd used the new white shirt she wore at dinner with Riley to mop up blood from the fight, tossing it from the speeding car somewhere along Route 17. She waited for the hammering to subside.

Her cousin was hunched over, mouth breathing. She had on an oversized men's *In Between Evolution* sweatshirt, a souvenir from a show they'd seen together at the Grapevine ten years ago, thick thighs poking out, mottled with cellulite, grim expression contorting her pug face. Tommy and Nick each took a side, trying to calm her down.

Alex stepped from the room with her things and Linda started toward her again. Alex met her head on, and her cousin backed up, still shrieking and swiping, but from behind the safety of Tommy.

When you grow up as close as they had, you can't erase histories, especially ones where the younger, prettier cousin kicked the crap of her hapless older one. Alex didn't remember what started that particular fight, only that it involved their mothers. It was summertime, the day hot, air weighted with ragweed and humidity. They had been walking through a vacant lot overgrown with high grass and abandoned appliances. Someone said the wrong thing at the wrong time. Something inside Alex snapped, and she took out years of frustration and hate, anger and loneliness, thrashing her cousin so viciously Linda needed sutures to stitch together part of her jaw.

Their relationship had endured worse fractures over the years, but in times like this, where someone wanted to thump her chest and talk smack, the knowledge of that beat-down served as friendly reminder to back the fuck off.

"Get out of my house! Bitch!"

Alex didn't say a word as she zipped her bomber. She caught Tommy's eye, conveyed appreciation, then pulled Nick along with a head tilt.

The bright morning sun sneered cruel in the aftermath, the still-wet street blanketed with fat maple leaves dislodged by the rain. Linda lumbered to the front steps, long enough to call Alex a cunt and slam the door, rattling the whole rickety porch.

When they got to the sidewalk, Nick saw Alex staring at the

ground beside her car. "What's wrong?"

"Someone slashed my tires."

Nick came around. Both curbside tires were carved in an upturned, evil grin. He glanced back at the apartment steps.

"Linda isn't doing anything to keep me here longer."

"Let's grab a coffee," he said. "I'll call my uncle. He's got spares at the garage."

Java the Hutt drew triple the crowd on weekends, overflow jamming the parking lot. Not even the railroad tie seats were available. They took their coffee to his truck. Which was just as well. It felt like the seasons had changed since she'd been asleep. Winter was here.

"You want to tell me what that was about at your cousin's?"

Alex did not feel like having this conversation.

"Can you talk to me? I'm trying—"

"I don't know! Okay? I guess she was trying to wake me up and I wouldn't open the door and she got pissed. Linda has issues. With me. About me. Can we talk about something else? Or how about nothing?"

"I'm trying to figure out what's going on with you."

"Why? Why do you care what's going on with me?"

"Because we're friends?"

"Is that what we are? I just met you last week. I don't remember being in class with you, Nick. Like, at all. Sorry to burst your high school fantasies, but I'm a mess. Look at me. I'm sitting in a fucking truck, at some roadside, hipster coffee stand with a guy I barely know who hauls crap for a living. My cousin threw me out and someone slashed my tires. I'm fucking broke. I probably fucked up my bartending job. I'm sick of flirting for two-dollar tips. I'm sick of selling pills. My prospects are shit. I'm running ragged in a town I swore I wouldn't be caught dead in trying to solve a crime that had fuckall to do with me."

"Where did you go after you left my apartment?"

Alex groaned. "What?"

"I stopped by your cousin's to check on you."

"When? Tommy didn't mention you stopped by."

"I did. That night, morning. Like one a.m. You'd already walled yourself up, were incapacitated, wouldn't answer the door, whatever. Tommy said let you be."

"Why were you at my cousin's at one in the morning?"

"I went down to those dive bars along the pier."

Alex returned an empty stare.

"The cops were at Sweetwater. There was an incident. A couple pieces of shit got their asses handed to them by the Uniondale rowing squad. The police had the parking lot roped off. Whole bar was outside talking about it. Apparently the Uniondale team stumbled upon a pair of druggies trying to rape a girl, and they fucked them up. Bad."

"Sucks for them." Alex had a hard time suppressing a smile.

"The girl got away. The junkies, not so much. One of them has an orbital fracture. From the rowing team stomping on his head. Probably lose the eye. The police found a shit-ton of drugs. The two scumbags actually confessed, so the crew team is off the hook. Cops are looking for the girl, though. Guess she ran off before they got there." Nick appealed sincerely. "I'm trying to help."

"I don't need your help."

"How do you think this ends? Even if you learn something about Kira that the cops couldn't, what then? Where do you go? Who do you tell? Have you even thought about that?"

Alex shrugged.

"Why won't you let me in?"

"Let you in?" Alex laughed. "We're not in some romantic comedy, Nick. There's no misunderstanding to overcome. No one is learning a lesson. And I don't need saving from some guy who lugs furniture in the back of his uncle's pickup truck."

"How about a married cop?"

"Fuck you."

"He was at Sweetwater. Your pal, Riley. Your ex, your whatever he is."

"You jealous?"

"Honestly? Yeah."

"What did you tell him?"

"You mean did I say I sent you down to the pier to score drugs, to the same bar where a girl narrowly escaped being sexually assaulted?"

"Don't screw around with me."

"I didn't give you up, if that's what you mean. It was too dark for the crew team to give the police an accurate description. Although I'm guessing that had more to do with how drunk everyone was. Riley doesn't know it was you. Enough shady shit happens at that bar. And you don't have to tell me you were there. I know you were. I can see the swelling around your eye and lip."

Alex snuck a peek out the window, searching for a stealth side view but she couldn't get a good look. To hell with it. She pulled down the visor. Christ, she looked like shit. She had a fat lip, and the hastily applied makeup only made the discoloration more pronounced. She slapped the visor shut.

"What do you want me to say?" Alex was surprised by how exhausted she sounded.

"You can start by telling me why solving Kira's disappearance is so important to you. And don't tell me it's a job."

"Jesus!"

"It's a simple question."

"I don't have an answer for you, okay? My life has been a mess since Parsons. Maybe I thought if I could find out what happened to Kira, I'd understand what happened to me. That good enough for you?" Alex put her head between her knees. "Fuck! Me!"

"I talked to them."

Alex threw herself back against the seat, staring at the ceiling. "Talked to who?"

"Kira's friends. While you were sleeping. For two days. I figured I should do something before you got yourself killed."

"Who did you talk to?"

"Meaghan Crouse."

"I talked to her already. Goth wannabe poser."

"She didn't mention talking to you."

"I didn't give her my name."

"I also tracked down Patty Hass, Trista White, and Jody Wood."

"You didn't have to do that."

"Wasn't that hard. Patty's in town. Trista and Jody both work in Rotterdam."

"What'd they say?"

"The same thing: Dan Brudzienski was head over heels in love with Kira Shanks. Like obsessive, stalker shit."

"That's what Meaghan told me." Alex paused, thinking. "I saw him the first night I got back to town. Came to my motel room, said my car lights were on, some bullshit story. Then I saw him later at the Fireside, the night you and Tommy got into it. I think he's following me."

"Why would Dan Brudzienski be following you?"

"Tommy said people around town believe Benny was put up to it."

"What? You think some high school kid ordered his special needs brother to kill Kira because if he couldn't have her, no one could? A little extreme, no? Lots of guys have crushes on girls in high school and don't—"

"Do anything about it?"

"I was going to say have them murdered."

"Can you call your uncle? See if he'll be able to fix the tires?"

"Already texted. Waiting for him to text back."

"I need to find a check-cashing place." Alex plucked her shirt, sniffed it. Even after her midnight laundry session, she still stank. "And I need to pick up some things."

"Like what?"

"A new pair of panties. The pretty lacy kind. That okay with you? I've been wearing the same pair for days. I'm getting sick of ringing them out in the sink."

"Okay, okay, got it."

"And I'd like to take a shower when I'm conscious."

"We'll cash your check, go to...the panty store...hit my place so you can take a shower. Then what?"

"What I should've done before now. Talk to Dan Brudzienski."

CHAPTER FOURTEEN

Alex expected to find a ramshackle farmhouse with bowed planks and duct-taped doors, dried-up fruitless fields, emaciated horses, a foreclosure sign hanging in a broken window. She'd seen Dan Brudzienski's truck, which didn't scream new or expensive or special in any way. She remembered Farm Aid as a kid, figured all farmers hardscrabbled to get by. Instead she found a grand estate resplendent on the hill, a magnificent homestead standing proud atop thriving farmland. Massive John Deere machinery, windrowers, and sicklebar headers sat at the ready, ripe crops in robust pastures prepared for the fall harvest. A drift of cows grazed in the lush green grass. Tall rows of corn stalks vanished over the horizon, and mighty oaks peppered the brae.

As Nick steered up the long driveway, Alex recognized this wasn't a residence that had been designed this way. Rather, it had been erected piecemeal, part and parcel, extensions and new wings added after the fact. The closer she got, the more she saw a Frankenstein house. The outline of modest brick quarters remained but the rest had clearly been augmented, like a low rider tricked out, gaudy and garish, with fifteen-inch rims and colors too bold. Not that it didn't still look nice—it was probably the nicest house Alex had ever seen in Reine—but there was a grotesque, monstrous element to the home as well, like its architects had the means to do whatever they wanted but lacked the aesthetic acumen to pull off the job tastefully. Colors didn't quite match; styles didn't quite gel, the top floor tacked on, giving the house a childish, tree-fort feel.

Alex hopped out of the truck, standing beside the open door.

Nick didn't move. "We're just going to go up and ring the bell?"

"That's the plan."

On the way over, Nick fretted endlessly, warning Alex about Dan's brother, Wren. "He's rattlesnake mean. Seen him at the Fireside a few times. One of these good ol' country boys. He sits on the tailgate, showing off his hunting rifle to the rocker chicks, always ready for a fight. You know he used to play college ball? Almost went pro. Until this shit with Benny brought him back home."

Showering, shopping, and finding somewhere to cash Noah Lee's check on a Sunday had chewed up a good chunk of Alex's day. Now late-afternoon skies threatened to swallow what little light remained. She didn't have the luxury of sweating a red-ass farmboy.

"Maybe we should come back tomorrow."

"What's he going to do? Shoot us for ringing the doorbell?"

"We don't even know if anyone is home."

Alex pointed at the truck in front of the bay, then at the house lights illuminating the bottom floor. "Someone is in there."

"And I don't think he'll be happy to see us."

"Why?" Alex glanced down at her new jeans and pristine white tee fresh from the pack. After a thirty-minute scalding shower, with actual shampoo and soap, Alex felt scrubbed clean. "We're not the cops. Besides last I checked, the cops were on the Brudzienskis' side." Or at least Riley was. "We have a few questions. No big deal."

"You can't go up to random people's houses uninvited."

"You never had a *Watchtower* shoved in your face? You can wait here if you're scared."

"No," Nick said, defiantly. "I'm coming."

The truck parked in front of the garage looked like the same one Alex had seen at the Fireside the other night. It's hard to tell with trucks. She knew these farmboys took a lot of pride in their four-wheel drive but to her the goddamn things all looked the same. When she rang the bell, the man who answered wasn't wearing a trucker's cap. Not being nighttime, Alex was able to get a better look at his face. This wasn't the same man who'd come to her motel. He was much smaller, younger, not nearly as imposing.

Maybe she had left her lights on that night. Her driver's side door only locked with a key, sure, but what if she'd left the passenger's side unlocked? What if some good-hearted stranger just happened to be passing by, taking the time out to spare her battery? Linda had been drunk at the Fireside when she ID'd Dan Brudzienski. What if this entire past week had been the byproduct of one big misunderstanding?

"Can I help you?" the man asked. Although boy was more like it. Baby-faced, wholesome, innocent, a pup.

"Dan? Dan Brudzienski?"

The boy checked with Nick, who stood off to the side pretending to be preoccupied with the topiary choices in the hedgerow.

"What's this about?"

"Kira Shanks." Alex decided to go with blunt and straightforward, which were powerful weapons when it came to disarming the intimidated. And Dan Brudzienski wasn't holding up under questioning.

Hearing Kira's name, Dan didn't get defensive or grow combatant, and he didn't seem besieged with guilt. His eyes only saddened.

"I'm writing a story for the newspaper," Alex added. "If you have a few minutes?"

Dan turned and headed through the spacious foyer. Alex and Nick followed down the long hallway, into a massive living room, which sported the same mismatched décor as the outside of the ranch, as if two teenage boys with inflated allowances had been given carte blanch to decorate their own really big playhouse. A giant flat-screen television plastered the facing wall, hunting rifles mounted in the glass cabinet beside it. Two massive reclining leather chairs with cup holders sat inches from the TV. PlayStation controllers snaked from the chairs to a console on the floor. Surround-sound speakers angled down from the ceiling. Like an IMAX movie theater. Empty pizza boxes and crumpled two-liter Pepsi bottles scattered about. There was even a pair of life-size Fathead decals that had been slapped up, one of Ben Roethlisberger, the other a player Alex didn't recognize. She only recognized the Pittsburgh quarterback because they broadcast the games in the bar on Sundays.

Alex pointed at the decal on the wall. "Steelers fan?"

"My brother, Wren."

"Your brother home?" Nick asked.

"No. He coaches football. They have an away game this weekend. You wanted to talk about Kira?"

"I'm a reporter," Alex said. "The *Codornices*. We're doing a feature on the seven-year anniversary of her disappearance. You guys were friends?"

Dan waited, processing and still confused, like this didn't quite add up—and he was right, because it didn't.

"Can I get some water?" Nick asked.

Dan headed for the kitchen. Alex trailed. Nick on her heels, miming with his brows, flapping his arms, her shrugging response saying, *Give me a break. I'm new at this!*

Dan reached into the shiny chrome fridge. Dull pots and pans coated in thick layers of dust hung on an unused rack. Handing out the water, Dan noticed Alex staring at them.

"We don't cook much since our parents died."

"I'm sorry," Alex said.

Dan shrugged. "They made sure we were taken care of. Financially. Life insurance." He pointed out the window, around the boundless quarters. "Farm was falling apart. We used the insurance money to buy more plows, more tractors, hire more workers, built a silo to store the corn. Our mom had been fighting the cancer for a while. After Ben—I mean, after everything that happened, I think she just gave up."

"How'd your father die?" Alex asked. "If you don't mind me asking." She added that last obligatory part, which is what people do when they inquire about touchy subjects. How much you paid for a house. How much money you make at a job. How so and so died. If you don't mind me asking. Same thing as asking if you can ask a question.

"Heart attack," Dan said. "Why aren't you writing anything down?"

"Huh?"

"You said you're a reporter. But you're not writing anything down."

"Because we're not talking about Kira, are we? I'm getting to know you. Trying not to bulldoze you with endless questions right off the bat."

"Sorry," Dan said, checking again with Nick, who since asking for the water had returned to silent observer. "Didn't mean to—I don't talk about—her name doesn't come up much."

Alex patted her pockets, turning to Nick. "I think I left my notepad in the truck." She hoped he knew enough to play along. "Can you get it for me?" She got the impression Dan might be more willing to talk if she were asking these questions alone.

Nick hopped to it with a two-finger salute.

"Were you and Kira close?"

"I had a pretty wicked crush on her. Who didn't? Not sure she noticed. We hung out early on, but always in large groups. She ran with a different crowd. Faster, wilder kids. I was pretty focused on football in those days. Trying hard to get a scholarship like Wren. The farm didn't bring in enough money to pay for college."

"Didn't work out? Playing ball?"

"I didn't have the drive my brother did. Didn't love the game, I guess."

"What do you do now?"

"Not much." He laughed but it wasn't a joyful sound. "Sometimes I feel like an eighty-year-old man. I can go days without leaving this house. Since we hired the extra help, I don't do much around the farm besides shooting the occasional jackrabbit. I don't even do that right. I don't like guns."

"It's just you and Wren?"

He nodded. "He was selected in the draft. Wren. Not drafted but invited. To training camp. The Browns. Wide receiver. Never signed though. He was great. A lot better than me. When they died, he came back to run things."

"Where'd you say he was?"

"He's an assistant coach at North Valley State. Division II. They had a game yesterday down in Virginia. I'm sorry. What's this got to do with Kira?"

Alex leaned back on her heels. She had nothing to sweat with this boy. He was as menacing as a field mouse. No way he'd been involved in what happened to Kira, but as long as she was here, she might as well see what he knew. Anything he told her about Kira's friends would be more than what she had now. "This feature article I'm writing for the paper, it's informal. We want to know about the real Kira. Celebrate her life, not dwell on the tragedy." Alex sometimes surprised herself with how well she could slip into the role of someone else. She liked this, playing the part of a normal, well-adjusted person.

Dan was still tough to read, though. He didn't act like he had anything to hide. But his pain was profound. A deep-seated sorrow undermined attempts to smile and pretend everything was okay.

"Do you see your brother?"

"Of course. We live together."

"I meant Benny."

Dan's eyes grew mean, quiet indignation seething behind them. "We don't think of him as a brother. And we don't say his name. He was a mistake, an aberration. What he did...no, we don't talk about him. He's dead to us."

"You think he did it?"

"Of course he did it! Everyone knows he did it. They found his blood and—"

"Couldn't find your notebook," Nick said, reentering the kitchen, stopping short when he saw Dan's red face and clenched fists.

Alex motioned to stay calm.

"What is this really about? You aren't writing anything down."

Alex turned to Nick. "Did you find my recorder?"

"No. Sorry."

"You asked him to get your notepad. You didn't say anything about a recorder."

"That's what I meant. My notepad."

"Bullshit. You said notepad. You're lying."

"I'm not lying. Did you find my notepad?"

"Couldn't find that either."

"What reporter doesn't have a notepad?" Dan looked over her clothes, jeans and plain white tee, jangle bracelets on her left arm, biomech tattoo peeking out the sleeve on her right. "You don't look like a reporter." He twitched unstable, accelerating to unhinged in less time than it took to sneeze. "You're a liar!"

"Relax. The *Codornices* is a college paper. Uniondale. Look it up on the internet. Just have a few more questions."

"I don't want to answer them. You guys have to go."

"Do you know they're trying to move Benny down to Jacob's Island?"

"I told you. We don't talk about him! He's not our brother. Benny is a fucking retard rapist murderer. He's not a Brudzienski, okay? Now go! I'm serious. Or I'll call the fucking cops. I'll call Wren. Trust me, you don't want to be here when Wren gets home."

Nick tugged at Alex's sleeve. "Come on. We should get to class."

Dan was breathing heavy, worked up, overlooking minor details like no one goes to class on Sunday.

Alex decided Nick was right. Time to cut bait. They backtracked through the living room, into the hall, Dan Brudzienski standing there, watching, smoldering, a tiny time bomb ticking, fuse lit and ready to ignite.

They were almost to the front door when they heard the rumbling truck engine grind to a halt. Nick had already twisted the knob. Alex recognized the big man with the canvas sack bulling up the walkway in the sun-bleached trucker's cap. He was the same man who had knocked on her door at the Royal Motel, the same man she'd seen later at the Fireside. And he did not look happy to see her.

CHAPTER FIFTEEN

Wren dropped the big bag of football equipment he'd been shouldering, helmets spilling out the top, severed heads tumbling down the steps. He charged, backing up Alex and Nick inside the house.

"I thought you were in Virginia till tonight?" Dan said.

"Wanted to get an early start, get out ahead of the storm." Wren eyed Alex. "What's she doing here?"

"She's a reporter for some paper."

"The fuck she is."

Alex took a step toward the door, trying to slip around him, but Wren blocked her path and kicked the door shut with his muddy boot.

"That's what she told me," Dan said.

"*That's what she told me*," Wren sang back. "What the fuck is wrong with you? Sometimes I think you're as dumb as that retard upstate." Wren turned to face Alex. "That's who you're here about, right? The retard?"

"I have a few questions, yes."

"I bet you do. I've heard all about your questions. Bugging everyone to get a story that isn't there."

"I thought you said she wasn't a reporter?"

"She's not. That's Alex Salerno." He studied his little brother, searching for recognition that didn't come. "Five years before your little girlfriend disappeared—"

"She wasn't my girlfriend—"

"There was this sicko up by the lake. Kenneth Parsons. Abducted girls. Typical candy-in-a-van pervert shit. But good looking, blond hair, blue eyes, had money. Didn't take much to lure them back to his castle on the water. He targeted the needy ones desperate for attention. No daddies." A sneer cracked his lips. "He did...things...to them. When he was done, he'd bury them in his backyard. Except one of them got away."

"Oh, yeah, I remember that," Dan said. "This is the girl that got away?"

"This is the girl who got away."

Nick grabbed Alex's hand. "This was a mistake."

"Yeah. It was," Wren said. "You don't barge into people's houses—"

"We didn't barge in." Alex snatched her hand back. "Your brother invited us in."

"When you told me you were a reporter—"

"What difference does that make? You don't talk about that shit. Didn't I tell you to keep your mouth shut?"

Dan kicked at the rug, head hung, every bit the baby brother.

"What 'shit' would that be exactly?" Alex said.

"None of your fucking business."

"He means our brother, Benny."

Wren slapped him, a quick, open-palmed snake strike, hard enough to leave a welt on Dan's cheek. "What did I tell you about that? He ain't our brother. You don't say his name in this house. He's the state's problem. Mom and Dad didn't die and leave us this place so we could pay for that fat slob to get fed through a tube, you hear me? That money is for us. This farm. *Our* future. Got it?"

Dan rubbed the side of his face, bobbing his head.

Wren cupped his ear, leaning in. "What's that?"

"I said I got it."

"We're leaving," Alex said.

Wren planted his feet, widening his stance, a football move. He had a good seven inches on her, and Alex wasn't short by any stretch. Nick tried to wedge between them but the broad-shouldered Wren had little trouble boxing him out. Nick tried to push back, but if Tommy manhandled him, she hated to see what a guy like Wren could do.

"What's the hurry?" Wren said. "You just got here. You have an appointment to harass someone else?"

"I'm not harassing anyone."

"What do you call this?"

"You're the one following me. You came to my motel room. I saw you at the Fireside—"

"I'm not following you or anyone else, girlie. I happened to be meeting with your teenage fantasy, Riley, about this Benny bullshit the night you showed up. Thought I'd pay a visit, meet the infamous Alex Salerno, see why you were sniffing around after you got done throwing yourself at him. Fucking home-wrecker. You know he has a daughter?"

"Fuck you."

"Can everyone calm down?" Nick said.

"Fuck me? You're in my house, bitch." He reached around Nick, poking Alex in the bony part of her sternum. "Yeah, I know all about you, Alex Salerno. Whole town knows about you. But your story's played out. You don't matter anymore. Go down to the Jackal's Den. Suck off someone for blow, whatever losers like you do. But stay away from me and my family. You hear? Or maybe you want me to call Riley, huh?"

Alex pretended the insult didn't sting and that last part didn't concern her. Her silence betrayed the hurt.

"Didn't think so." He turned to his brother. "Get me a beer."

"But I—"

"I said get me a beer. This is my house. Mom and Dad left it to *me*. Not you. Me. I let you stay here, rent-free, no job—you don't do shit on the farm—I buy all the food, pay all the bills. Least you can do is get me a goddamn beer when I ask for it."

Dan slinked off toward the kitchen.

"And not the piss water in the fridge either. That's for you and your little friends. Get me a bottle of stout, from the basement."

When Dan was out of earshot, Wren stepped to Alex and Nick, who still hadn't left her side. Even banded together the two of them didn't constitute half of Wren Brudzienski. "The Galloway Institute of Living pays for that retard up north. And it's going to stay that way. I am not shelling out good money— *my* money—to keep that brain-dead potato breathing. And I sure as shit am not bringing him here."

"I don't understand why—"

"It's not your job to understand." He didn't even consider Nick, clocking Alex. "This is your last warning. I hear any more bullshit about you nosing around, asking about Kira Shanks, I swear to God, I won't call your make-believe cop boyfriend. I will gut you like a fish, nail you to the barn wall, and dry you out like jerky. We clear? Now get the fuck out of my house."

A long bank of storm clouds encroached from the northwest, ushering winter's silvery chill on its wings. Nick drove, apprehensive to broach what Wren Brudzienski had said. Alex wasn't a delicate flower. She considered herself more a tough-to-kill weed. She wasn't like Denise. She didn't sit in showers, sobbing with all her clothes on. And she wasn't going to let some 'roided-up jackhole push her around. Denise never would've survived that bunker. Denise fell apart every time the lights went out, the gas got shut off, rent was overdue; her mother's entire life had been a never-ending slew of dire straits and epic meltdowns.

When Alex looked over at Nick, he was reading a text on his phone. "My uncle towed your car to the shop. Won't be able to get you new tires until tomorrow. Guess you're stuck with me till then."

"How much is that going to run me?" Two thousand bucks wasn't going to last long if she had to fork out for new radials.

"Don't worry about it."

A hard rain riveted the windshield. Strong gusts bent boughs, snapping twigs and limbs, shredding remnants of maple leaves.

"Back to my place?" Nick said. "Hole up till your car is ready? We can watch movies or something."

"Can we snuggle too? Maybe make hot cocoa? Do you have a cat I can pet? Maybe an oversized fluffy sweater I can wear?" Alex batted lashes. "Ooh, something that smells like you?"

"What do you want to do? Go back to your cousin's?"

"I want to check out the Idlewild again."

"You're kidding, right? You heard what Wren said."

"Like I give a shit what Wren Brudzienski says."

"You see the hunting rifles on the wall?"

"If you're too chickenshit, drop me off."

Nick had the wipers on high but nothing helped. "Come on, Alex. It's pissing rain. What do you think you'll find at the Idlewild? I talked to all of Kira's friends. All fingers pointed at Dan Brudzienski. You saw that kid. He isn't issuing any code reds. Wren's the one you need to be worried about."

"Right, but not for the reasons you think." She'd assumed that Riley and Wren were fighting the same fight, to exonerate Benny. She now saw they weren't. "Wren doesn't care if Benny is charged or found guilty." She didn't know Riley's real motivation in this. But Wren had tipped his hand. He was worried about the money, being on the hook for Benny's continued care. Cold, hard cash.

"He's guilty. They found his fucking…jizz…at the motel."

"Wren wants to keep his brother locked up in Galloway because then the state foots the bill. Charges result in a trial, a trial a guilty verdict, then Benny goes to Jacob's Island."

"So? Why would Wren all of a sudden have to pay? Jacob's Island is another state-run facility. Galloway. Jacob's Island. What difference does it make?"

"The Brudzienskis have money now. They didn't when Benny was sent away. If Benny is found guilty, the family could be liable for civil suits. That money—life insurance, will, trusts, whatever—becomes fair game. You think Wren wants to risk getting tossed from that ivory tower he's built?"

"How do you know that?"

"Because that's how the law works?"

"No, I mean, how do you *know* that?"

"I read?"

"What's this got to do with Kira Shanks?"

"Nothing. Absolutely fucking nothing. That's my point."

"You are one of the most confusing girls I've ever met."

"I'm twenty-nine years old, Nick. I'm not a girl."

"Why are you doing this? You don't have a horse in this race. You are putting yourself in serious danger—"

"Do you believe in serendipity?"

"Serenwhat?"

"It means that sometimes God, the Universe, whatever you want to call it, delivers you to the place you are supposed to be."

"Now who sounds like a romantic comedy?"

"I saw something when I looked in Benny Brudzienski's eyes."

"That's what this is about? The vacant gaze of a vegetable?"

"He's not a vegetable."

"Then he's faking it."

The downpour relentless, brackish waters gurgled out storm grates, rushing rivers carrying away detritus and fallen twigs. Nick used his hand to wipe the condensation, peeking out the base of the windshield. "I can't see a fucking thing."

"I know what I'm supposed to do. I know why I came back." She pointed straight ahead. "Idlewild."

"Oh come on—"

"Idlewild."

That was Alex's last word on the subject.

By the time they got to the motel, the worst of the squall had passed, but the rain still fell dark and slow.

Nick punched it in park. "What now? Please tell me you don't want to see the room where it happened? Seven years later, I'm pretty sure they've cleaned it by now."

Alex hopped down, mud slopping beneath her Chucks. She headed around back, Nick trailing, muttering. Half the motel was under renovation. Or it had been. Efforts to resurrect the dump had been abandoned a while ago. Empty paint cans rusted in the weeds. A rotting ladder lay splintered on its side. Blue tarps rippled along the edge of the property, unfurled flags flapping on unpatriotic seas. Big black trash bags were piled beside waterlogged, stained mattresses propped against the wall, bellies sagging under the weight of a thousand rainstorms. Alex stared into the forest, imagining all the places a body could hide.

"What are you two doing back here?"

A stout, middle-age woman stood beneath an umbrella, smoking a long, skinny cigarette. Alex could see her pores, wide as rice grains, from ten feet away.

"You can't be back here. This is private property. I'm going to call the cops."

"We're looking for—"

"Scrap metal to sell. I know. All the copper got stripped long time ago. There's nothin' left to steal. Whole motel ain't worth squat. Now get."

Alex shielded her eyes from the rain. "We're not stealing anything. I'm looking for Cole Denning. I heard he works here."

The old woman drew on her Virginia Slim, scowl fading. After a moment, she waved for them to follow.

Inside the tiny check-in office, the old woman handed them each a towel, warn so thin they might as well have been drying off with cheesecloths.

When they were done, the old woman held out her hand, snatching back the rags as though they were prized possessions. The lobby was choked with stale cigarette smoke and the burnt singe of vending machine corn nuts, assorted junk foods that came in single-serving bags. A small TV, the ancient kind with aluminum-foil rabbit ears, played behind the counter, which was done up like the inside of an RV, cheap wood paneling culled straight from the seventies.

"I'm Alex." She offered a hand, which the old woman accepted, begrudgingly.

"Evie Shuman. Motel used to belong to my husband, John. He's dead. Now it's mine. Until they tear it down. Fuckin' gummint wants to build a freeway. Least they can do is pay me what the land's worth. You said you was a friend of Cole's?"

"Not exactly."

"What you want with 'im then? He owe you money?"

"This isn't about money. Just want to talk to him."

"He don't work here no more. Fired him last week." Evie Shuman's expression washed empathetic, an odd emotion for a woman so hardboiled. "Didn't give me no choice. I knew he drank on the job. I didn't care about a few beers. He was good at fixin' stuff. Not as good as the last guy I had, but no one was. That big dumb retard could jigger PVC flappers like nobody's business. Didn't have to pay him nothin' neither. Give him a few treats, settle up with his dad, work it out in trade. Great arrangement. Till he went and mucked it all up."

"Are you talking about Benny Brudzienski?"

Evie Shuman's face coiled tight as a copperhead. "What you asking about Cole and Benny for? Why you snoopin' 'round my property?"

"I, um…"

"Because," Nick said, picking up the ball, "we are reporters for Uniondale University. We are writing a story on eminent domain."

"How the government seizes valuable property," Alex added, grateful to follow Nick's lead. "How they can make you sell but don't have to give you what it's worth."

"Goddamn right. Takin' advantage of people is what they do." Evie Shuman waited. "What the hell you want to talk to Cole for?"

"The paper doesn't have the most up-to-date resources," Nick said. "We had Cole and Benny listed as working here."

If the old woman had taken a few moments to think about it,

she would've asked why a school newspaper considered two handymen contacts, but she was too fired up about the government stealing her land.

"They think they can do any goddamn thing they please. Vultures. I know my rights. I'm gonna lawyer up."

"Do you know where we can find Cole?" Alex asked. "Since our editor told us to talk to him."

"Don't know what anyone would want to talk to him for. Damn fool has water on the brain. I had to fire him. Showed up here Friday, could barely stand."

"You have an address?"

"Got one of those trailers by the turnpike." Evie Shuman thumbed out the window. "He's at the bar most the time though. Man seems intent drinking hisself to death."

"Any bar in particular?"

"Try the ones down by the river."

"What was wrong with Benny?" Alex said.

"What you mean what's wrong with Benny? He's a retard."

"You said he was really good at fixing things, and if he worked here, he must've been able to follow instructions. I'm just wondering what his actual diagnosis was?"

"How the hell should I know? Ask Lawson."

"Lawson?"

"His doctor. What's this got to do with that imminent domain you was talkin' about?"

"Thanks. I think that's enough for now." Alex backhanded Nick's shoulder, their cue to leave.

"Don't you want some documentation or somethin'?" Evie started to walk into an adjacent closet. "I got all the letters they sent."

"We have everything we need," Alex said with a smile.

CHAPTER SIXTEEN

The nighttime changeover at Galloway usually went off without a hitch. Part of the reason Tracy Karas liked the late shift so much, the stillness. During the day, patients got riled up. Especially during thunderstorms. They'd wail and thrash in their seats, fighting against the restraints. Then you'd have to sedate them. Nighttime, though, was a different story. The institute aggressively applied phototherapy, using light to combat sleep disorders, implementing phase advances, delays. Doctors at Galloway believed a good night's sleep was the first line of defense against neuroses. Worked out well for Tracy. By the time she got there, natural circadian rhythms had kicked in, all fight drained out. Like baby lambs. Tracy was taking abnormal psyche classes at North State. Part-time, one class a semester, which was all she could afford. But she'd been steady about it, consistent. That's the key to anything in life. Consistency and technique. She'd already earned her associate's this way, and in another three, four years, she'd have her bachelor's. Then she'd apply for a job far from this place.

Tonight when she slid her security card, Dontrelle, the exballer with the bum knee, hopped up, happy to see her, a little *too* happy, waving both arms from the observation desk.

"Enjoy your weekend?" she said.

"Guess who I caught running around causing trouble while you was gone?"

Tracy set down her reusable mesh bag, which contained her e-reader, textbooks, and tonight's special: week-old meatloaf.

Tasted like brick and poverty. She wasn't in the mood for riddles or progress reports on psychopaths. Plus, Dontrelle was full of shit. Most of these men were strapped in twenty-four seven. No one was running anywhere.

Tracy hoisted a dense textbook out of her bag, so thick it made *Infinite Jest* look like a pamphlet. "I have a lot of studying—"

"Benny Brudzienski."

Benny Brudzienski didn't have to be restrained. Because he couldn't move. He had to be rolled over hourly to rotate bedsores. The large man had been this way so long, he'd loss most of his muscle mass. Anytime you sat him upright in a chair, he resembled Jell-O devoid of a mold, absorbing into the contour.

"I'm sure."

"Honest Injun." Dontrelle raised his hand, and grabbed Tracy by the sleeve, tugging her toward the window. "Put him there. Come back later." Dontrelle pointed five feet away. "He here."

Tracy wrinkled her nose. Dontrelle always smelled like weed. She didn't care if he was getting high on the job—she wasn't his boss—but he had to be blitzed out of his skull if he thought Benny Brudzienski had moved.

"Like De Niro shit," Dontrelle said. "Y'know, that movie where all the patients wake up at once? Was on TV the other night. I forget the name."

"*Awakenings.*"

"No, I don't think that's it."

Tracy walked across the floor, to Benny Brudzienski's room. She peered through the little window in the door. Dontrelle came up behind her.

"And I wasn't high," he said. "I mean *that* high."

Tracy stared inside Benny's room. Moonlight shone through the window, brightening his blank, doughy face. She didn't like looking at him. He slept with his eyes open. Freaked her out. Of course she never unlocked the door to check to see if he was actually sleeping. For all she knew, he could be awake the whole time.

BENNY BRUDZIENSKI

I have not been cleaning the football fields, or doing any of my other jobs in town. I have been staying at the farm, even though I am not wanted. Dad will not let me help. They could use my help because money has been a problem since Wren came home and Mom got sicker. Mom does not get out of the bed much these days.

Wren cannot keep playing football because they are not paying him to play football anymore. I hear them fighting in the kitchen when I come home. I am surprised to see Wren because he usually does not come home during the season. Dad and Wren are yelling. Mom is there too but she is not talking. I sit on the stairs and listen. I do not mean to spy. No one notices me half the time, no matter how big I am. So maybe I am not doing anything wrong after all.

The school said Wren can keep playing but they cannot pay him because they have to use the money for new players. Dad says he will find a way to pay the school. Wren says he cannot afford to do that. Wren is right. We have a big farm but it does not bring in the money we need. I overhear Dad talking to men from the bank. They want to buy the land. Dad says it belongs to the family. Wren says he will help out. I want to help too. But they do not let me. They do not trust me to do a good job. I wish they did. I am still ox-strong. I can lift and move things around the farm as good as any machine.

Later I try to tell Dad this when he is alone in the kitchen, drinking from his special bottle, but the words do not come, and every time I try the sounds get jumbled in my throat. They stumble over my tongue and spill out in grumbles and moans. He says, "Not now, Benny. Not now." I want to tell him that Wren should go back to school and I should stop working for men like Mr. Supinski and Mr. Miano because they do not pay what I am worth. Let me help the family. Our family, our farm. I can see Dad wants to be left alone, I should leave him alone, but I want him to know I can help out too. He pays men to do the same things I can do for free. I cannot drive tractors or plows but I can lift heavy things, grain and feed, like I used to lift those pieces of firewood, back when Dad and Mom were proud of me. I do not mean to make Dad angry. It is my fault when he balls his fist and punches the side of my head. I am hard to move. He wants me to leave. He does not punch me hard.

I see the way the men punch the cows when they have to get them down. It is not out of anger but necessity. It does not hurt. Even when Dad does it again. I will stand here until he hears me. But I am not talking. I am hoping he will understand my thoughts. I am his first-born boy. That must mean something. I am still his son. When I try to hug him, he pushes me away. When I come back he hits me harder. This time he plants his foot and drives his fist deep up into my gut. He punches the side of my head like those men punching steer. It is not his fault. It is the bottle. I know what is in there. I have smelled it on his breath, sour and rotten. I have smelled it on Wren's breath, and on Mrs. Shuman's breath, even Kira's. People drink it to not feel pain, but it seems to make them hurt more. It can make people mean too. That is why Dad is doing this. Pushing me away, calling me names, hitting me. He is a good man. He loves his family and wants to provide for them. He keeps pushing, and I keep putting up my hands. I try to wrap my arms around him. I want to tell him it will be okay because he is crying the whole time he is hitting me and I do not want to see him hurting. I open my mouth to speak but the harder I try the louder I moan. This makes him wind up and hit me harder. It is okay, Dad, I say in my brain. You can hit me. I cannot feel anything. Even when my legs buckle and I fall to the ground, I keep trying to speak, tell him it is okay.

"Why did you have to born?" Dad says. "Why couldn't you be like other boys?" He is crying so hard he barely gets these last words out, and for once we are the same.

The next day I look at my big, swollen face in the mirror, and the telephone rings. I hear Dad whispering over the line. He is upset about more than Wren and football and me stuttering. Sick. Cancer. Hospital costs. I understand Mom is dying. The white skin, the dark circles, the sadness when she pats me on the head. Everything is changing, like the seasons switching over. The drafty old house gets colder like the house can feel it too. She is leaving us, and there is nothing we can do.

I hear Dad talk about selling the farm to those men. I have never heard Mom raise her voice, but she does tonight. She makes Dad promise he will not sell. She says the land is for the boys, Dan, Wren, and Ben. It has been a long time since anyone has called me Ben. Back when they thought I was a regular boy, they called me Ben. When they discovered I was broken, I became Benny.

I refuse to go to work. I will let not Dad touch me or put me in the truck and bring me to the rail yard. I do not peddle my bicycle to the football field anymore. I stay in my room and wail when anyone comes near me. Dad thinks it is because he hit me, but I do not blame him for that. When he was finished the other night, he knelt beside me to help me up and was crying so hard. He let me hug him and he hugged me back. He kept saying, "I'm sorry, Benny. I'm sorry." I was not angry then. I am not angry now.

I watch the men out in the drying fields. There are less of them, thinning out like the dying herd. I understand why Dad does not let me help around the farm. Seeing me out there reminds him of his failure, so they rent me out for pennies, let me do the grunt work of strangers so they do not have to look at me. This is why I am upset. But I cannot tell anyone this. The frustration eats away at my insides. The days pass this way. Wren and Dad fight because of football and school. Dan is at class with Kira, and I miss her. I take the pictures she gave me, the poems I cannot read, and make a book. Mom does not look well. I stay in my room, close my eyes, and hope to make these problems go away.

The first snowfall comes early, around Thanksgiving. Wren does not go back to school. He moves into his old room. I do not leave mine. After a while, no one remembers I am there.

When the end comes, it comes fast. They take her away.

Dad used to say I could crush the life out of a cow. I never knew if that was true. I never thought of trying. But sometimes, on these dark days, I think about going down to the killing fields to try. I want to crush the life out of something to see if I can.

CHAPTER SEVENTEEN

Nick brought Alex to get her car in the morning. They'd spent the previous night searching for Cole Denning, scouring the sleazy bars along the waterfront, staking out his mobile home. They'd deliberately avoided Sweetwater. The search proved exhausting, disheartening, leaving a thousand unanswered questions whirling around Alex's mixed-up mind.

"What are you going to do?" Nick asked, handing her the keys he'd retrieved from inside the garage, where Uncle Jimmy barked about a delayed shipment into an old-fashioned landline.

"What was the name of that doctor Evie Shuman mentioned at the motel?"

"Why do you want to talk to Benny Brudzienski's doctor?"

"Lawson," Alex said, answering herself.

"Even if you can hunt him down—even if he is still in town—no doctor is going to talk to you. You know that, right? Not without the family's approval. Doctor/patient confidentiality."

In the yard, hulls and casings peeled off machinery like damp matchbook covers. Shredded tires stacked high in a pyre, awaiting the flame.

"Don't take this the wrong way," Nick said, slipping a house key off his ring. "But you look like shit. Kick back at my place. Watch some mindless TV. I'll be back later this afternoon. If you want we can go down to the narrows together, pick up where we left off, hunt down Cole, all right?"

A trash barge floated by, big white birds dive-bombing breakfast.

"Promise me you won't go looking for Cole on your own."

"I can take care of myself. It was two on one last time. That won't happen again."

"Just promise me. Please."

"Fine," Alex said, snatching the key.

Back at Nick's place, she tried to unwind, let her brain go limp. She knew he was right. She *was* worn down, torn apart. Even after Nick gave up his bed last night and took the couch, she hadn't slept well, the night too cold, apartment too hot. She flipped, flopped. The gray-scape clawed behind her eyelids, calling her back to hell.

Curled beneath the comforter, Alex flicked on the television, hoping to catch an episode of *Law & Order* because nothing killed the hours faster. He only had basic cable. Even with the TV off and overcast skies, it was still too damn bright.

Alex snatched her phone and did a quick search of every doctor in the area named Lawson. A long shot and no doubt waste of time. Except that she hit on a Dr. John Lawson in Reine right away. Just the one. Called the number. Disconnected. Scrolling pages, she learned the private practice had closed years ago, the doctor retired, but she got his home address. Stratford Road. Up in Schenectady.

Alex hated that city almost as much as she did Reine. Schenectady was where her mother grew up, making it the place where everything started to go wrong. She thought about calling first but decided she'd have better luck in person. She didn't want to confuse the old guy or have to shout. Subtracting the practice's inception to its closure, Lawson had to be pushing eighty by now.

As Alex shifted the Civic in gear, she felt that creeping sensation return, like someone was watching her. When she turned around she found the same banks of passenger-less cars, pulled along the curb. A mailman pushed a cart, cruising the block in shorts and high socks despite the frigid temperature. She tried to shake off the creeping malaise. Like with Benny Brudzienski's haunting gaze, she had a tough time.

The drive from Reine to Schenectady was a short trip, fewer than thirty miles. Denise had dragged her there plenty when she was a kid, back when her mother still had family in the area willing to house them for a night, relatives dumb enough to loan Denise money they'd never see again. Alex couldn't recollect the names of these people, second cousins, distant aunts, gray-faced, scraggily strangers she wouldn't recognize if she passed them on the street. What she remembered most were the expressions of disgust when they opened the door, the disdain her mother's mere presence invited.

Less than thirty miles took more than sixty minutes. Morning traffic trudged, everything damp, dreary, drawn out. Alex could do nothing to pass the time except smoke and think about all the bad decisions she'd made in her life. She kept checking the rearview, waiting for headlights to rise up like the night Tommy fetched her from the insane asylum. She reassured herself that all the monsters were locked up. None roamed free. But each cigarette only augmented the lunacy.

The doctor lived in a part of Schenectady called The Plot, one of the oldest and most desirable sections in the city. The name derived from the early 1900s, when General Electric designed subdivisions for its executives to live in. There weren't liquor stores on every corner, no hit-and-run vigils with flowers, candles, balloons tied to mangy teddy bears missing an eye. Just quiet streets with strategically placed trees concealing two-car garages and three-story houses. This was a part of town Denise never had reason to be in.

Alex sat in her car. No one peeled curtains. No nosy housewives peeked out blinds wondering what the tatted girl in the crappy car was doing in their cozy community. But she still felt self-conscious.

Alex ground out her smoke in the ashtray. Normally she'd flick the butt in the street but the neighborhood was so pristine, with its fenced-off plots of green grass, ornate flowerbeds, and unique mailboxes, she didn't want to sully the illusion.

Dr. John Lawson answered the door. Slight and frail, he might've been closer to ninety than eighty. But his face was kind, warm, and welcoming. Unlike when she was dealing with Evie Shuman, or anyone else back in Reine, Alex experienced no hostility or aggression; therefore, she saw no reason to lie.

"I was hoping to speak with you about Benny Brudzienski." Even after Alex acknowledged doctor/patient confidentiality, the doctor brushed aside any such concerns, inviting her inside.

"I'm not practicing medicine anymore," Dr. Lawson said, shuffling to the kitchen. "It's been a long time since I was the Brudzienskis' family doctor. After everything that happened, I'm not sure it would matter. Can I offer you some coffee? Tea?"

"Coffee would be great. Thank you."

Lawson told her to sit down at the breakfast nook while he poured a cup from a pot already made. The house was immaculate, organized, and homey. The only thing out of place: a newspaper on the table that the doctor had been reading when she showed up, pair of glasses upended atop the world news.

"My wife passed away three years ago," the doctor said, bringing Alex a mug, along with a tiny spout of half-and-half and bowl of sugar with miniature spoon.

"I'm sorry," Alex said, because that's what you say when someone tells you their wife has died and they live alone, waiting for their own end to come.

But he dismissed those concerns, too. "Been a long time." He slowly creaked into the seat opposite her, a bleached-white wooden chair with pastel cushions tied around the back. The sort of accouterment only an old person would have. No one under seventy adds pastel cushions to their kitchen chairs.

"Now what can I do for you?"

"What can you tell me about Benny?"

Dr. Lawson shook his head, pensive and heavy-hearted. "That boy didn't have it easy. Although I suppose he's not a boy anymore."

"Do you think he did it?" Alex was surprised how fast she jumped in, got right to what she wanted to know. She hadn't explained why she needed to know any of this. She offered no cover story, no con about being a reporter. The doctor didn't seem to notice. Or care.

"Does it matter what I think?" His eyes crinkled like onion-skin when he spoke. The doctor sipped his black coffee.

"What was wrong with Benny? I mean then more than now."

"His technical diagnosis?"

Alex nodded.

"In layman's terms, Benny has a form of degenerative retardation. Medically speaking it's a type of aphasia."

"Aphasia?"

"The symptoms are similar to a stroke victim."

"Benny had a stroke?"

"No. The symptoms are similar because of a cerebral vascular injury or impairment. It's hard to say when that damage occurred or how serious that original injury was, whether it was one incident, or a series of aberrations that grew worse over time. A bad fall can trigger it. Blow to the head. More than likely it started in utero or something went wrong during incubation. Benny is much older than his two brothers. He began life a normal boy, so the reaction was slow to evolve, or at least his handicap wasn't as evident."

"How long were you the family doctor?"

"Can I get you something to eat?" Dr. Lawson said, pulling himself up before she could answer.

"I'm okay—"

But the doctor was already rummaging cupboards. "Please. It gives me an excuse to cook. I don't get much company, and I like to have prepared oats on hand." Alex appreciated he didn't say anything corny like she needed to keep up her strength, or hurtful like she looked too skinny. He pulled down a giant canister of stone oatmeal. It was brutal watching him crane for shelves and bend for pots. Alex would've done it for him but didn't want to seem rude. When she got to be his age, she wouldn't want someone implying she was helpless and always offering to do mundane chores for her. It was insulting. Then again, she was lousy with social graces.

The doctor measured a couple cups, painfully slow. He ran the pot under the faucet with shaky, liver-spotted hands, before setting it on the burner and creaking back to the table. She waited for him to ask what they were talking about, as if his mind must be going too, but he picked up right where they'd left off.

"They were a happy family. The Brudzienskis. In the beginning, anyway. I used to go out to the house frequently. Doctors don't make house calls anymore, but that was a different era. Ron Earl and Dot—that was Benny's parents—I think they were self-conscious about bringing Benny into town. Benny being the way he was, Reine being so small."

"I thought you said Benny was normal when he was younger?"

"Maybe that's not the right word. Normal. Who's to say what is or isn't normal? Just by looking at him, you could see something was wrong. Eyes too close together, forehead broader, expression duller. He was able to communicate. A few words here and there. Single syllables. He was slow but could draw pictures. Simple, but they conveyed meaning. He grew very fast, abnormally large." The doctor laughed to himself. "That boy was otherworldly strong."

The pot started to boil, and Dr. Lawson headed back to the stovetop. He turned down the heat, letting the oats simmer, occasionally stirring with a wooden spoon while smiling in fond remembrance. "I was out the farm once. Ron Earl was changing a tire on a tractor, and the jack started to slip. Benny was there.

Caught the front end of that machine, held it right up. Never seen nothing like it."

The doctor stared out the window, then switched off the burner and grabbed a bowl, ladling goopy, steaming oats. He brought the bowl along with honey, nuts and raisins in mason jars.

"People always thought Benny was stupid," Dr. Lawson said. "Benny wasn't stupid. Oh, he had a condition, and it was tougher for him to process information. The pathways from his brain to his hands and mouth didn't work as well as other folks. There was a short circuit in there somewhere, and his IQ was stunted. But I spent a lot of time with that boy, and he could understand you. He knew right from wrong." The doctor paused to make sure she caught his meaning. "Benny has a kind, good-hearted soul. I misspoke earlier when I told you I couldn't comment one way or the other. Whether he did it or not. I don't know what happened up there at that motel, not the particulars at least. But I know Benny didn't kill that girl. He was big, strong. But a gentle giant. Wouldn't harm a woodland creature."

"Did you tell the cops that?"

"Cops never asked me. Neither did the papers. Then again, there were other doctors besides me. You're the first person to ask my opinion about any of this."

"What are his brothers like?"

"Dan and Wren? I didn't know them as well. Benny's almost fifteen years older than Wren, and Dan's a few years younger than that. As time went on, I saw less and less of Benny and the family. He needed specialized care. When he started to go downhill, he went downhill fast. I know Ron Earl was considering institutionalization. Of course then Dot got sick with the cancer. Not enough money to care for them both."

"How old was Benny when you stopped being his doctor?"

"Let's see." The doctor counted and subtracted in his head. "I've been retired eleven years, and I hadn't been his primary for a few years before that. Fifteen? Maybe longer?"

"How much do you think he understood?"

"They put his IQ comparable to an eight-year-old. I always thought it was higher than that. But I didn't administer those tests. I know when I talked to him, I didn't talk down to him like most folks, and he followed along just fine."

"What about now?"

"After the accident, you mean? You'd have to talk to his current doctor."

"I don't think that's happening."

"No," Lawson said, laughing. "Probably not."

Alex dug into her oatmeal. Even with the honey, the breakfast was bland, tasteless. Needed salt. She didn't want to offend though. "What happened to Ron Earl?"

"After his wife passed, Ron Earl didn't last long. I don't think he had the heart to go on without her." The doctor gazed out the steamed-up window, condensation gathering, droplets rolling down the pane. "I'll always have a soft spot for that family."

"Was Wren bitter about having to quit football?"

"I couldn't speak to that. But I'll tell you this. That farm was in shambles when he took charge. Ron Earl was a good man, but he didn't know how to run a farm, at least not the business end of things. He was always one bad crop from ruin. Not sure how good Wren was at football—from what I hear he could've gone pro—but he was a *very* good businessman. The Brudzienski farm is now one of the biggest in the state. The insurance money helped—Ron Earl had a sizeable policy—but Wren had a good head for farming. He hired the right people, contracted what he had to, kept in-house what was needed. Formed partnerships with the right vendors and banks. Did a helluva job."

Alex finished her oatmeal, scraping the walls clean. The doctor made to stand, but Alex gestured to stay seated, bringing the bowl to the sink and running water. She thanked the doctor for his time and for the meal.

Dr. John Lawson insisted on walking her out. She thought he had something else to say, his face gathering urgency, but he only smiled and wished her luck.

Wasn't until they said their goodbyes and Lawson closed the door, after Alex had walked down the front steps and was halfway across the stone garden that she realized he never asked her name. A circumstance she might've found more peculiar if not for the car idling down the block. She couldn't see who was behind the wheel but she knew they were there for her.

CHAPTER EIGHTEEN

Alex slid in the driver's seat, hands unsteady as she pretended not to be spooked by the car up the block with its eyes on her, doing her damnedest not to give into fears she was being hunted again. Who would tail her all the way out here? Maybe it was the cops, someone sent by Riley. But would Reine PD really allocate limited funds to tail her? For what? Even when they'd been together, Riley had never been the possessive type, and it had been a while since they'd been together. She was kicking stones but hadn't uncovered enough to warrant attention. She'd made zero headway, either in exonerating Benny or proving he'd done it. No one knew where Kira's body was, and seven years later there was little chance of it popping up now. That car sure looked like an undercover's. Dark, boxy, meant to blend in. Cops usually did a better job when they wanted to remain inconspicuous. Whoever this was didn't mind being seen. The car sat there, making no effort to hide.

The singing phone jolted her out of her seat.

"Jesus, Nick. What?"

"You really know how to make a guy feel wanted, you know that?"

"Sorry. Wasn't expecting a call." Alex kept watch in the rearview as she fired up the engine, battered Civic coughing to life.

"Where are you?"

"Visiting Benny Brudzienski's old doctor." Parked too far away, she couldn't make out any impactful detail, not even a definite color for the vehicle—dark blue? brown?—the driver's face a blur.

"I thought you were going to get some rest?"

"Yeah, I don't do well with men telling me what to do."

"I was trying to help. Whatever. What did he say?"

"Not much. Mostly he talked about what Benny was like as a boy. How he wasn't always so screwed up. His condition is degenerative."

"Did he give you an actual diagnosis?"

"Begins with an A."

Alex couldn't think, preoccupied with the car down the block. It just sat there. Watching her. Which made her think of Denise. Anytime her mom smoked crack, she'd start rambling about being shadowed. Once she got on that ledge, nothing could talk her down, not logic, not reason, nothing. "They changed drivers and they changed cars," Denise would say, crouched on the floor, peeping out the slats, "but they're still following me."

"What are the symptoms?"

"Loss of motor function, cognitive ability, communication. Same as a stroke. But Lawson made it sound like Benny still comprehends." Alex hated giving into paranoia like this. Over the years, she'd met a lot of people like her mother, people who'd get jacked on coke and become convinced the authorities had sent in a task force, NSA spy planes, DEA agents. The truth was no one cared about people like her. What was that car doing there?

"So it's possible Benny is faking it?"

"Lawson meant before the accident. Nick, I think someone is following me."

"What do you mean 'following' you?"

"There's a car outside the doctor's house. Same car I saw the other day."

"I thought you saw Wren Brudzienski's truck?"

"I did. This is a different car." *They changed drivers and they changed cars but they're still following me.* "I'm sure I've seen it before. After my first trip to Galloway. Might've been outside your house this morning."

"What are they doing?"

"Nothing. Just sitting there. Idling down the block. Watching me."

"Shit. What are you going to do?"

"Don't worry. I'll be fine." Alex thought for a second, eyes never leaving the mirror. "Why are you calling?"

"I wanted to see if you were up for lunch?"

"Impromptu midday date? Don't ever change, Nick. You're adorable. I can't. I'm still up in Schenectady."

"What are you doing up there?"

"I just told you. Benny Brudzienski's doctor. He lives in Schenectady now. I have to go."

"Wait. Hold on. I don't feel comfortable leaving you on your own."

Through the rearview, the driver slowly pulled off the curb, K-turned and headed in the opposite direction. At a stop sign, the car hooked a right and was gone.

"If you're being followed—"

"Never mind," Alex said. "They're gone."

"You should get back down to Reine. I'll cut out early—"

"I appreciate the concern. But I have some business to take care of up here."

"Like what?"

"Like none of your business. Don't worry about it. It's personal. Christ."

"You don't make it easy, Alex."

"To do what?"

"Be your friend."

After Alex hung up on Nick, she rang Noah Lee but he didn't pick up. She left a message telling him to look into the Brudzienski farm. Something wasn't right. Call it a red flag. A cause for concern. Or flat-out common sense. A family on the

155

brink of financial ruin, a business going under—lender's ready to swoop in and foreclose—and magically everything is restored, flourishing, better than ever, the farm incorporated into one of the most lucrative in the state? And all it took was two people dying to make that happen. Alex wasn't implying Wren was guilty of murder. Cancer grows from mutated cells, and unless Wren spiked his father's drink with nightshade, heart attacks are hard to predict. But when you hear the words "large insurance policy" ears prick up. If nothing else, the timing was strange, the angle worth pursuing.

Alex knew she could lose chunks of time, and a serious disconnect existed between her endgame and points of origins, intentions perverted on their path to execution. Pathways fractured, Point A didn't always arrive at B. At least not in a straight line or cogent fashion.

She'd wanted to talk to Benny's doctor. If he'd been in Reine, she would've had no reason to drive up here. How was it her fault his practice had closed, or that the doctor had retired and moved back to her mother's hometown? But she knew it didn't matter where Dr. John Lawson lived. Alex would've made this trip eventually.

She'd lied to Riley the other day. She hadn't gone to Albany to arrange the funeral after Denise died. She'd gone up there to collect her mother's ashes.

Alex had been popping pills all morning, drinking hard. Looking back, she'd later wonder why they let her drive away from the funeral home, why no one stopped her, sat her down, called the authorities. She could barely stand and had no business being behind the wheel of a car. Maybe the director gave her the benefit of the doubt because she was grieving. Maybe they had another customer in the waiting room and had to keep the line moving.

She knew Riley was around, and she wanted to get in touch. As soon as she got to Reine, she changed her mind. She couldn't let him see her like this, didn't want to be on the receiving end of his pity. Instead she drove around visiting old haunts. The crappy apartment. The Fireside. The pizza place where Parsons snatched her up. Like the world's most depressing sightseeing tour, her dead mother in a cardboard box in the passenger seat beside her.

Denise's dying hit her hard. But not for the reasons most people thought. She didn't hate her mother, she'd long ago accepted what their relationship was, and there had been some good times in between the letdowns and disappointments. Alex didn't blame Denise. They still talked a couple times a year. She certainly didn't wish her mother dead. When the news came over the phone, Alex felt so little she feared something was broken inside her, as if she were missing the mechanism that allowed her to process feeling like a normal human being. Alex had been at a party with friends, acquaintances from the bar. After the call ended, no one asked if she was all right. Nothing about the news had unnerved. Like an automatic notification that a prescription is ready for pick-up. The party carried on.

But she knew it affected her, on some level, the loss of any chance at reconciliation. Because even if Alex managed to swallow her own bullshit about acceptance and forgiveness, she had to lament the loss. Not just for her mother, but for all of it, the missing years. Denise was the key to understanding parts of her life, the men, the abuse, the cutting and self-destruction. Someday Alex might seek out another therapist at the clinic, a Dr. Jane or a Margaret, an Abby, someone whose last name she wouldn't remember week to week but who'd work for sliding scale, and they'd probably have questions, right? And it would've been nice for Denise to stick around long enough to help answer them. It's call restitution. Comeuppance. Payback. Fucking karma. It was only fair. Alex was owed that much. Now Denise was gone. Of all the shitty things her mother had done, for as piss-poor a legacy as she'd left behind, checking out this early was the most inconsiderate.

The decision to drive up to Schenectady that day wasn't

planned, a bad idea fueled by good whiskey. Or maybe the other way around. Searching for a poignant moment, some poetry, Alex had driven along the 146, searching for that dirt road her mother had pointed out once long ago, the winding path gouged in the hard clay and stone around the gnarled wolf tree, the one that led to a tiny house atop a hill, the shelter Alex had never seen, only heard horror stories about. Cycles of violence passed down, generation after generation.

Denise had been drunk that afternoon. Her mother was always drunk. Like Alex was drunk now. She thought she'd found the turnoff, and pulled over, squinting through the thatch, searching for a home she could not find. As good a place as any for a funeral. Alex opened the box and cast her mother's cremated ashes to the wind, waited for them to be carried away on its wings. But the winds abated, stopped sudden, and the ashes dropped like stone, deposited in weeds and mud.

Alex unceremoniously tossed the empty box, a takeout container of mediocre Chinese, because, fuck it, Denise was what Denise was, and she might've been a mother but she'd never been a mom. Alex told herself that in some perverse way Denise would appreciate the sendoff, like pissing on Jim Morrison's grave, a fitting end to a raunchy, unconventional life. Besides, Alex wasn't rewriting narratives just because someone was dead. Death doesn't change who they'd been when they were alive. Death doesn't translate to some magic get-out-of-jail-free card.

In the following months, which slipped into the following years, Alex tried to convince herself she'd done nothing wrong. How much more did Denise deserve? A formal funeral would've run Alex at least a couple grand she didn't have, and for what? No one to show up? Far as Alex was concerned, death was for the dead, and it didn't matter what happened when you were gone. Burned to powder. Food for worms. All the same. You're done.

Alex didn't know if she had the same spot after all this time.

Trying to recollect a bend of branch, a crook of tree, a fool's errand. She'd been wasted that day. It had been summer, lush green leaves and ripe pollen instead of stripped bare trees on the cusp of winter.

She drove up and down the stretch of 146, hoping scent or sight might trigger memory, but she recognized nothing, feeling lost all over again. She flipped a bitch and backtracked. The more she drove, going in circles, remorse sneaking in, no pharmaceuticals to help push those feelings back down, the worse the world weighted.

Until, unable to squash the regret, guilt, confusion, whatever was going on inside her, Alex pulled off to the shoulder, onto a dirt path unlikely to lead to her mother's childhood house or any final resting spot, and slammed the car in park.

Alex gripped the wheel and screamed until her voice frayed hoarse.

Then she put her head in her hands and cried.

On her way out of Schenectady, Alex hit the 76 gas station, parking by the air pumps. She needed cigarettes and caffeine, a minute to collect herself. Drained and depressed, trapped in her head, she didn't see him standing outside her door until he knocked on the window.

Of all the people Alex suspected might be following her, she hadn't once considered Yoan Lee. After Noah boasted about his famous father, Alex had dug up information on the journalistic icon. The bylines and awards. Hall dedicated at the college. A sandwich named after him at the local deli. Which in these parts was as famous as famous got. It didn't leave a lot of time to play hide and seek. Although sitting in the passenger seat, Yoan quickly dismissed the notion, explaining that he hadn't been the one actually driving around spying on her.

"I had an intern keep an eye on you once I learned what Noah was up to. I hope I didn't scare you? I wanted to know what trouble my stepson was causing now."

"Stepson?"

"He's my second wife's child from a previous marriage."

"No, you didn't scare me," Alex lied. "But you could've called instead of creeping up on me at a gas station."

"I did call you. Several times. You didn't answer."

Alex thought about the missed calls from those two days she was passed out at Linda and Tommy's following the incident at Sweetwater, the blocked number without a voicemail. "Ever hear of leaving a message?"

"My apologies," Yoan Lee said. "You need to understand Noah has done this before. It's very frustrating, and I'm fed up at this point. Don't get me wrong. I love Noah as one of my own, and I have tried to give him every opportunity to prove himself. Uniondale's tuition isn't cheap. But he cuts corners, takes the easy way out. Every time. This is a last straw, hiring someone to complete a term paper for him."

"It's not exactly like that, Mr. Lee," Alex said, unsure why she was covering for Noah, since it was exactly like that. A part of her knew, without the excuse of the job, she'd pack it in. Even at her resolved best, Alex excelled at self-sabotage.

"You're not working for my son?"

"No. Yes. But not like you think. Noah contacted me to help conduct interviews because of my, I guess, history."

Yoan studied her, and Alex felt victimized by the interrogation. Despite conflicts in ideology, there wasn't much difference between detectives and journalists. Both possessed tunnel vision when it came to their version of the truth, and neither minded circumventing due process to get it.

"I'm not writing his paper for him," she said. "I'm a pretty lousy writer, if you want to know the truth. I'm a source. My history is part of the story."

"Making a subject part of the story is a gross violation of ethics. Noah, above all, should know better."

"Noah isn't focusing on Parsons, just the Benny stuff."

Something changed in Yoan's expression. It wasn't understanding and it wasn't disappointment.

"Can I be honest with you, Alex?"

What was she supposed to say to that?

"My stepson, my son, Noah, has always had a morbid fascination with cases like this. The macabre. Serial killings. Murder. Sexual assault. Which would all be well and fine if there was an underlying quest for justice. But I'm sad to say he simply elicits enjoyment from the gruesome, the sensational. And right now that interest is counterproductive."

"Maybe not for Benny Brudzienski."

"You're not telling me you think Benny is innocent?" Yoan looked like she'd just called the moon landing a hoax or said lizards ran the government.

"I'm not saying that. I mean, I don't know. There seems to be inconsistencies."

Yoan Lee smiled, an expression both comforting and patronizing. She could see why he excelled in his field. He commanded the discussion. Even when casting suspicion, Yoan projected endearing charms that made you want to tell him secrets.

"I'm going to share something with you, Alex, something that I hope you'll keep between us. This business with Benny— the decision about whether or not to bring formal charges—has further reaching ramifications than you know. It's a landmark case. A battleground, if you will, being fought by the bureaucrats in Albany. He's being used. Outside interests are lobbying for prison reform, at the cost of people who can least afford it. People like Benny."

"I'm trying to help Benny."

"Then let him get the treatment he needs. Galloway is not equipped to provide long-term care. Without formal charges and sentencing, a loophole is cast wide open, allowing men like our friend Ken Parsons to potentially go free."

"How does Benny Brudzienski's case affect Ken Parsons?" The idea was ludicrous, laughable. Alex's heart did summersaults inside her chest. "Those two have nothing to do with one another."

"Sorry. I don't mean that literally. I'm only saying that in the future, resulting legislation *could* impact such cases." Yoan Lee's phone buzzed. He glanced down, lips pursed, then tucked the cell away, reaching for the handle. "It was nice talking to you, Alex. Please, if my son calls you again, do me a favor and tell him to do his own classwork, okay?"

CHAPTER NINETEEN

"You talked to my father?!"

"He ambushed me in a parking lot." Alex stood on the muddy banks of the river. Backlit by the bar, her towering figure threw shade across choppy waters.

"Why did you tell him you were helping me?"

"I didn't tell him anything. He's an investigator. It's what he does."

"Do you know how much you fucked me?"

"I backed your play. I said I was assisting with research. A source. That's it."

"A technicality. You think my father cares?"

The storm had passed, hunter's moon high and bright, but stiff winds still gusted, angry waves slapping the pier. A chipping sparrow trilled in the distance.

"Did you listen to my voicemail?"

"I don't give a fuck about a fucking farm. I wanted information about Benny."

"I know what you want."

"It doesn't matter now, does it? My father is cutting me off. I sent you money. And you fucked me. You were supposed to get me quotes, something I could use for my assignment. I paid you. You fucked me. It's been almost a week, and I don't have shit."

"Relax. I'm giving you way more than you're paying me for."

"You're fucking me."

"Did you get my texts and email?"

"I got all of it. Texts, emails, voice messages. What do you think I can do with any of it? Why do I care what Wren Brudzienski does with the family farm? I needed to know why the cops suddenly think Benny Brudzienski is innocent. I don't give a shit about property management."

"Maybe you should."

"I paid you to find out why your boyfriend is itching to get the charges dropped. That was going to form the basis of my paper. That was my launching point. That was how I planned to get the *Codornices* to run the goddamn thing, the angle, hook, lead, what I was parlaying into a summer internship, a foothold in the industry, and now my plans are all shot to hell."

"Stop calling him my boyfriend. And that isn't what's happening. Riley isn't trying to get charges dropped. He doesn't want charges filed."

"Same difference!"

"No. It's not. Charges filed mean a trial, and if Benny is found guilty, he goes to Jacob's Island. It's a very violent place. Benny won't get the help he needs." Which contradicted what Yoan had said earlier, how a conviction netted better care.

"Did Riley say that? Can I quote him?" Noah spat a nasty laugh. "I'm out."

"No. You're not. You're not quitting on this."

"Excuse me? Yes, I fucking am."

"Wren doesn't care about his brother. He doesn't want to be on the hook for restitution." Alex didn't know if Riley really thought Benny was innocent, but this overlap, preventing formal charges, at least explained why the two, Wren and Riley, would be working together.

"None of that helps! This isn't what I hired you for!"

"You can do some work yourself, y'know? Your father is this hotshot reporter. You have his last name. Use his connections."

"I can't! That's the whole point! Why else would I have

asked someone like you if I had access to his contacts? He wants me to make my own name, not ride his coattails. Even if I wanted to keep going with this, which I don't—even if I could survive without his money, and I can't—you think my father will give me his contacts now?"

"Then work harder. Get creative."

"I. Don't. Care. Alex, I paid *you* to do it, good money for *this* paper, *this* class. And it's called Beats and Deadlines. Not Shady Real Estate Deals. I was very specific—"

"You need to check out Ron Earl's will. From what the doctor said, the farm only became profitable *after* Wren took over the reins—"

"Are you not listening to me? I'm out! I don't give a shit about Benny Brudzienski's finances. I don't give a shit about any farm. Quotes, copies of reports, evidence. About the *Kira Shanks* disappearance. The rest of this Nancy Drew crap, you're doing on your own—with *my* money!" She heard Noah collecting himself on the other end of the line. "I want my money back."

"You have to think bigger."

"It's a term paper. I don't need bigger. I need a grade. I'll be eating Top Ramen till winter break. Send me back my thousand bucks."

"Even if Benny did it, word on the street is, someone put him up to it. Which means someone else, every bit as guilty, is out there walking around."

"You don't know that."

"I've seen Benny. I've looked into his eyes."

"Hold the presses! Alex Salerno has looked into Benny Brudzienski's eyes!"

"While you've been sitting on your ass, I've been busting mine, and I'm telling you, something isn't adding up."

"And while I'm looking into some farm bullshit, what exactly are you doing?"

"For one, I'm talking to Kira's friends."

"Oh, that sounds real helpful. Going to get some pics, make a scrapbook?"

"It's called covering all your bases. Jesus, what do they teach you in school?"

"This is bullshit." Noah huffed, a bratty child's response to not getting life handed to him in the order he wanted. "I'm going to have to beg my professor for an extension, and pray he lets me pick a new topic."

"Listen to me, Noah. You look into the farm. Find out whose name was on the life insurance. The exact beneficiaries. Was there escrow? A trust? How much money are we talking about? That material has to be filed with probate. The farm is a taxable business, income reportable. I'll talk to Kira's friends. Someone has to know something about the night she went missing. Someone has to have seen her at the motel. I need you to trust me, give me a few more—"

"No."

"No what?"

"No, I don't trust you, and, no, you can't have a few more days. No, I am not pursuing this further. I want my money back."

"No."

"No what?"

"No, you can't have your money back. Man, I spent it. How do you think I'm eating up here? Paying for a place to sleep?"

"I don't care."

"You better care. Because we made a deal. And you still owe me another grand."

Noah mocked an exaggerated laugh. "You are crazy! If you think—"

"You're going to pay me. Every penny. Forget Daddy. You welch on me and I am going to the dean of your school and telling him that you paid me to do your work for you."

"That's not true. I wanted—"

"I know what you wanted. Me. To do your work. For you.

Which violates about eighteen rules of journalism. And education. And life. I'll tell the dean and you'll get expelled. How do you think Daddy will feel about that?"

"Like you know how higher education works. *You* went to college?"

"You don't have to go college to know what cheating is. Forget cheating, asking me for *any* help is a breach of ethics because I'm part of the story. Dumb fuck. So, yeah, you are going to pay me the rest. But here's the thing. You paying attention?"

Noah groaned. "I'm listening."

"Lucky for you, I take keeping my word seriously. I am going to earn this money and send you something you can use. You're going to grow a pair and stand up to your father. You write the paper, put your name on it, call me an anonymous source, and call it a day. You get your grade, the story runs. I get paid. That's our deal. But we're also going to figure out what really happened, because nobody up here believes Benny acted on his own. And if Benny didn't act on his own that means someone else got away with murder. And, Noah?"

"Yeah?"

"Try bailing on me again, and after I'm done with the school and Yoan, I'll rat you out to every newspaper in the tristate area. You'll be lucky to find a job writing copy for shopping flyers."

"Alex, hold on, wait—"

Alex ended the call as Nick headed over.

"Everything okay?"

"Peachy."

Nick motioned back at the bar. "This is the third place we've checked out tonight. No one's seen Cole for days. Tell me again why you want to speak with him so bad?"

"Cole works, worked, at the same motel, had the same job Benny did. If Kira was killed at the motel, where's the body? Someone had to help clean up that mess."

"Why would Cole help Benny cover up a crime? Besides, no one cleaned up anything. They found all the evidence in the room, right?"

"Except a body." Alex looked over the Mohawk, which drained into the Hudson, a river more than capable of selling secrets to the sea.

"Maybe we should stake out his trailer? If the guy got fired, he isn't out drinking."

"We tried that last night."

"Maybe he split town." Nick glanced around the lot, hugging himself with a shiver. "Let's piss or get off the pot. I'm freezing my balls off."

Alex was ready to take Nick's suggestion, try the trailer park again or call it a night, start fresh tomorrow, when she saw the stooped-over figure sloughing toward the bar. Even without seeing his face, she knew who it was. She'd seen him before, that first afternoon at the Idlewild, the man with the big eyeglasses and bushy mustache carrying the ladder around back.

Cole Denning was not a small man, but the way he moved—back hunched, shoulders rounded forward—made him seem small. His body appeared in danger of caving in on itself.

Alex slapped Nick on the elbow, pointing.

As Cole crossed beneath the moth-eaten awning, he peered over his collar, squinting in their general direction. The porch-bulb reflected off his giant glasses, lighting up a weathered face.

"How much older than us is he? Dude looks fifty."

Cole Denning ducked into the Jackal's Den. After her night at Sweetwater, Alex wasn't looking for more trouble. True, she had Nick with her this time. But she'd seen him fight. She considered waiting till Cole was done for the night, question him on his way out. Except she hadn't known many affable drunks. They were quick to take things the wrong way, and people seldom walked out of a bar more sober than they walked in.

"What's it like inside?" Alex asked.

"Alkie bar. Not much of a crowd, mostly old men slumped over shot glasses. Hard drinkers. Couple rough-looking bikers playing pool. Bartender didn't look too friendly."

Alex started for the door.

"Maybe we should catch him on the way out? If Cole's got friends in there, they won't like us getting nosy."

"Stop being a pussy, Nick."

She heard him fall in line behind her.

The Jackal's Den wasn't much different than Sweetwater, either in layout or prevailing mood. Dank, desperate, dirty. With one glaring exception: no Uniondale students. Since being back, Alex hadn't found a single bar immune to the college's influence.

Cole sat at the counter. Drawing nearer, they got a better look. To say Cole Denning wasn't a handsome man short-changed the ugly. An unruly yellow mustache overwhelmed his soft chin. A thick pair of glasses, the kind they make you wear when contacts aren't an option, swallowed his eyes, relegating his irises to two tiny slits. He drank alone, nothing about the man inviting. Like sharp quills on a rodent, or the bright, blistery skin on a red hot pepper, nature's way of saying to steer clear.

Alex and Nick took a seat on each side. Nick ordered a beer, Alex a whiskey. She asked Cole what he was drinking but he didn't answer. Not sure it would've mattered; he was already feeling no pain. Or maybe he was feeling too much of it.

The bartender set down their drinks. Nick paid cash. This wasn't a place where you ran a tab.

Alex spun her stool sideways. "You're Cole Denning. We went to high school together." Alex didn't remember people in her own class, let alone a guy who wasn't even in high school when she graduated.

Cole didn't take the bait, or maybe he wasn't used to pretty girls making the first move, not unless they wanted to sell him company for the night. And even those girls had their standards. Not enough money in the world for some things.

"You were friends with Kira Shanks," Nick said. "I remember you."

Cole glanced at Nick, then looped around to Alex, before

drooping his head.

"Hey!"

The bartender stomped over. Big slab of gut, hairy forearms, miniature baseball bat in hand, the kind they give away on minor league baseball promotional nights.

"What are you bothering him for?"

"No one's bothering anyone," Alex said.

The bikers stopped playing pool.

"I think you two might be more comfortable with your own kind."

"Our own kind?"

"I've had enough of you Uniondale kids coming in here." The bartender slapped Nick's cash down. "I don't want your parents' money. Go slumming somewhere else."

"I don't go to Uniondale," Nick said.

"No," he said, nodding at Alex. "But she does. Boys like you are their charitable contribution to the lower class."

"You think *I* go to Uniondale?" Alex looked down at what she was wearing, tee shirt out of a ten-pack, ripped jeans, and Chuck Taylors, ratty black hoodie, bracelets jangling on her wrist, and realized she didn't look all that different than Noah Lee, or any of the other kids at Uniondale acting poorer than they really were. Who was appropriating whose culture? She didn't know whether to be offended or feel pride for finally having passed as one of them.

Cole Denning lifted a languid hand. "It's okay, Lou."

Lou the bartender grunted, before retreating to the other end, one eye on the tiny television under the counter, the other stuck on them.

"You want to talk about Kira?" Cole said, not giving either a chance to answer as he pulled a wad of crumpled bills from his pocket, sifting singles from the lint. "Kira Shanks was the only real friend I ever had. Not a day goes by that I don't think about her. I miss her more than you could possibly know."

Cole swilled his drink and staggered off. He threw open the

doors, jamming shaky hands in pockets, returning to a cold, uncaring world.

"What you think?"

Alex stole a peek at the bikers, who still hadn't resumed their game of eight ball, at Lou, choking up on that bat, tapping the barrel impatient against his meaty palm. "Probably time to leave."

When they got outside, there was no sign of Cole. A second later Alex's cell buzzed with a text. Not the message she was expecting.

She showed the screen to Nick.

Meaghan Crouse.

"What's it say?"

"Party tonight in Rotterdam. We're invited."

CHAPTER TWENTY

Apparently the party was in the middle of nowhere. They'd veered off Route 5S a while ago. Past Schenectady, beyond Rotterdam, deep into the forest. Streets turned darker, signs ebbing less frequent, until they were deposited in this no-man's land. More than once, Alex considered turning around, insecurity getting the best of her. She flashbacked to painful elementary school memories when Linda and Jennifer Swanson invited her over to Jennifer's house and then refused to let her in, stifling giggles behind the door. Silly now, but in fifth grade, those're the kinds of wounds that leave deep and lasting scars.

How had Meaghan gotten her number anyway? Alex didn't remember leaving her name at the pharmacy, let alone a phone number. When Alex got the text (*Wazup? Its Meaghan. Party tonite. U shud stop by*), Alex played it cool and asked for the address (*Cool. Addy?*). No reason to risk spooking her. Alex knew Meaghan wasn't looking for a new best friend, but whatever her angle, this was a chance for Alex to get a closer look, perhaps glean something about the night Kira went missing. Alex felt excited but wasn't sure why. A job was a job, and two thousand bucks didn't hurt. But aside from her current "boss" being an affluent piece of shit (who was threatening to pull the plug), Alex could only ignore the obvious for so long: she needed this to mean something more.

"You sure that's the right address?"

Alex held up her phone for Nick to read.

"Don't you think it's strange? Meaghan inviting us to a party in the middle of the woods?" Nick scanned the surrounding wilderness.

"I'm not worried about some high school poser."

"She's not in high school anymore."

Alex squinted at the GPS overview.

"What the hell? Are we going camping?"

"Says seven minutes."

They'd been on the same dark, twisting road for a long time. No streetlights. No street names. Just the skeletal outlines of bare-boned trees. There was nothing in the remote vicinity. Briar patch flourished by the roadside, dry, thorny blackberry bushes minus the fruit. Cloud cover drifted across muddy skies, obscuring moon and stars.

"This sure isn't Rotterdam," Nick muttered.

Alex fished her smokes.

"At least roll down the window."

"Fuck that. It's cold."

"Then don't smoke. Christ, Alex, I have to sit in this truck all week. If you're not a smoker that shit stinks. Have a little consideration. I'm going on this mission with you—"

"Okay, okay. Like you had anything better to do. When I stopped by your place the other night, you looked like you were already in bed. At nine-thirty."

"I get up early for work."

"What do you do, exactly?"

"Thanks for taking an interest in my life. We've only been hanging out a week."

"I figure I might as well get to know you in case we die tonight."

"Funny."

Alex checked her phone. "Take the next right. Fox Hollow Road. Half a mile."

"Oh, boy. An actual street name. My uncle runs a hauling company. Among other things. Side business. I move the sensitive stuff. TVs, computers, artwork."

Alex craned over her shoulder, out the back window, to the dirty flatbed cluttered with a toolbox and moving blankets, gunny straps, and bungee cords. "In this thing?"

"I've got a gentle touch. People feel better having sensitive items personally transported."

Nick turned onto Fox Hollow. Paved asphalt surrendered to dirt and gravel. Alex jostled about the cab, back teeth chattering with the jarring bumps. The road splayed open and the skies parted, naked stars brighter than the sun. Still waters glinted in the moonlight. Coming to a fork, they saw the sign for the Plotter Kill Preserve, and drove further into the hidden jungle.

Birthwort and wakerobin threaded tall pines and oaks, slippery elms covering the basin, valley floors caged by rockwall, slabs of stacked stone. Soon the big Queen Anne cottage came into view. Nick peered over, nonplussed. Loud rock music bled through the bulrushes. Half a dozen cars peppered the torn-up lawn, people sitting on the hoods, drinking beer in the cold moonlight.

Thin Lizzy blasted out the bottom floor. Despite the chill, windows had been thrown wide open. And why not? No neighbors to complain. The trip was a haul but Alex could see why they'd party out here. On the edge of the preserve, there wasn't a soul for miles. In the summer, when days don't end, Alex imagined no one ever went home. It was that kind of place—a communal crash pad where everybody comes to hang out and get wasted. Pills and powders, powders and pills.

Nick killed the engine. Alex dipped low to look out the clear part of the windshield. Everyone appeared college-aged. Although Alex knew none of this bunch was in school. Reine comprised two distinct groups. The boys and girls who went to Uniondale. And everyone else. This was everyone else.

As much as she could use a drink or drug, Alex quickly regretted coming. Like attending music festival after twenty-six, Alex was too old for house parties.

Nick picked up on her unease. "They aren't much younger than us."

"Yeah," she said, "they are."

Walking up to the front door, the pair received odd looks, but that had less to do with age than it did their outsider status. The community projected insular, guarded, a secret club. The boys all retained that hard look, miscreants with something to prove; the girls, like they peaked in high school.

The inside of the house was torn to hell, holes in the drywall and empty kegs tipped on their sides. Crap everywhere—empty liquor handles, flattened chip bags, random articles of clothing, wet underwear from midnight swims. A nitrous tank leaned against the wall like a discarded Christmas tree waiting to be hauled to the curb.

Weaving through narrow halls, Alex squeezed between garbage bags leaking pools of fetid liquid. Extension cords wriggled along molding, opposite ends connecting lifelines. She peeked in various bedrooms. Each one, the same listless scene: three or four blissed-out kids copping feels on floor mattresses, milk-crate end tables safekeeping valuables. Chain wallets, lighters, pipes, condoms. Limp hands pawed body parts, trying to grope tit, wriggle down pants for uninspired rubs, half-hearted tug jobs, reciprocation unlikely, recipients damn near passed out. Alex could smell chemicals burning, the unmistakable preparation of harder narcotics wafting down the hall—acetone, paint thinner, ammonia, baking soda. This was what she wanted, right? Something to take the edge off, make her forget. Suddenly the thought of getting high had never seemed less appealing.

At the back end of the house, the noises grew louder, voices booming, music cranked higher, laughter more raucous. Alex realized what she'd thought was the front was actually the back. She'd gotten it all mixed up. There was an actual driveway, from an actual paved road. Somehow she and Nick had gotten turned around, going in through the backdoor.

The front porch was more like an observation deck at a museum, extended and spacious. The landing overlooked a picturesque pond. There was even a little waterfall beyond the reeds. The party up here was reserved for the cool kids, who all lounged on tattered couches and gashed leather La-Z-Boys, the air a haze of marijuana smoke. To hang here, you had to be invited. Soon as Alex stepped foot on the deck, a couple guys cut her off, burly bouncers at an uptown club.

"Hey, Alex," Meaghan Crouse said, like they'd been tight for years. She was sitting on the lap of a boy who had his face nuzzled in her neck. She was smoking a joint, which she held out for Alex, who couldn't say no.

Alex took a hit, then passed it to Nick, who succumbed to the peer pressure, or what he perceived as peer pressure since no one gave a shit whether he took a hit or not. Alex made a mental note not to call him a pussy again.

Meaghan nodded toward a couch in the darker shadows, where three other girls sat in silence. "Patty, Jody, Trista."

Patty, Jody, and Trista returned the silent head bob. The too-cool-for-school crew. A handful of dudes loomed past their shoulders, drinking beers and taking turns sparking a broken light bulb, sucking thick white smoke through a straw. Another boy sat on the porch railing, aiming a shotgun at an imaginary target in the trees, lifting the gun in slow motion with each report, making soft exploding sounds like a twelve-year-old playing army. Meaghan nodded, and one of the boys stepped forward, offering Alex the light bulb.

"No, thanks. I'm cool."

"I thought you partied?" Meaghan said.

"Sometimes I do. Sometimes I don't."

Patty, Trista, or Jody whispered something, and all three giggled.

The dishwater blonde, Trista, was bigger than the other two. Not fat, just taller. Hard to tell with someone sitting down, but Alex wouldn't be surprised if Trista White topped six feet.

"I had to call your cousin," Meaghan said. "To get your number. In case you were wondering how I got your cell."

"I wasn't."

"You don't live up here anymore," Trista said. It wasn't a question.

"No," Alex answered anyway. "The city."

"The city," one of the girls repeated.

"Shut up, Patty," Meaghan said.

Patty had on a vintage Zeppelin tee, *Houses of the Holy*, naked urchins crawling up stone stairs to an altar. "What's your boyfriend's name?" She was looking at Nick.

"He's not my boyfriend."

"Hi. I'm Nick." Nick took a step into the circle in case anyone wanted to shake his hand. No one did.

"Not him," Trista said. "She means that detective from Reine. What's his name?"

"Sean Riley. But he's not my boyfriend either. Beer?"

Meaghan nodded to a boy in the back who reached into a cooler without ice, tossing Alex and Nick each a warm Miller Lite.

"Whose place is this?" Alex asked popping the tab. She could feel more feet step onto the porch behind her, taking up position. She wasn't turning around.

"Mine," Jody said, speaking for the first time. She had a high, squeaky voice, like a balloon with a teeny pinhole leaking air.

Alex didn't ask how a girl her age owned a house this big. If she had to guess, someone left it to her when they died. Jody Wood didn't strike Alex as an overachiever, let alone someone with enough credit to secure a mortgage.

"Why are you up here?" Jody asked. "In town, I mean."

"She's looking into Kira's disappearance," Meaghan answered. Facial expressions said the girls already knew that. "Newspaper article, right?"

Alex nodded.

"What paper did you say you worked for again?"

"Uniondale's."

"You go to college?" Patty relieved the boy of his light bulb cooker, bottom charred black, holding flame to glass until it glowed hot and billowed smoke.

"No," Alex said. "I don't."

"She's helping someone," Nick said. "On a piece."

"A piece of what?"

"You want to ask us questions about Kira?" Trista said. "Go ahead."

Someone switched off the music.

"Yeah, ask away," Meaghan said. "You drove all the way out here. What do you want to know?"

"Why is she here again?" Jody said.

"She's working on a piece, remember?"

"Oh, yeah. Right."

Nick tensed. She could feel it too, the circle tightening. Whoever stood guard behind them had one purpose: make sure they didn't try to bail before the girls made their point.

"Since you don't feel like talking," Meaghan said, "let me start. We think it's real fucked up that you would come back here and start stirring up shit. You think because of what happened to you that you're special? Kira was our friend. Not yours."

"Yeah," Patty chimed in. "It's fucking rude."

"No one likes strangers poking their noses where they don't belong."

Alex pulled her Parliaments, footsteps encroaching. They were almost on top of her. She fought to keep her hands steady as she lit the cigarette.

When someone bumped her back, she whipped around. Three men stood there, older, more seasoned, Buscemi eyes extracting the price of long-term drug use.

"Hey. You mind? There's such a thing as personal space."

Alex was surprised when they retreated.

"No one is stirring up anything," Nick said. "She told you. She's working on a newspaper story with another reporter."

"Not stirring up anything?" Meaghan said. "What do you call stalking Cole?"

"We weren't stalking him. I had a few questions."

"Cole isn't too good with words."

"He's got water on the brain."

Alex caught the girls on the couch exchange a look.

"He seemed fine to me."

"Yeah?" said Trista. "And what did Cole say?"

"Sorry." Alex drew on her Parliament. "Can't reveal my sources."

"I'm sure." Patty took her turn on the light bulb. The acrid stench of cleaning chemicals hit Alex from across the porch. The smoke tasted like bleach and dentistry, making her light-headed. If the drugs were impacting Alex ten feet away, she could only imagine the damage being done to Patty's brain.

Another set of heavy boots landed on the porch. Like at the bar, Alex knew whom they belonged to before she saw his face.

"We were just talking about you," Meaghan said. "You need a drink, Cole? Looks like you can use a drink." Meaghan gestured to the cooler boys. "Get Cole a drink. And not that schwag beer. Get him a shot of something." She turned to Cole, his turtle shoulders calling him back to the shell, oversized glasses absorbing his face. "Bushmill's good? You need a fix? Load that baby back up and pass that shit to Cole."

Cole's gaze crossed Alex's.

The look was not unlike Benny Brudzienski's.

It screamed: help me.

CHAPTER TWENTY-ONE

They got back to Nick's a little after midnight, neither of them sure what they'd seen at Plotter Kill. Other than they'd been warned off in big way, and that Cole Denning knew more than he was letting on.

Alex fell on the couch, splayed out, wrecked. Nick brought back a couple beers from the fridge, dropping beside her.

"That pot fucked me up."

She snagged a beer, laughing. "You took one hit."

"What can I say? I'm a lightweight."

"Not that first night at the Fireside. You were pounding them back."

"I told you. That was because—"

"You liked me." Alex pulled her legs underneath, sitting on her heels. "Poor Nick. So sensitive." She reached out, brushing his hair behind his ear. He flinched. She laughed.

"Why do you have to be like that?"

"What?" Her fingertips lingered on the back of his neck. "The other night you said you didn't want to because I was too wasted. I'm not wasted now."

"That's not what I mean. You treat everyone like a game. Looking for leverage, some play. You're playing me now. People have feelings."

Alex returned to her side of the couch. "Jesus, Nick. Lighten up." She grabbed her beer, bracelets jangling with the faraway sound of a lone car racing up the boulevard.

"You're not helping yourself acting like that."

"Thanks, Dr. Phil."

"I think you pretend you don't care because it's safer. I think you push people away because it's easier than taking a chance. I think you want what you can't have because then there's no way you get rejected and feel the hurt. I think you run so fast and so hard so you won't get caught—because if you did, if you stopped moving, even for a second, let your guard down, allowed someone in, they'd glimpse the real you, and the thought of that terrifies you."

Alex stared off into space, killing time till the sting abated. Those initial seconds after the tip pierces the flesh? Sure, you feel it. After that? No big deal. Numbs over quick. Nothing but tiny white crosses buried among scar tissue.

"That was precious." She patted his knee. "I'm going to bed."

That's when he made his move. The kiss caught her by surprise. What surprised her more was how much she wanted it, someone to take charge, call her on her bullshit. She was tired of running. She wanted to stop. No one had bothered trying to catch her. He pulled her lower on the couch, crawling on top. She liked feeling his bulk pressing down on her. His hands cradled her face. He kissed her, urgent but without desperation, tender without hesitation. There were no games this time. Alex wasn't fucking around, killing time because she was bored on a random weeknight. She wanted him.

Nick traced her collarbone, lifting her hair, kissing her neck, eliciting chills, inciting heat. Hands up the backs of shirts, hips rising off the cushions, body against body. He wasn't frantic and he didn't rush. His hands stayed right where they belonged. He didn't try to speed through this part, making out as a pretense to get on to the fucking. His patience forced her to be present, exist in the moment, feel the now. Too often Alex tried to escape the present. Regret yesterday. Dread tomorrow. Never have to be here and deal with today. The way he kissed her,

slow, impassioned, possessed, full of yearning, she felt connected, which thwarted her usual defense mechanism of checking
out, taking no risk. When their eyes opened and they stared at
one another there was none of the usual awkwardness. No one
stifled giggles or felt overtly self-consciousness. The way he
touched her, exploring every inch of her body, like he could do
it all night long. And she wanted him to do it all night long.

Alex's cell buzzed in her pocket. She tried ignoring it at first,
but the ringing was nonstop; as soon as one call ended, another
started back up. Whoever it was wasn't giving up.

"Seriously?"

"Sorry," she said, slipping out from beneath him, pulling the
phone from her jeans. She turned it over but didn't answer, staring at the name on the screen.

"Who is it?"

"Riley."

Nick sat up, snaring his beer and cracking the tab. Whether
or not she took the call, the moment was gone.

She took the call. "Yeah." Pause. "How do you even know
where I am?" Pause. "Okay." She clicked off.

She grabbed her hoodie and bomber. "He wants to talk."

"What? When?"

"Now. He's downstairs. He sounded different."

"Different."

"I don't know. Not himself? Something's wrong."

"I'm coming with." Nick started to stand.

"I don't think you're invited."

"Right. Got it."

"Nick—"

But he was already up, headed for the bathroom, slamming
the door.

When Alex slipped in the passenger's seat, she knew what was
different about Riley. He was drunk. And not a couple-beers
buzzed but six-sheets-to-the-wind hammered. She could smell

the booze on him three feet away.

He didn't look at her when she climbed in, didn't acknowledge her at all. Which didn't make her feel all that talkative. They hit 90 North toward Albany, Riley pushing the needle, threatening triple digits. Alex gripped the Jesus bar. He was daring her to tell him to slow down. Of course Alex wasn't doing that.

Exiting the freeway like an afterthought, Riley ran a pair of red lights, swinging a hard left into the hotel parking lot, finding a spot far enough away where no one needed to respect lines, which was good since the forty-five-degree angle he ended up at would've banged the hell out of any vehicle in the vicinity.

At a fourth-floor room, Riley slapped his key card and splayed open the door. Alex stopped in the entranceway and peered inside. Men's clothes and complimentary *USA Today* sections lay strewn across tangled sheets. The TV was on, sound off. The view out the window overlooked the dirty Hudson, downtown lights twinkling without promise. Empty liquor bottles littered the floor.

"Get in here," Riley said, finally speaking. "I don't want to have this conversation with you in the hallway."

Alex stepped inside. The rank room overpowered with the ripe tang of body odor and takeout Italian food left too long in tin beds. She could almost taste the acid reflux.

Riley bent at the little fridge. "Want a beer?" Alex shook her head. He closed the door, taking nothing, opting instead for whatever was in the paper bag on the dresser. He cracked the seal, poured a couple fingers in a ceramic mug, then abandoned all pretense and brought the bottle with him to the small, round table, loosening his top button, kicking his feet out.

"What are we doing here?"

"What? You don't like my new place? Make yourself at home."

"You want to tell me what happened?"

Riley dug in his pants' pocket, retrieving a metallic token, a poker chip. The bronze coin gleamed in the overhead lights. Riley tossed the chip on the dresser. Or tried to. The chip missed its mark and clinked off the edge, falling to the floor, which prompted manufactured laughter. "How funny is that?"

Not funny at all, she wanted to say. Alex felt sorry for Riley. And not because of what he said, this being his new address, or the years of sobriety he'd apparently wasted. She felt sorry for him because he didn't know what wrong steps he'd taken to end up here, which meant he couldn't find his way back home.

"Meg threw me out," he said, addressing the elephant. Although Alex had figured that out by now. This was why he'd brought her up here. He wanted her raked over coals, ass planted in the front row to bear witness to his shame. "Found out you were in town, and then the last ten years of couples therapy, nodding yes like a naughty pup that had crapped the bed, the nonstop apology tour, all of her shit I had to take, out the window." He took a long swig from the bottle, rage coursing off him in waves, the indignant, self-righteous kind of the wrongly victimized, a proud captain only too happy to go down with his ship if it meant drowning the rest of his ungrateful crew too.

How had she missed this? He must've already been on the wagon when they met. Now that she thought about it, she couldn't remember his ever drinking when they were together. He didn't talk about AA. Then again, she was underage and he was a cop.

"You going to say anything?"

"What would you like me to say?"

Riley closed his eyes tight. "Why did you have to come back here?"

Alex stepped closer, standing over, looking down on him. She reached out and put her hand on his head, stroking his hair. He grabbed her hand, but not to stop her.

"Oh, Riley," she said.

He staggered to his feet, pulling her close by the waist, grappling, pushing her back to the wall, trying to shove his tongue down her throat.

She ducked his stranglehold. Riley stumbled, laughed, swiped his bottle, keeping his back to her. "I thought that was what you wanted."

"So did I."

"Fuck you, Alex."

"No, I don't think so. Not tonight."

Riley returned to his drink and liar's throne.

"Whatever you got going on in there," she said, "it isn't about me. Or your wife. You were waiting for this excuse."

"What the hell would you know about it?"

"I grew up with an alcoholic, remember? Alcoholics always have a tragedy on hold, ready to dial up disappointment whenever they need license to run their life into the ground."

"That's funny coming from you. I deal with burnouts and addicts all day long. I know the look."

"You're right. I drink too much. And, yeah, I might lean too hard on pills sometimes. Maybe I need to take a hard look at my life and make some changes. But I'm not the one feeling sorry for myself in a fucking Extended Stay in downtown Albany, blaming the high school girl because I couldn't keep my dick in my pants."

"Why don't you get out of here? Call a taxi. Need some money?" He pulled his wallet, fingered a pair of twenties, flinging them with a violent gesture. The paper bills fluttered to the floor. "That should cover your time."

Alex wasn't offended, and she wasn't scared, and she wasn't leaving.

"I talked to Wren Brudzienski yesterday."

"No shit. What do you think started all this? I've known everything you've done the minute you got back into town, every move you've made. How'd you think I knew you were at your boyfriend's?"

"You're investigating me now?"

"I tried to play nice. All it's gotten me is a pain in my ass and a thankless fuck you."

"I'm sorry Meg threw you out—"

"I bet you are."

"But it's got nothing to do with me."

"Not now."

"Not then either. I was seventeen years old."

"Yeah, well you aren't seventeen anymore."

"No. I'm not." She paused, slowed down, made sure she had his complete attention. "But I was. You were almost thirty years old. As old as I am now."

"And?"

"And if I slept with a seventeen-year-old boy, they'd call it rape."

"Don't! Don't!" Riley jammed a finger under her nose. "You wanted that!"

"I did. And so did you. That's why it happened. I don't regret it, and I'm glad it happened. But here's the thing, Sean. You were the grown-up. You're the one who should've known better. If your marriage is still feeling the effects, if you're still dealing with the fallout, that's on you, man." God, it felt good to say that. Riley made for the bottle. She stopped him, moving it out of reach. "Why aren't you convinced Benny Brudzienski is guilty?"

He slumped back in his chair. "Why can't you let this go?"

"I told you. I'm getting paid."

"A few hundred dollars? Christ, Alex, I'll pay you that much to leave. Go back to New York. I have enough problems. I don't need you adding to the shit pile."

"It's two thousand dollars."

"Two thousand dollars? Fuck, that's my monthly mortgage payment."

"I'm sure. But it's mine. I'm earning it."

"Doesn't matter. I told you I'm going to call that reporter, pull the rug out—"

"Except you haven't."

Riley spread an arm over his new hotel home. "Sorry. Got a

little distracted."

"It's not about the money anymore."

"Whenever someone says it's not about the money, it's about the money."

"The day I met Noah Lee up at Uniondale for the interview, he was trying to get under my skin, shooting in the dark, talking out his ass, trying to rile me. He asked if I thought I started something. Me and all those other girls. Because of Parsons."

"Started something? Like what?"

"Like a curse on this town. A hex."

"That's ridiculous."

"That's what I said. Except I've been wondering if maybe he wasn't right. Not the way he meant it, not exactly. I don't believe in curses or voodoo. But I don't think I was supposed to escape that basement. I think I was meant to stay there. Maybe if I had, the circle would've closed, been complete. No one else would've had to die."

"That is the dumbest thing I have ever heard."

She took his hand, patting it, soothing. "You were like a superman to me. Because you got to me in time. That's what I thought. But you didn't. It's not your fault. No one could've. Something happened to me down there."

"And you think, what? Learning Benny Brudzienski didn't act alone is going to cure you? That if you discover Kira Shanks alive and well, living under an assumed name in Binghamton, you're gonna be fixed, whole, happy?"

"I don't know if I'm ever getting that," Alex said. "But I know I can't keep living this way."

Riley leaned back, sobered by the conversation. "You're right. I should've known better. And I have to live with that. My daughter Sam will turn seventeen someday. You don't think I know what I did? I could send you a thousand more emails and letters telling you I'm sorry, that I overstepped my bounds, abused my authority, but it wouldn't make a difference. We live with our mistakes, and if you live long enough, all you have is the regret. But you weren't some shining example of well-adjusted when I found you. You were seventeen going on thirty." He tried to laugh. "You were like you are now. But it played a lot better back then."

"Why are you partnering with Wren?"

"I'm not 'partnering' with Wren, except to keep Benny from getting killed. Wren Brudzienski doesn't want his brother down south because then he'd be on the hook for a lot of money. If the DA brings official murder charges, Wren could get stuck with the bill from Galloway, all the cash the state has invested in Benny's care. And New York would come after him for every red cent. You better believe it."

"Yoan Lee said Benny needs to go somewhere with better long-term care."

"Yoan Lee is full of shit. He's got his own agenda. Everyone does. His lawmaker buddies up in Albany want their puff piece. He's tossing them softballs. The guy used to be a real journalist. Now he's another corporate shill."

"And charges automatically put Benny in Jacob's Island?"

"There's always a chance Benny gets assigned to another hospital. I doubt it. Either way, Wren would still be the one writing the check, and he doesn't want to roll the dice. Neither do I."

"Guess Wren is lucky Benny can't say what really happened."

"I know what you are thinking, and, no, Wren had nothing to do with Benny's accident. Wren was a hundred and fifty miles south coaching football when Benny was attacked. I've spent a lot of time with the man. Wren can be an abrasive prick but he wouldn't hurt his brother, and he wouldn't dishonor his parents' memory by letting Benny live on the streets."

"What aren't you telling me? Come on, Riley. There's a reason you are trying to give Benny a break beyond concern for Wren's financial wellbeing. You've never been a bleeding heart. I know they found Benny's DNA at the motel."

Riley scratched his ornery beard, reclining further, kicking his feet out. Superman status on permanent hiatus, he accepted he couldn't put her off any longer. "That college reporter's right about one thing. After Parsons, Reine couldn't survive another tragedy. The politicians and powers that be up here—including your new pal Yoan—wanted someone held responsible. You don't get rezoning ordinances passed and new shopping centers built with murderers on the loose. Benny's blood was found in the room. Benny was found speechless in a ditch. Same end. Different means. Crime, punishment. Deal done."

"What are you saying?"

"I'm saying semen was found on the sheets. More blood. DNA not belonging to Benny. But no one wanted to explore those avenues. Those streets were too goddamn dirty. A rumor leaked the semen belonged to Benny, and that was good enough for the higher-ups. They leaked that detail to the press, whipped the masses into a frenzy, let them do their jobs for them. Fuck the jury, screw the judge, bring on the execution. They wanted the mess cleaned and off the books. I went along with it because that was my job. Might as well have joined the lynch mob myself. The least I can do now is let the guy have a nice view, some fucking trees and birds to look at while he craps himself. That's not bleeding heart. That's basic human dignity."

"How many other people's DNA?"

"The Idlewild's not the cleanliest of places. Truckers, transients, hookers. People fucked there on their lunch breaks. Bring in a UV flashlight, you're looking at the goddamn Milky Way. Who the hell knows what went on in that room?"

"Did you get a sample from Cole Denning? Because I met that guy, and he's hiding something—"

"Yes. We did. Stop playing cop."

"And?"

"And wasn't a match."

"Dude's sketchy. He's drinking himself to death—" Alex stopped, glancing at the bottle a few inches from Riley's hand.

Who knew what drove a person to destroy himself like that? Denise ran her liver in to the ground. So had her aunt, Diane. Linda was well on her way. Alex had always considered herself better because she switched it up, never stayed with any one drink or drug too long, was always on the move. Like her life. Nick was right. Can't get attached to anything if you're always running. She was tired of the race. "Don't you find it a little weird, Cole Denning working as a handyman at the same motel?"

"Cole is practically Evie Shuman's stepson, her boyfriend's kid, so no. And coincidences don't hold much water in a court of law."

"Have you talked to Kira's friends? Meaghan, Trista, the others? Been out to their clubhouse in Plotter Kill?"

"I've done my job, yes. I've been to Plotter Kill. I've interviewed all her friends. Every alibi checks out." Riley swept his mangled, sweaty hair back off his brow. "Right now I have one concern: keeping the DA from shipping Benny Brudzienski down to Jacob's Island. Do I think Benny killed Kira Shanks? I don't know. His blood is in that room. So is hers. The only two positive IDs we could make. Besides a couple long-haul truckers halfway across the country when it happened."

"How'd you get Kira's DNA if you never found a body?"

"Body?" he spat. "No one's ever finding a body. Kira Shanks was dumped in the river and dragged out to sea. You know how many bodies fishermen snag each month? There was a lot of rain that November. If she had been buried in the ground, we'd have found her. Once we didn't recover Kira's remains after a few weeks, I knew we'd never find them."

Riley reached around her for the bottle. "We got Kira's DNA from her parents. And Benny spent so much time with doctors, hospital practically had his blood on tap." Riley turned away, as if he had to think about whether to disclose this next part. "There's no nice way to say this—Kira was promiscuous. She slept around, bedded half the men in this town. Even if we had found her body, I don't know what it could've told us. And before you ask, yes, every one of these men has been cleared."

"Any names you want to share?"

"Why don't you start with your cousin's boyfriend?"

"You're kidding, right?"

"There are no saints in this, Alex. You should know that better than anyone."

BENNY BRUDZIENSKI

I hear Dad talking on the phone. It is the hospital. They want to ship me off and make me someone else's problem. They use big, long words to describe what is wrong with me. Dad says I am getting worse, and I know it is true because I cannot do the few things I used to be able to do. My hands do not always move the way I want them to. I can still walk, sit up, use the bathroom on my own, but it is getting harder, all of it, this life. Sometimes I get stuck in time, and it feels like I am living the same day over and over. I want to quit. I feel alone. They are scared of me. Not because I would ever hurt them but because I remind them of the parts of themselves they do not want to see. We are family and share the same blood. They worry my sick will get on them.

Mom was sick but it was different from the sick I have. I miss her. When I am gone, they will not miss me. They will be relieved. Speaking has become impossible for me. Even the one or two words I used to be able to sputter out. I do not try anymore. No more stuttering, no more stammering. No more standing and staring into space like a fool. There is nothing I can do about it. Thinking too hard makes my eyes roll up into my head. My eyeballs flutter so far back I can almost see my brain. I wish I could. Maybe then I could see what is wrong back there and fix it. I am good at fixing things with parts and gears, but the human brain does not work like that.

No one tells me Mom is dead. They think I would not understand, that my days could continue and I would never notice my mother is gone. Even if the words do not always follow the right path, get jumbled and mixed up on their way to my brain, eventually I can put them in the right order and reassemble the pieces. I can make sense of things in my own crooked way. I know what cancer is. I know what dying is. When you live inside your head you have nothing but time to figure these things out.

I often lose track of time. I do not know if this is a new problem or if it has always been that way, because that is how time works. It goes forward. Sometimes I feel like I am in two places at once. I am still young carrying firewood, or I am with Kira under the bleachers, or I am watching the bad men do bad things, even though I am not there now. I am here. Outside my window, I watch the men on tractors till the fields. I watch the big black crows.

I miss my friend. I will go see her.

I find my bicycle, wrapped like a pretzel around the old oak tree by the barn. It has been smashed with a rock. The chain is broken and the tires are slashed. Wren did this. He hates me, and he is mad I stopped working my jobs in town. Now he has to see me all the time. He thinks because I am sick that I am weak. I am not weak. When he was playing football at the school he did not have to look at me. Now he cannot escape me. Sometimes when he looks at me I know he wants to smash my head with a rock like he did my bicycle. It makes me sad because I knew him first. Wren does not know this but when he was a little baby, Dad and Mom used to let me hold him, play with him, take him outside, and we were like regular brothers. He loved me then. He would laugh if he knew that he used to look up to me. There are many years separating us. His first word was "Ben." No one talks about that anymore, and he would not believe me even if I could tell him these things. No one wants to be reminded of the things they cannot change. I used to put him on my shoulders, back when Dad and Mom trusted me and still thought I might become whole. We would run through the fields, Wren and me, and he would howl with laughter. I held his legs tight so he would not fall. I never let him fall. Sometimes when he is staring at me, I see the murder in his eyes. I wonder if a part of him, way down deep where you cannot see, remembers me from before, if only in flashes of light you cannot describe because the words for that color do not exist.

It is raining and I walk slow along the old roads. I am wearing a tee shirt underneath my bibbed overalls but no jacket. I keep my pine oil toothpicks and spearmint chewing gum in the pocket. The cloudburst erupts. It was not raining when I left and it did not smell like it would. I can usually smell when it will rain or snow. The air tastes different. Maybe that is another part of my brain that is not working anymore. I should have worn a coat. I want to see Kira. I miss her. I do not want her to think I forgot about her. There is scratching at the base of my skull, like rodents gnawing holes in the grain sack. How many times have I made this trip?

The winds begin to blow and electricity fills the air. Then comes the thunder and lightning. Runoff water gurgles along gullies, carrying twigs and broken sticks. My boots and socks get wet. I see a tunnel and sit inside until the storm passes. There is a dead raccoon, fat and waterlogged. The water rushes past fast but the bloated body does not move. It must have been hit by a car and then crawled in here to die. No one will come to look for it. I could die in here too. No one would look for me either.

When the rains stop, I start walking again, and I make it to the center of town, past the Dairy Queen and Dollar Store, past the church on Alling Street with its statues of angels carved in the stone. I keep shuffling along, past the library and the bank and the Price Chopper. In the grocery store parking lot, a group of boys sits on the back of a pickup. Even though it is cold, they are drinking beer and playing their radio loud. I am freezing, shivering so hard my teeth keep chattering and clamping on my tongue. They are laughing at me. I wonder what it feels like. Being normal, belonging, laughing at something lesser. One of the boys throws a bottle at me. To see if I will move. Then they all do because I am standing there staring. I am an easy target. It does not bother me, and I do not get sad when they call me names. I am different. Everyone fears the things they do not understand.

Day switches to night. The storm clouds have rolled away. Over the hills and mountains, the sky washes purple and pink.

I hear a familiar rumble beside me. My brothers get out of the truck. Through the bare branches, I can still see the boys in the parking lot. Lamplight falls on them too. They think it is funny, the way I am loaded on the flatbed, like cattle. I will try again later to remember their faces.

After my brothers unload me at the farm, Dan leaves to tell Dad they found me. Wren stays behind. He tilts his head curious, like he can see what others do not.

"I know you can hear me in there, Benny," Wren says, and he pushes his forefinger hard into the center of my forehead, twisting it, like he is squashing a bug. "Yeah," he says slow, "I know you do."

I can feel my mouth move, my lips quivering. I slobber like a big dumb dog, moaning louder and louder. I want to tell him I can hear him. I want to tell him that I understand. I try to nod but my head does not agree with what I am trying to do, and rolls without direction, flopping as I flap my arms like a farmed turkey too fat to fly.

"Here's the thing, Benny, you stupid, fat fuck. I am getting tired of having to hunt you down. That is the third time this week. I'm sick of it."

I know he is right and I am wrong. My order of things gets scrambled like the eggs Mom used to make in the morning. Everything happens to me today. It is always today. It never changes.

Now he smiles. It is not a nice smile. "I know what you're doing." He winks.

Wren squeezes my shoulder and leans in close next to my ear. I know what he is going to say. I have heard it before, and I do not want to hear it again. It is going to be a bad thing and make me angry. But it also makes me wonder: how many times have we had this conversation?

"You're looking for your little girlfriend, aren't you? I know all about her. She's bad news, Benny. You'd do well to steer clear of that one. That girl is a whore, the town bike. Everyone gets a ride."

He is talking about Kira and I do not like it. I do not like it at all. I can feel my skin get hot and my hands ball into fists. But my hands will not move like I want.

I cannot remember when he was my little brother anymore, when he rode on my shoulders through the fields. If my hands moved the way I wanted them to I would punch my brother in his yellow country teeth.

CHAPTER TWENTY-TWO

Of course Nick wanted to talk about what Riley said—he'd asked a hundred questions when he picked her up from Albany. Given how much he'd helped her out, what had happened between them before Riley's call, Alex knew she should be straight with him. And she wanted to be. But finding the right words wasn't easy, and whatever she said only seemed to make things worse. She was still processing everything Riley told her, the confession and circumstance of their conversation. How could she be expected to filter all this crap and be sensitive to someone else's needs and wants? She asked Nick to please table the discussion till later. Nick said forget it, he had to get to work anyway. A kiss goodbye did little to soothe hurt feelings.

Only a day had passed since Alex's cousin called her a cunt and told her to never come back. Then again, if Linda wasn't at work, Alex wouldn't be here.

Tommy answered the door in his filthy white robe and mossy slippers. He held a pot of coffee, chugging Extra Strength Pepto Bismol straight from the bottle, expression wan, skin gray. He waved her inside.

Alex recalled the running joke, how Tommy never called in sick, no matter how late he'd been out drinking, even that time he did Jägerbombs on top of the Boilermaker Bar roof. She felt compelled to poke the bear.

"Can't hold your liquor these days, old man?"

"Bad baked chicken. What'd you want to talk about?

Sounded important on the phone."

"Kira Shanks."

"Still on that kick, eh?" Tommy poured her a mug of steaming coffee, plopping down at the kitchen table.

"I couldn't find the coffeemaker when I was here."

"Keep it under the sink. No counter space."

She grabbed the milk and sugar, swirling clouds, trying to figure out how to word her question without crossing lines or sounding ungrateful.

"There's no way to ask this without—"

"Just ask, Alex."

"Did you ever hook up with Kira? I know you and Linda have been together since forever, and this is a weird question coming from me. When you talked about Kira the other day, how she got around, it sounded personal. A little too personal."

Tommy thumbed his eye, stalling. Alex wondered if he was going to deny it, because she already knew it was true.

"Yeah. Once. Linda and I were going through a rough patch, and Kira—"

"Was hot?"

"Made it easy. I've made a lot mistakes but that was the only time I ever cheated on your cousin. And Kira, she had, I don't know, this thing."

"What thing?"

"She liked to fuck other girls' boyfriends."

"How is that a thing?"

"Everyone's got their thing, right? What gets them off? Know a guy at work. Wants a girl to piss on him and stick things up his ass. Dude's straight as an arrow. It's his thing. That was Kira's thing."

"Having sex with other girls' boyfriends?"

"No commitment. I think it was safer that way. Fuck guys who are already attached, no chance they get attached to you."

"Where'd it happen?"

"The hook up? A party. One of her friends has this old

house out by the preserve."

"In Plotter Kill."

"That's the place. Glorified flophouse. They always threw parties out there. I don't even remember where your cousin was. Shit. This is going to make me sound like a bigger asshole. I think she was visiting Diane in the hospital. When the new liver wouldn't take."

"Who else knew about this?"

"About me screwing Kira Shanks? Not your cousin, that's for sure."

"No, I mean, about her getting off on doing other girls' boy-friends?"

"I don't know. Everyone? She was a sad girl, Kira. I hate talking about her like this because of what happened, but she was fucked up. And because of the way she looked, prettier than all the others, it made it worse. She was eighteen, but that body...Jesus, I sound like a pig."

"I'm not judging you. You know any other boyfriends she seduced?"

"I don't think I'd call it that. Seduced. Didn't take a lot of convincing. Happened often though. In fact, that night I was out at Plotter Kill, she'd gotten into it with another girl, because she'd fucked her boyfriend, too."

"Remember any names?"

"Are you kidding me? This is, what, eight, nine years ago? They were in middle school when we graduated. I can't remember how I ended up at that party. I think Cal Miller dragged me there."

Alex took a courtesy sip of coffee, then stood to go.

"That's it?"

"That's it." Alex fanned her hair out of her collar. "Don't worry. I won't say anything to Linda."

"I know."

Alex was almost to the door when she heard Tommy mutter something. She turned back around.

"Trista," he said. "That was the girl's name. Trista White."

Alex thought a moment. "You know *any*one from Kira's graduating class? Enough to ask a favor?"

"Couple guys. Maybe. Why? What are you looking for?"

"Yearbook."

Alex drove out to Java the Hutt's, grabbed a good cup of coffee, and sat on the railroad ties, staring into the never-ending forest on this edge of town, the gray, black, ashen stalks of a wasteland. That's what this town was to Alex, despite its shiny coats and newly erected façades. It was ground zero, the day after, like one of those old movies of the week they aired trying to scare the hell out of everyone. How one day they would drop the big one and there was nothing you could do about it; we were all doomed. Circles of scorched earth, a post-apocalyptic horror show with hordes of survivors fighting over cans of powdered milk.

"Alex?"

She squinted up. Casual sports coat suit sans tie, bike messenger leather bag slung over his shoulder, pointy helmet tucked under his arm, the kind of guy who worked in finance downtown and rock climbed in a gym on his lunch break.

"Greg," he said. "Greg Judd." He reached into his shoulder bag and extracted the brown pleather book, passing it along. "Don't hold the popped collar against me, okay? Or the Pink Floyd yearbook quote."

"Not a problem. I'll get it back to Tommy."

"No rush." He glanced around, unsure whether to stay or go.

"Can I buy you a coffee?" Alex nodded toward the pop-up shop. "Place is amazing."

"I heard about it. Been meaning to check it out." Greg checked the time. "Sure."

Who says no to a pretty girl buying you coffee?

It was a smart move on Alex's part. Greg wasn't tight with

any of Kira's friends, having been part of a different clique, but graduating the same year, he had no problem picking out photos from a lineup, and he had plenty to say about them.

"They were trouble." Greg sat on the railroad ties, sipping his small half-caff soy macchiato. "Like I said, I hung with a totally separate crowd. But everyone knew about those guys. Burnouts, screw-ups, druggies. Weird sex parties." He stopped. "Who knows, right? Like heavy metal and Satan worship in the nineties. I don't know how much of that stuff was true, but that entire bunch came with a reputation. I remember when Kira got here. She was so good-looking, so nice, sweet. There was a fight over her. There were guys like me on one side, guys who played football, wrestled, were part of student council. And then you had that group. I never understood why she picked them."

Alex flipped open the yearbook. Greg instantly pointed to Meaghan Crouse, and had no problem identifying Trista White, Patty Hass, and Jody Wood, as well.

Alex located a picture of Sharn DiDonna. "How about him?"

"Sure. Sharn DiDonna. We called him Sharn Prima Donna. Family was loaded, but he'd go undercover for the weekend. Get ripped on whatever new designer drug was trendy, then go home and sober up beneath satin sheets at his dad's mansion in Bethlehem."

"Do you know if he dated anyone? Trista? Kira?"

"If I remember right, everyone sort of went with everyone."

Seven years, the girls hadn't changed much. Meaghan was a little heavier now, but she'd been thick back then too. Trista towered above the rest, the four of them together in almost every picture, like a little gang.

"You know Cole? Cole Denning?"

Greg shook his head. "Wasn't in our class."

She flipped through the book, searching for Kira, who didn't arrive on the scene until much later. There were a couple shots of her with the color squad, at the county fair in an oversized varsity jacket. Then there she was, another troublemaker with too much eyeliner, smoking cigarettes, posing tough against a brick wall.

Alex tapped a photograph, where a boy sat on a picnic table, arm draped around Patty Hass. "Who's he?"

"Jeremy Fisk. Dude's a lunatic. Joined the army after high school, came home freaked out. Tim McVeigh conspiracy shit. The events of September eleventh were an inside job, you know the type. He's still in Reine. A buddy ran into him at the Fireside. Got in a fight about gun control. His family used to own that shooting range in Rensselaer, Locked and Loaded. I think they shut it down a couple years ago."

Some of the boys looked familiar. Alex wasn't sure if any of them had been part of the Plotter Kill club last night. Might've been. Lurking on the porch, rattling chains, inhaling chemical concoctions from jagged light bulbs. She hadn't gotten the best look. Was Jeremy the one taking phantom pot shots with the shotgun?

"Sounds crazy," Greg said, "but I always wondered what would've happened if we'd tried harder to pull Kira over to our side."

"You think her friends had something to do with what happened?"

"No. Not directly. I don't know. I mean, everyone knows Benny Brudzienski killed her."

"Dan Brudzienski was in your class, wasn't he?"

"Dude was weird. Wren's a real shit, too. But Dan, even though he played football, he didn't have many friends, kept to himself, scribbled in journals in the library. Then I think, man, how hard that must've been? Having your mom die so young, your dad so soon after, forced to take care of someone like Benny? That family was cursed. We'd be hanging out in the supermarket parking lot after practice, and here would come Benny, shuffling down the road, all cross-eyed, hunting for his French-fried potaters. Sometimes he had a bicycle, but he didn't peddle any faster than he walked. He'd putz along until Wren and Dan would pull alongside him in the family truck, load him on the flatbed. You know Wren came back to help around the farm, right? Gave up a football scholarship. Could've gone pro. Dan wasn't half the size his brother. Looked like he'd blow a gasket trying to haul that tub of lard up there." He waited. "He was in love with Kira."

"Dan?"

"Benny. I remember early on, back when she still hung around with us, she'd go out of her way to be nice to him at the games. Like how some people adopt the mangiest, ugliest dog, Kira always made sure to wave to Benny, smile, give him a hug if we were close enough, treat him like a regular person. Benny swept the football field before Friday night games. The rest of the town knew better and steered clear of him. But I think Kira felt sorry for Benny, which sent the wrong message."

"Because Benny thought they were in love?"

"Or whatever a guy like Benny calls it." Greg laughed. "Then again, who *wasn't* in love with Kira Shanks at some point?"

"You know how I can find any of these guys? Jeremy, Sharn?"

"Jeremy's still around. I think. But I couldn't tell you where to look other than the Fireside. I know Sharn's in some lame local band."

"You got a name?"

"Of the band? Jesus, what're they called? Something ridiculous. The Groove Guppies. Used to play that big college bar off campus. A joke band. I hate the shit. Half the songs are about erectile dysfunction, pigs in space, crap like that. Dudes like Sharn take nothing seriously. It's easy to make fun of everything when you don't stand for anything. But he has money, so he knows a lot of that Uniondale crowd too. Operates both sides. Cool Moose, that's the name of the bar. Went there once and his shitty band had just finished a set. That was, like, ten, eleven months ago? Maybe longer?"

"How well did you know her?"

"Kira? A little. We had biology together. We didn't talk about what her childhood was like or anything. Once she started hanging with Meaghan Crouse and that crew, the Sharn Prima Donna dipshits, she didn't come around much."

"What about the reputation she had?"

"For sleeping with every guy who walked? Sure, I heard that. But you know high school. It's vicious. Once rumors get started, they're hard to stop." Greg finished his macchiato and shook his head. "I don't know what went on with that bunch, but like I said, when Kira hung around with us? She was a real sweetheart. What happened to her was a travesty." Greg thumbed over his shoulder. "Thanks for the coffee. I have to get to work." He climbed on his bicycle and strapped on his helmet, then stopped.

Alex looked up from her railroad tie seat.

"I wasn't going to say this, but I know who you are. I remember that story from when I was a kid, and I think it's pretty bad ass that you survived, got out of here, moved on to something better. I don't know why you're asking these questions. I've heard the rumors too, how someone egged Benny on, put him up to it. I don't know. Maybe that's what happened. But if you really think it had something to do with that crew? Be careful. This crowd you're asking about? They were trouble then. And they're trouble now."

Greg slung his bike bag in position and disappeared between the sardined cars, wheeling through the trampled weeds, back on the road.

Walking to her car, Alex scanned the yearbook, judging proximities, hand-to-hip ratios, mouth placement, studying snapshots as if each one potentially held all the answers.

Her cell buzzed. Nick. She hoped he wasn't still butt-hurt over last night. She didn't have time to deal with boyfriend drama right now.

"Hey," she said. "Got my hands on a copy of the Reine High yearbook from seven years ago—"

"You know the football field? By the turnpike?"

Alex had to think. She wasn't much into sports but, sure, she knew the spot.

"My Uncle Jimmy and I have to be in Saratoga Springs after lunch. We'll be gone all afternoon. Won't get back till late. Anyway, I'm over here at the football field now, hauling these old speakers. Worth like six bills each—"

"Okay…"

"Sorry. The guy my uncle is having me pick them up from, Stan Supinski, used to be Benny Brudzienski's boss, back when Benny cleaned the football field before games. He has some interesting things to say about that time. I think you're going to want to hear this. I mean, see this."

"See what?"

"Benny kept a diary."

"I didn't know he could write."

There was a long pause on the line.

"Nick?"

CHAPTER TWENTY-THREE

On the way over to the football field, Alex tried the Cool Moose, inquiring after Sharn DiDonna, about his band, the Groove Guppies, a show that may've taken place there "maybe ten, eleven months ago?" The guy who answered the phone had no idea what she was talking about, didn't know anyone named Sharn or anything about any band, and he didn't appreciate being bothered, slamming down the house phone to hammer home the point. Alex looked up the number for Locked and Loaded in Rensselaer, hoping Greg Judd had been wrong and she'd get a bead on Jeremy Fisk, find out if he was, indeed, the same hillbilly cleaning the shotgun on the porch. But Greg was right about it being closed down. He just had the dates wrong. The shooting range had been out of business since before the murder. She couldn't fault Greg for screwing up the timeline— she'd be hard pressed to recollect the names of anyone from her graduating class, save the ones she'd had sex with—she was lucky he had given her any names at all.

Reine High played its home games at Forsman Field, the park on the north side of the turnpike. Alex had been there a few times, mostly to get stoned and screw around under the bleachers. But that had been fifteen years ago. Since then the town had pumped a ton of cash into athletics, and Forsman Field looked better than ever. Big, paved parking lot; brand-new, high-tech scoreboard; a concession stand to rival the pros.

Alex spotted Nick's truck, crested on the dirt hill leading up to the storage shed and equipment trailers. He was kneeling in the flatbed, straining to tighten yellow canvas straps around a pair of massive speakers, securing hooks to the tailgate as he cranked the ratchet. The autumn winds chewed with an icy bite but he'd worked up a good sweat, muscles wrought underneath the tee shirt he'd stripped down to. No matter what else she thought of him, the kid was a hard worker. His apartment was a dump, his truck a piece of shit, but he wasn't lazy. She'd never had that work ethic. If the job didn't benefit her, right here, right now, Alex didn't play. No wonder she was losing the game.

"Where's your uncle? I want to thank him." Things had been too chaotic the other morning. Alex didn't even get to meet Uncle Jimmy, let alone tell him how much she appreciated the new set of tires.

Nick jumped over the railing, wiping his hands on an oily rag, snagging his sweatshirt and jacket. "Already on his way north." He started toward the trailer above the equipment sheds, waving for Alex to follow, waiting till she caught up. "I was talking with Stan Supinski this morning about Benny. You'll want to take a look at this."

"A look at what? A diary? How could Benny have kept a diary if he can't write? And why wouldn't the cops have it?"

Nick motioned for her to keep her voice down as they approached the trailer door. "Supinski is a mountain man from out west. He still rodeo circuits in the summer, old school. He's pretty distrustful of the media. I wouldn't mention the story or newspaper."

A stocky cowboy—snakeskin boots, embroidered shirt, Stetson buffalo hat, the whole wrangler nine, an odd look for Upstate New York—opened the door, all howdy ma'am smiles but still retaining an air of distrust, like Alex might be working for the Man. He might've busted a button if he knew anything about Alex.

Nick introduced her, and Supinski wedged past for a handshake. "Friends call me Smitty." He even had the yokel twang when he spoke. He motioned to a little sofa covered in home-made quilts. The trailer obviously doubled as a residence. "So Nick tells me you don't think Benny did it?"

"I wouldn't say that. Still trying to figure stuff out." Even if Alex had told Nick that, she wanted to appear impartial before Supinski shared whatever he had to show her.

Nick dropped into the sofa, happy to get off his feet, but Alex remained standing.

"I get you a beer or anything? Might have some pop in the cooler."

"No, I'm good. You wanted to show me something?"

Smitty picked up a mud-stained, weathered shoebox from the table and passed it along. Alex stared down at the closed, crumpled lid. The box looked like it had been buried deep in the dirt.

"Go on," Smitty said. "Have a look."

Alex peeled the top. Inside the box was a leather-bound book, the kind you find at indie bookstores or flea markets, with stamped gold leaf and unlined pages. It stank of mildew. Inside the book were photographs. Old photographs. A lot of Polaroids, yellowed by time, edges taped, surfaces bubbled from the heat, like they'd been stored in the attic during muggy summer months. She recognized Benny, even though he was younger. His parents had probably taken the photographs since Benny stood alone in most of them, the fashion firmly rooted in the 1970s, denim one-pieces and Dorothy Hamill bowl-cuts. Benny still had hair then, and his eyes and face didn't look so smushed together. If you looked closely, you could tell he wasn't all there mentally, but if you just glanced at them, he almost appeared normal. Then Benny disappeared, replaced by newer pictures of a girl, separate setting, locale. These were actual photographs taken with a good camera, cut from sheets of polished paper, as if they'd been stolen from the internet, dragged, cropped, printed out. Alex had a good idea who the girl in the pictures was but showed them to Nick anyway.

"Yeah, that's Kira."

They weren't scandalous pictures but wholesome ones. A young, pretty girl with blonde hair and blue eyes, dressed in big sweaters, oversized sweatshirts. In the stands at football games, laughing at the Dairy Queen, reclining on the hood of a car. There were other pictures when she was younger, too. Family holidays, church steps, Fireman's Bazaar. The last couple photographs featured ripped jeans and too much eye makeup, the angry, wounded expressions. But there were only a couple like that, tucked way in the back, a postscript. On several pages, even the ones with Benny, someone had scrawled snippets of verse in the margins, poetry or song lyrics. Alex didn't recognize the source material—they weren't from any musicians or authors she knew. Even if Benny could write, the penmanship was definitely feminine. There were flowers pressed between the pages. Dandelions.

Sifting through the pictures, Alex glanced over at Smitty Supinski. "How'd you find these?"

"Nick tell you Benny worked for me? Worked for a lot of folks around town. He was kinda, you know, special, but he could do a job once you showed him how, if it was repetitive enough. He was good at patterns, repeating them. Couldn't beat the price neither. Ron Earl wanted him off the farm, being a productive member of the community. Pay the boy a few apples, he was happy as a pig in shit."

"You think this book belonged to him?"

"How else them old family photos get in there?" Smitty said, before interrupting himself. "Sure I can't get you anything? I got some pop in the cooler—"

"We're good, Smitty," Nick said. "Tell her what you told me."

"One day Benny doesn't show up for work. Now even though he was a retard, er, what folks call special nowadays, he never missed a day. Regular as rain in March. I call out to the farm, and his dad, Ron Earl—he was a good man—he says Benny's been having a hard time, slipping a bit, 'specially since Dot, that's the mom, died. Docs think he might need to be hospitalized, get 'round the clock care. Now I don't know what was wrong with the boy, exactly. If he was a run-of-the-mill mongoloid, but he *had* been a little slower of late. I thought it was because of that girl."

"Kira?"

"Oh he was star-struck with that one, over-the-moon in love with her. Caught them two beneath the bleachers plenty."

"Caught them? Doing what?"

"Oh no not like that. I don't think that boy would know where to put his pecker if you gave him a honey pot and drew a map." Smitty's face winced red. He took off his rancher's hat. "I beg your pardon. Don't get much company up here. Sometimes I forget how to talk. I ain't from here, in case you can't tell. Come from out in 'rado. No, I mean, I'd catch her petting his head, being nice to him, feeding him kibbles like you do a barn animal. After that, I had to tell him to stop plucking them damned dandelions. Poor fool gave her a bouquet of dandelions every time he saw her. Those kids laughed at him. But not Kira. It was her fault, giving him the wrong idea. You can't expect someone like Benny to know the difference."

"When was the last time you saw him?"

"Maybe a few weeks before it happened. Benny used to ride his bike here or else he walked—that boy loved to walk, could walk for miles and miles, from one end of town to the other, all day long—Wednesdays and Fridays were his schedule. In the fall. Before the football games. After Dot died he didn't come as regular. You had to use a separate standard with Benny. A big bird flying by could distract the boy." Smitty Supinski shook his head. "But I tell ya, you get that boy to focus, he wasn't a total ret—specially challenged, mentally deficient individual—could put a tractor back together blindfolded. You see those speakers Nick's loading up? Benny hardwired those bad boys from scratch. And he was stronger'n a field ox."

"Benny had a key, I take it? To the equipment sheds?"

"He did, and I never got the key back." Smitty looked away, overcome with grief. "That poor boy. That poor family. When Deidre—that's the mom—everyone called her Dot—when she got the cancer, it was hard on them all. Benny couldn't express himself too good. If he really put his mind to it, he could squeak out a yes or no, but I'm tellin' ya, some things he could do as good as a regular person. Same as you or me." Smitty appeared pained. "I hate to admit it, but I wasn't always very nice to him. He had a tendency to daydream and we don't get a lot of time to get the field ready. I drank more than beer in those days, and I could get whiskey mean. Maybe if I'd been nicer..."

"Why didn't you show the book to the cops?"

"Two reasons. One, I don't trust the po-lice. Never have. Never will. But the other—and this's where things get weird—I found the box in the storage shed about two weeks *after* that girl went missing."

"Two weeks?"

Smitty Supinski nodded.

"They'd already found Benny beaten to hell by then," Nick added.

"That doesn't make any sense."

"I'm telling you the God's honest truth. Damn box was in plain sight so I don't know how I'd miss it. I go in that shed every day. Wasn't there until *after* that girl got killed, Benny run down, after everything. Someone dug it up, left it there for me to find."

Alex turned over her shoulder. Nick shrugged, as unsure as she what any of this meant.

"Who had keys?"

"Me and Benny. Although I'm sure parks and rec kept a duplicate set somewhere. Nothing in there but sod and fertilizer, mowers, weed whackers for field upkeep. I've been doing this job almost thirty years. No reason for anyone to go up there. A goddamn mystery, that's what this is. When cops come around, they searched the areas Benny had access to, so if that box and book had been there, means they didn't do their job neither. 'Course could mean the po-lice planted it. But no one ever came back, and I wasn't volunteering the information."

"Why'd you show me?"

Smitty pointed past her shoulder at Nick. "He seems fond of you, and holding on to them pictures wasn't doing nobody no good. This town ain't been right since that happened. Sounds wonky, but—you believe in ghosts, spirits?" Smitty shook himself off. "Sorry. Like I said. I don't get a lot of company. Sometimes my brain gets screwy ideas."

Alex tried to reconcile what Greg Judd said about Dan Brudzienski keeping a journal. But this book didn't belong to him. This was Benny and Kira's diary. Two independent lives coalesced into one large keepsake, kept in a shoebox, preserved for posterity.

"You can keep it," Smitty said. "Maybe give the pictures to his family. Benny's brothers might find comfort seeing life on the farm before everything went to hell."

Stan "Smitty" Supinski obviously didn't know the Brudzienski brothers.

Alex thanked him for his time.

Nick followed Alex, who toted the shoebox and diary under her arm, outside into the nippy fall air and gusting gray winds. "What are you thinking?"

"There was a time discrepancy, right? Between when Kira went missing and Benny was run down."

"A week or so."

"He never returned to the farm. I'm betting that's where he was hiding out."

"Why would he be hiding out if he didn't kill her?"

"I don't know. Maybe he saw who really did? Knew they were coming for him?"

"You heard Supinski. He said he checked those sheds every

day. No book. Certainly no Benny."

"He also admitted being a drunk. Alcoholics forget things, overlook what's in plain sight, get dates wrong. I'm just glad he gave it to us and not the police. They could use it to say Benny was a creeper."

"Maybe he was. Ever think we got it wrong?"

"We?"

"I'm right here with you, Alex."

She shook the shoebox. "What this shows me is that there was more to Benny Brudzienski. You saw the pictures. He cared about her."

"What are you doing now?"

"Waiting on phone calls. Trying to track down one of Kira's exes. You?"

Nick pointed at the speakers. "Gotta bring these bad boys up to Saratoga. In the slow lane. I won't be home till late. Should be able to catch a late bite before bed, if you want to wait up."

Alex laughed.

"What?"

"Sounds like we're living together."

"I didn't mean it like that."

"I know. Sounds nice." She felt her cheeks flush and turned toward the speeding cars on the turnpike.

"You have the keys," he said. "Make yourself at home. We can figure out something when I get back." Nick made like he was going to hug her goodbye, then turned quick and climbed in his cab, rolling out of the park.

Alex was almost to the turnpike when her cell buzzed with a restricted number. Her only thought was Yoan Lee must be calling again with more demands. But it wasn't Yoan.

"Why are you asking about me?" the man snapped. "If this is about the money that bitch ran up on my card, I've already talked to my bank, I'm not on the hook, call her—"

"Who is this?"

"Who's *this*?"

"Alex Salerno."

There was a long pause on the other end as if the man were weighing all his options, trying to figure out if admitting his name somehow snagged him, got him on the hook or into further trouble, like being served an official summons.

There must've been no angle he could find, because he said, "This is Sharn DiDonna. What do you want?"

CHAPTER TWENTY-FOUR

IHOP was an odd choice for a meet and greet. Given the recent improvements in Reine, there were better places to eat, tastier food, stronger drinks. Alex had suggested Java the Hutt's, but Sharn DiDonna dismissed the pop-up coffee bar as "hipster bullshit."

Alex arrived first, watching from her booth as he pulled up in a shiny sports coupe. With the weather and how far away he parked, Alex couldn't tell what kind of car it was. Only that it cost more than any car she'd ever drive. The Idlewild's half-lit yellow sign glowed weakly in the gloaming.

With his slicked hair and ironic shirt collar popping out of thrift store sweater, Sharn DiDonna didn't come across as a townie or someone who worked in the mills. And he was far too flippant for Uniondale. He projected a guy who chameleoned at will, slipping in and out of whatever world he needed to occupy at that particular moment for the greatest personal gain. Alex knew he had chosen this restaurant because of its proximity to the murder scene. It added to the kitsch appeal.

"I know you aren't a reporter for the *Codornices*," Sharn DiDonna said, sliding opposite and immediately snapping at the waitress.

"Yeah? And why's that?"

"Because the guy who edits the goddamn thing crews with a good friend of mine." Sharn picked up sugar packets, shaking the contents and snapping the bottoms like they were gram bags. "Noah Lee is a privileged, lazy fuck. Did he mention his father is Yoan Lee? From the *Post*?"

"He said his dad's a famous journalist, yes." She wasn't giving him more than that. "I'm not a big newspaper reader."

"Yet reporter is the cover story you went with?" Sharn shook his head. "Noah has a morbid fascination with the Shanks case. Like some people obsess over the identity of D.B. Cooper, or whether Frank Morris and the Anglins made it out of Alcatraz alive. I don't know what fairy tale he sold you. But every word out of his mouth is a goddamn lie."

The waitress poured a cup of piping black coffee. Sharn smirked and waited till she was gone. Then didn't say anything else. The entire time he refused to meet Alex's gaze, he spun the condiment carousel, glanced at his cell phone, anywhere but her eyes. He wasn't intimidated. More hyperaware of his own person, like a celebrity scared of being recognized in public. There was no one else in the restaurant. Alex got the impression of an actor playing a character, one he'd embodied so long the performance had become a permanent part of his person. Like Johnny Depp after *Pirates*.

"Why are you talking to me?" she said.

"You called me."

"Yeah, but why make the drive? If you know I'm not writing any article. It's clear you don't give a shit about unsolved mysteries."

"I hate this town. Hate the phony pricks at Uniondale almost as much as I hate the posers I ran with in high school." He laughed, spreading his arms in a show of magnanimity. "I'm a man without a country. I don't know why I agreed to meet you. I like to stir the pot? Some people call me a contrarian. Maybe I'm bored on a Tuesday afternoon. Why? You want me to leave?" He pretended the threat was genuine but didn't move. "You want to know about Kira's friends? About Trista and Meaghan and those Plotter Kill kids? Sure, I know things. But I'm not helping Noah Lee."

"I couldn't care less about helping Noah. Or the paper. Or the college." She stared through the rain-rivered window. "Or this town."

"That," Sharn said, pointing a finger, "is why I agreed to talk to you." A grin crept up his pretty-boy face.

Alex felt for the phone in her pocket, wishing she could open a recording app without him noticing. Sharn would never consent to going on record but she wanted to capture it all. She knew this was going to be good.

"When Kira got to town," Sharn began, "she was all anyone could talk about. You know what she looked like, right?"

"I've seen pictures." Yes, Kira Shanks was beautiful, with long, wavy blonde hair and baby blue eyes, the composite sketch of a million teenage boys' fantasies.

"If you've only seen pictures," Sharn said, tapping into brainwaves, "they don't do her justice. There are some girls, women, whose beauty cannot be contained by a camera lens. I've also known women who look fantastic in photographs, but when you see them in person, they disappoint. Kira had it both ways. Gorgeous in pictures, and radiant in person."

"I didn't know you were such a poet."

"I play in a band. What can I say? I'm a hapless romantic. Beauty cut down in its prime is always tragic."

"You act like you know she's dead."

Sharn creased his brow, reaching for more sugar. "Of course she's dead."

"What makes you so sure?"

"Um, because Benny Brudzienski killed her? Everyone knows that. No one's seen Kira Shanks in seven years. Someone dumped her body in the river. She's far out to sea by now, fish food, baby. What other possibility could there be?" There was a winking smile in his eyes, like everything he said was both a joke and the gospel truth at once.

"You wouldn't be here if you really thought that."

"I don't go for conspiracies."

Sharn DiDonna was exactly the kind of guy who went for conspiracies. Otherwise where was the challenge? Winks, nudges, elbows on the sly. And shame on you if you believed a word he said.

"When I was dating Trista, I was also fucking Kira."

"Seems to be a common story."

"Yes. It is. While Jeremy Fisk was dating Patty, he was fucking Kira. Same with Peter, Mark, Rich, and, well, you get the point. Kira was *very* popular. You talk to her parents?"

"I heard they moved out of town."

"Doesn't mean they can't be tracked down? Maybe journalism isn't in your cards after all. Kira was a troubled girl." Sharn picked up a butter knife, drawing it achingly across his wrists and forearm, etching tiny crosses. "Cutter," he whispered, glancing at the long-sleeved hoodie Alex still wore inside.

The waitress headed over to see if anyone wanted food, but Sharn shook her off. A pro used to high school kids ordering French fries and ice water without leaving a tip, the waitress turned on a heel, resigned to the lost cause. Sharn was just getting warmed up.

"Benny was in love with Kira," he said. "As much as a thing like him can love. I'm sure you figured that out by now."

"I've figured out a lot of things. I'm more interested in what you think."

Sharn threw a loose arm over the backrest of the adjacent, empty booth, kicking a foot in the aisle. He jumped the salt shaker like it was a chess piece. "I think those girls—Meaghan, Trista, Patty, Jody, a couple others whose boyfriends Kira was fucking on the side—I think they all got together, waited till Kira was in a room with one of these guys—" He stopped like he knew what she was thinking. "Hey, it wasn't me. I mean some *other* guy, someone not part of that crew, a stranger, long-haul trucker, random lay from the bar, whatever. I think they waited till Kira and this dude are getting it on, tell Benny to go to the room—everyone knew Benny was in love with her—they say there's a surprise waiting for him." Sharn pointed out the glass, toward the Idlewild and number eight. "Benny goes in, sees Kira and some guy bumping uglies—she liked it freaky—he loses his shit. Might've been an accident, maybe he didn't mean to do it. Who knows? But here's the deal: Benny couldn't cover up a murder of that magnitude. He's too stupid. What did he do with the body?"

"You said he dumped her in the river."

"No. I said *someone* dumped her in the river. Someone helped cover it up."

"You got any proof?"

"If I could prove anything, I would've told the cops."

Or not. Alex couldn't picture Sharn going to the authorities. But he was aching to share just the same. All she had to do was sit back and listen.

Sharn returned to real cool customer, fingers tapping a smooth beat against the booth. "Everyone I saw in the aftermath acted odd. I was already done with Trista and the rest of those losers. But I remember seeing them around town, huddled together, nibbling nails, biting tongues, shushing any time I got within ear distance. Not hard to put two and two together. At least not for someone who used to be a part of that scene. Those girls were jealous as hell of Kira. This was payback."

"Okay," Alex said, buying in while reserving doubts—Sharn made no bones about axes to grind. If she could weed out the personal vendetta, a lot of what he said rang true. "And then what? These girls chase Benny down, beat him half to death?" A few post-graduation pounds aside, those four weren't getting the jump on a man the size of Benny Brudzienski. "Or are you saying they had their 'dopey boyfriends' do it? That's a lot of people expected to keep a secret. You know what they say about keeping secrets in a small town?"

"Yeah. Only way to keep a secret is if one of you is dead." He winked. "If I were you, I'd be looking at Cole Denning. You know who he is?"

Alex had to admit the name had flashed on her radar once, twice, or half a dozen times.

"He was older, worked at the motel too, used to rent rooms to high school kids, buy them booze to party. He was desperate for them to think he was cool. Cole's old man had been bagging Evie Shuman for years. She inherited the place after her husband died. That's why Cole always has a job, doing repairs and shit. Been working there for forever. Hardly dependable." Sharn tipped back an invisible glass of booze. He pointed around her, out in to the murky gray, where gravel lot met winding road, face feigning whimsical. "Maybe that was an accident, too, Benny getting run off the road. No streetlights along that stretch. It had been raining, dark. A car clips him, sends him into that ditch. Where Benny bashes his own head against a rock. Repeatedly. Stranger things have happened."

"I thought you said you don't believe in conspiracies?"

"I don't." Sharn set down his coffee. "I know who you are. I know what happened to you." He panned around the empty restaurant as the light rain began to fall harder. "That's why I'm telling you all this."

"Why?"

"Because you care about the truth more than the cops. You know what it's like, don't you? The cops around here, they aren't interested in solving squat. A town like Reine rakes in tourist dollars whenever the leaves change color. Get a bunch of morons up from Connecticut to watch something die so they can sell more maple syrup. Why else is anyone coming up to this shitburg? Better to blame one bad apple than the whole damn tree. Ken Parsons. Ben Brudzienski. Lone gunmen are easier to stomach than systematic patterns of violence."

"You sound like a college student."

Sharn held up his hands. "Guilty. Criminology and urban statistics. But not Uniondale. Fuck those bourgeois pricks. But it doesn't make what I'm saying any less true. There is something wrong with this town. You grew up here. You must've seen it."

"What's that? An evil hanging over the place? A harbinger of doom?"

"Nothing so esoteric or gothic, please. I'm talking about the kids, today's youth, the bleak landscapes, no faith in the future. The despondency. The sickness. You travel a lot?"

"I wouldn't say a lot."

"Take it from me, then. I've been all over, okay? I grew up in Reine, but Dad's family has money. When my folks split up, they took him back, we got paid, and I did a lot of sightseeing. Up and down the coast. Overseas. Backpacking to Ibiza." He swung his arms wide. "Counting cars on the New Jersey Turnpike, all across America."

"Then back to college."

"Education is important. My point—there's nowhere like Upstate New York. It's a dirty, ugly place that's never possessed the hope to lose. Look at this town. I'm telling you, it breeds cruelty, nastiness." Sharn glanced down at his buzzing phone. "And on that note."

He hopped up, pulled his money clip, plucked a five spot. "Nice meeting you." Bluetooth to ear, he held out a finger. "Yeah. Hold up." He looked her dead on. "Be careful."

As Sharn talked business down the aisle and out into the monsoon, she knew he meant more than Benny, Kira, or even this town. He was cautioning against something far more sinister.

CHAPTER TWENTY-FIVE

The rains kicked up when Alex stepped out of the restaurant, that distinct wind and raw howl you only get in Upstate New York. Dead, wet leaves lifted off the ground, swirling, infused with the charged scent of decay. She may not have traveled much but Alex knew these storms were germane to the region. You didn't get storms like this in the city or Connecticut or anywhere else for that matter. Of course Alex didn't have an umbrella with her. Though her car was a few feet away, she saw the yellow Idlewild sign, beckoning with answers. She lifted her hoodie and collar and made a run for it as the skies opened in earnest.

Pushing through the door, rainwater sloshing the mat, Alex saw the broad back of Evie Shuman camped out in front of the blue-gray glow of her television. With the powerful shudder blowing through the open door, you'd think the old woman would be incited to sneak a peek. But she remained frozen in front of her TV, back turned, even after Alex offered a courtesy cough. Alex had started to creep forward, wondering if the old woman was dead, when Evie Shuman shot around.

With the motel just across the way, Alex wanted to take the opportunity to verify Sharn's claims. The guy oozed smarmy charm, with plenty of balls to bust, but something about his version carried more weight than any other story she'd heard. As soon as Alex's eyes met Shuman's disapproving scowl, she regretted that decision. Any trace of familiarity gone, the only thing left in its place: hard-country mean. Alex noted the bottle of rye clutched in a clenched fist, like a desperate Baptist and a Bible. The way Evie Shuman greeted her—hissing at the intruder in the nest—Alex felt the need to reintroduce herself. Maybe the old woman had forgotten who she was?

Alex extended a hand, pulling it back as fast when she realized the feeling wasn't mutual. "Remember? We talked the other day? I was here with—"

"I know who you is. You said you was with the newspaper."

No question in the accusation, statement of fact. Evie Shuman had obviously done her homework.

"I said I'm working on a story *for* a newspaper, helping with the research. But, no, I'm not an actual reporter or anything."

"You said you was a reporter. You said you was going to do something to help me keep my property."

"I apologize if you thought that. I may've misspoken."

"You may've misspoken," Evie Shuman parroted. She poured rye into a smudged motel glass, holding up the bottle for Alex to see. Alex shook her head. The offer felt like a last cigarette before the firing line.

Alex glanced over her shoulder. The now-torrential downpour fell in sheets, flooding the lot, muddy ponds filling potholes and divots. "Raining cats and dogs out there."

"No shit. I can see. What do you want?"

"I was hoping to ask you some more questions."

"You told me I was going to be on the TV." The old woman sneered, tossing back her rye. "I ain't gonna be on the TV."

"I never said you were going to be on television—"

"Yes, you did. Dirty little liar."

When Alex was in her early twenties she went through a phase where she got in a lot of fistfights. The brawling didn't last longer than a few months, a chapter she later regretted, though looking back on that time now, she understood what it was all about. Parsons had taken control from her. Fighting strangers was her way of taking it back. So that's what she did.

Instigating fights at bars and clubs, on sidewalks after closing time, in the heat of a party. Man, woman, didn't matter. Alcohol, drugs, late nights, perceived slights, real or imagined, and it was on. Immature and lamentable, sure, but her antics won her legions of fans, which led to more shots and freebies. There was something about a pretty girl who could throw a punch. The real benefit from that time: Alex wasn't afraid of physical confrontation. The other night at Sweetwater she'd been distracted, reckless; she'd put herself in a dumb situation, tunnel vision clouding judgment. She had nothing to worry about with a sixty-something alcoholic, even if Evie Shuman acted ready to throw down. With the hard rain and drastic change in barometric pressure, old thing would probably break a hip if she made any sudden moves. There were easier ways to handle this.

"You're right," Alex said. "I owe you an apology. I misrepresented myself. I'm sorry to bother you again—"

"Then why are you? You're interrupting my programs."

"I was hoping you might show me the room."

The old woman cocked her head. "Why you want to stay at this dump?"

"Not to rent. I'd like to see the room where it happened."

"Where what happened?"

Damn this old fool. She was going to make her say it.

"Where Kira Shanks was last seen."

"Rooms are twenty-nine dollars and ninety-nine cents. I ain't running no sightseeing tours."

"No problem." Alex reached in her pocket.

Evie Shuman pointed at a sign on the wall, the novelty kind you can pick up along the highway, in the gag section of truck stops, the kind aimed at blacks in the rural South. "You see that?"

"Yes, I can read."

"Says I reserve the right to refuse service to no one I don't like."

Alex pulled out forty bucks. The motel was falling down, in

need of serious repair; Evie Shuman wasn't in any position to soapbox.

She snatched the cash, stuffing the bills in her front pocket.

Bypassing the keys hanging on the wall, the old woman creaked below the register. Alex heard a lockbox unclasp. The sounds of metal against metal, scraping, clanking, Marley's ghosts rattling. Shuman popped up holding a key.

"That's one of the rooms we don't rent no more. I'll give you fifteen minutes."

Alex wanted to say she paid forty bucks, she'd take all day if she wanted to, but she could worry about that part once she got inside.

Walking out the office, the two kept beneath the overhang, following the L shape of the motel. Rainwater gushed out gutters, overflowing in a waterfall. The room she wanted was all the way at the end. The storm came in fits and bursts, and soon even the overhang didn't offer protection. The rain slashed sideways, splattering off stone, soaking ankles.

When Evie Shuman unlocked the door, years of sealed-in mustiness rose up and smacked Alex in the face. It was more than mildew trapped in damp carpets and the wet, rotten wood. The pungent stench carried the echoes of death. Soon as Alex entered the room, any questions of whether Kira Shanks had survived her ordeal went by way of the wild winds. That girl had died in here.

The low lights flickered on. Wasn't much to see. Alex didn't know what she'd hoped to find. The room, unoccupied for years, spread out like any budget motel, minus a TV, an empty spot on the dresser where one had once lived. Everything else of value had likewise been removed. There was no chalk outline of an invisible body on the carpet, no yellow police ticker tape. Blood and bodily fluids had long been wiped cleaned, room sanitized, sterilized.

"Did you rent it out after she disappeared?"

"I said you could look at it. Didn't say I was answering any more of your questions." Evie Shuman paused a moment, before whispering, "Dirty little liar."

"How long had Cole Denning been working here?" Alex asked, scouring the room for clues.

"Told you. He don't work here no more. Fired him last week."

Alex bent down, craning her neck to check under the bed. "I heard he was like family."

With the door still open, rain and wind wailing, Alex couldn't say if the cold alone was responsible for the shiver down her spine, the goose bumps on her arm. She felt a presence in that room. Not Shuman's. Not hers. A separate one altogether. Like a living, breathing third person were standing right there with them. Alex didn't buy into ghost stories, and she had no use for the supernatural, and don't even get her started on organized religion. But she didn't dare turn around, for fear of validating all the things she didn't believe in.

Alex shook off the creeps, straightening up, making for the sink adjacent to the bathroom. She could feel the old woman in the doorway, swigging from her bottle, seething impatience, waiting till Alex got her money's worth because no way was she leaving Alex unsupervised.

"When did Cole Denning start working here?" Alex asked, rephrasing the question, stepping toward the closet, which was now an open space, doors taken off the hinges. She flipped on the lights above the sink. Bulb burned out. The mirror was filthy, opaque, covered in a thick layer of scum.

Alex went to wipe the mirror, like clearing steam after a hot shower.

That's when she saw the bottle crashing down on her head.

The bottle was not in Evie Shuman's fist.

It's really hard to knock someone out, no matter how hard you hit them. Except in the movies. The man who hit Alex had hit her hard—hard enough to send her face first into the dresser; hard enough to make her chomp down on her tongue and tear out a chunk of meat; hard enough for her to taste her own blood. The back of her head burned with sharp, searing pain, like someone had lodged a pick axe at the base of her skull, but she never lost consciousness. The blow did make it tough to think straight though, eyes unable to focus, bearings too scattered to gather. She heard voices.

"You idiot," Shuman shouted. "She's still awake. Hit her again!"

Clodded steps approached. Flipping onto her back, she expected to see Cole Denning, or at least someone she knew. Instead, she came face to face with a stranger. She did not know this fat, old man coming at her, had never seen him before, had no idea why he cocked the liquor bottle above his head or why he wanted to kill her so bad, but she didn't plan to stick around and find out. As the fat man readied the bottle for a second strike, Alex curled her leg to her chest, kicking her sneaker out, a clean, straight shot to the groin. He dropped to his knees, both hands covering his junk, bottle clunking off the bathroom linoleum. Shuman bellowed to grab her. The old man wobbled like a walrus rolling to get upright. Alex scrambled to her feet and sprinted into the pissing rain.

Spinning mud and gravel, Alex peeled out of the parking lot, and drove straight into the storm.

CHAPTER TWENTY-SIX

She checked her face in the mirror, gingerly touching the back of her head, scouting the damage. The skin felt shredded, like a butterfly cut of poultry, underside wet and gummy. She brought back slick bloody fingers. Alex tried Nick but couldn't get through. Why had that man attacked her, and when had Shuman summoned him to do so? The way the man appeared, like a demon conjured, Alex couldn't shake what Noah Lee said about the evil she cursed upon this town. Maybe she never escaped that bunker after all. She'd died down there in Parsons' basement with the others, and somewhere the girl the world knew as Alex Salerno lay on a cold, concrete slab, stuck in time, daydreaming storylines while her organs calcified; or maybe time worked the same in the afterlife. Her body had been dumped in the woods, the worms fed on her, feral animals picking bones clean. With the sweet release of death, a chemical reaction sparked neurons, firing a final fleeting thought into the ether, conspiring to create this fantasy of a girl with a bloody head, driving around her hometown, trying to solve the mystery of her own murder.

Alex didn't decide to drive to Linda and Tommy's. With Nick gone, she didn't want to be alone, and she didn't have anywhere else to go. If she were thinking clearly, she'd have checked the clock, known Linda would be home from work by now. She wasn't up for another fight. Alex wasn't thinking clearly.

Pulling in front of their place, she didn't see Tommy's truck, only her cousin's car. Linda was already at the door, dressed in sweats, holding a can of beer.

"Great." She held open the screen. "It's you."

Blue smoke ribboned through the messy living room. The place stank with a mix of hopelessness and musk, like every bar before they banned cigarettes and professional drinkers had to ply their trade elsewhere. Without Linda having to say it, Alex knew Tommy was gone. And not simply because his truck wasn't parked outside. Closet doors and drawers remained opened, hangers ripped to the floor, evidence of all things gathered in haste. Alex knew she was going to get blamed for this latest rotten turn in her cousin's life.

"You got a towel? Some ice?" Alex held out her hand, covered in blood after holding together her skull.

"What the hell happened?"

Alex sat on the couch. "Got jumped."

Linda lumbered to the kitchen, grunting to access lower drawers and a dishrag. She packed ice from the box, running it under the tap, twisting the rag into a hard, bulky ball.

Her cousin handed her the homemade icepack, breathing heavy through her mouth.

"Tommy?" Alex had to ask.

"I think you know the answer to that."

Linda's face pulsed, a torrent preparing to unleash a lifetime of resentment, and not just for Alex's role in Linda's failures, but her mother's too. As if Denise hadn't been around, maybe Linda's mom, Diane, wouldn't have been such a fuck-up. But Linda shook her head, ire abating, like only now she recognized how pointless it all was. Storing years of hostility hadn't done her any good; and truth, in its various forms, has its limitations. Any attempt to repair the damage at this point was too damned little, too damned late.

"Want to tell me what happened?" Alex asked.

"He admitted fucking Kira Skanks. After your little heart to heart."

"I didn't mean to cause you any trouble."

"Not your fault, coz." Linda sounded like she almost believed it. "You didn't stick your tiny dick in her."

"You won't want to hear this right now, but he loves you."

"Yeah," Linda said, sitting on the couch beside her. "You're right." She lit a cigarette of her own. "I don't want to hear it."

The two sat in silence listening as the rain slowed to a steadier rhythm, beating against the asphalt and concrete, the hardest parts of this brick and mortar town.

"Why did you have to come back?"

"Just blame me for Tommy and let's get this over with."

"I don't blame you." Linda sucked on her Marlboro, a wheeze rattling deep in her lungs. "I think in some ways I already knew." Linda looked down at her shapeless body, the oversized tee shirt soiled with mustard and pizza sauce, beer dribble, the unflattering sweat pants stretched too wide at the hips, the protruding belly that might've been understandable if she'd had kids. But Linda didn't have any kids. She wouldn't have any kids. And everyone knew that was for the best. "I can't say I blame him."

"Don't do that."

"I'm not like you, Alex. Men don't fight over me. I'm no one's prize. I'm the girl they take home at the end of the night when all their other choices are gone. I'm last resort."

"Tommy took you home. Picked you first, if I remember right."

Linda grumbled and guzzled her beer.

"What are you going to do?" Alex said.

"Get drunk for a few days. Might go down to the bar, catch a dick. Then I'll call Tommy, and we'll patch things up. Truth is we're both too tired to start dating again. Neither of us can be alone."

Alex had nothing to add to that statement, which might've been the saddest thing she ever heard. At least since yesterday.

"I know. Not terribly romantic. But you know what? Romance dies pretty quick, and people ain't perfect. I can count on Tommy to be there, and he can count on me, and we'll get through this."

"That's good, I guess."

"What about you? Someone jumped you?"

She shook her head. "I went to the Idlewild to talk to the woman who runs the place. Someone didn't like me being there."

"Why do you care so much? You didn't know Kira. Or Benny. You don't live here anymore, and when you did, you hated this fucking town. Neither one of us has happy memories of this place. I wish I could get away. Growing up here was awful. Our mothers were drunken whores. What happened to you—you should've died. Why? Why come back here and relive it?" Her eyes brimmed earnest, a last-ditch effort to bridge unbridgeable chasms. "Is this about Riley?"

"No, it's not about Riley."

"Benny ain't Parsons. They have nothing to do with each other. You know that, right?"

Alex turned to face the wall. Wet brakes, grinding gears, the distant sound of retreating thunder.

"I'm sorry," Linda said.

"For what?"

"I haven't been very nice to you."

"I haven't been very nice to you either. Not sure it matters. We're blood."

No one spoke for a long time. Then Linda pushed herself up and said she had to be somewhere. Alex knew her cousin didn't need to be anywhere, other than not here. Only so many times you can talk about where it all went wrong and not do anything to make it right.

"You can crash if you need to."

"I'm fine."

"Well, you can still stay." Linda was almost to the door

when she stopped. "How far do you plan to follow this?"

Alex thought about laying it all on the line—the farm, Wren and Dan Brudzienski, Riley getting thrown out of his house and falling off the wagon, the tiny parts of her heart breaking all over again. She thought about confessing that even though she knew Parsons acted alone, a part of her still lived in fear that he hadn't, that someone—or something—else lay in wait, a monster in the closet, a beast hiding under the bed, preparing to steal her back just when she got comfortable, and so her only defense was to never be comfortable, worry constantly, pay penance in advance like layaway. She wanted to share the rest of it, too. Sharn DiDonna's theory. Noah and Yoan Lee, the politics of parenting and punishment. Cole Denning. Evie Shuman and Stan "Smitty" Supinski. A photo album filled with flowery snippets of poetry. Meaghan Crouse, Trista White, Patty Hass, and Jody Wood—the list of possible suspects endless—either guilty as sin or wrong place wrong time, complicit through inaction. Alex was desperate to trust someone other than the guy she met last week in a bar, and who better than family? She missed her mom.

But by then Linda had already walked out the door.

Alex woke in the dark, unsure where she was, smells of damp, sodden earth overpowering, then that old familiar panic set in, the claustrophobia that the air was going to run out soon. Took her a moment to remember she'd passed out on her cousin's couch, that the torrent had passed. She filled her lungs with after-the-storm calm. Her head felt as if it had been riddled by the business end of a Howitzer. She recalled the Idlewild, Sweetwater, the burden of an unexpected week that had thrust her into the past, forcing her to face demons she thought had been laid to rest, only to be reminded that demons don't go to sleep so easily.

Linda hadn't returned. Alex knew her cousin wouldn't come

back until she was gone. In the kitchen, Alex filled a paper cup with cool tap. The cut still felt tender to the touch. She soaked the cloth, dabbed at the gash, wiped away the crusted blood, tried to free the matted hair, but the wound had fused, become a permanent part of her. The clock on the stove said she'd lost half a day. She checked her phone. Nothing from Nick. But there were several calls from a number she didn't know. Not blocked like Yoan or Sharn but an unfamiliar local number. She checked her voicemail. Nothing but dead air. A text dinged in.

At house in Plotter Kill. Come alone. Cole.

CHAPTER TWENTY-SEVEN

After the Idlewild, Alex knew she shouldn't brave that house alone. But Linda was gone, and it wasn't like she'd be any help anyway. She couldn't reach Nick, who was still trapped up north in the storm's path. Alex contemplated calling Riley, but what would she tell him? Would he still be drunk and raging? Some things you have to face alone. Alex grabbed the Louisville Slugger by the door.

Hitting the highway, she pulled up the address for the secluded, creepy house on the edge of the Plotter Kill Preserve. She tried Nick again, but once more the call went straight to voicemail. She left a message, explaining where she was going, whom she was meeting, and what she hoped happened next. Even at her most optimistic—and hopeful was not a trait Alex Salerno naturally possessed—she knew there was no guarantee the text had even come from Cole. That crowd the other night had been rough. She needed a plan. If she saw cars, any other people, she'd err on the side of a setup. From the perimeter, she'd be able to tell if Cole was lying about being alone. If it looked like he had company, she'd come back later with Nick, maybe Tommy too. Even Riley, if he was sober by then and she was up for dealing with that.

Compulsion and curiosity pulled her along, the burning need to learn the truth. Even before Sharn, Alex felt Cole had been hiding something. She could see it in his face, his eyes, the way he carried his body, a man tormented. A man with a confession he was dying to get off his chest.

Alex's cell rang as she raced. It wasn't anyone she wanted to talk to now.

"Forget about the farm," Alex tried telling Noah Lee, who kicked off the conversation in high gear, prattling about the Brudzienski property. "Dead end," she said.

"Maybe not," Noah said. "Did some digging. I took your advice and called the probate court where Ron Earl Brudzienski's will was filed. Wren is potentially on the hook for a lot of money—"

"I know. I talked to Riley." Alex searched for the signposts up ahead. "If Benny gets moved to Jacob's Island, the state can seek restitution. And if Benny were to somehow get cleared, Wren has to decide whether he lets his brother die in the streets. I don't think he's looking forward to facing that dilemma."

"No dilemma. He doesn't have a choice. There's a provision."

"What provision?"

"One that mandates Benny's continued care. A percentage of the profits from the farm. Hard and fast numbers. In writing. Legally binding."

"How much of a percentage?"

"Thirty-three and a third."

"A full third?" Alex asked.

"Three kids, so yeah. Every cent has to be accounted for. It's very thorough."

Alex hated admitting she'd come to view Benny as less than human, assuming his parents would have done the same. Which made her the shittier person.

"So we have a motive," Noah said.

"For what?"

"Who put Benny in the hospital. You know how big the Brudzienski farm is? They have more property than just the one in Reine."

"Hold on," Alex said, trying to read exit names. "You're

getting a little ahead of yourself."

"You think, what, it was an accident? Bad timing? Benny was already headed for inpatient hospitalization. Ron Earl had started arrangements before he died. Found that out too. If Benny isn't brained in that trench, he's shipped to Brattleboro Acres. Wren is executor of the estate. You know how much Brattleboro costs? Let me tell you, it isn't cheap. As long as his big brother stays in Galloway, Wren is pocketing a fortune."

"First off, there's no foolproof method for beating a man to within inches of his life." Alex didn't know what finally shorted Benny's circuits, but the provision cemented Wren and Riley's partnership. Riley had admitted as much, just without the hard stats to back it up. If Riley was trying to prevent formal charges against Benny because he had lingering doubts of culpability, Wren had no choice but to get behind him. A third of all profits explained the expansion and diversification of the family farm, as well—why, for instance, Dan didn't work there. The more outsourcing, the greater the rotating overhead, the less technical "profit."

"This is *huge*, Alex. You were right. This story is turning into something much bigger than just Kira Shanks."

"There's no 'just' about it. A girl is still dead." She slowed to make sure she had the right turn. "What about your father?"

"What about him? He wanted me to stand up for myself. *You* wanted me to stand up for myself. This is me standing up for myself." And Noah was off and running, citing additional research he'd done, figures, stats, projections, the cost to run a farm, how much money they made, lost, spent on advertising, electricity, refrigeration, upkeep and maintenance, interstate shipping—the kid swelling with pride over a job well done. She let him drone on, her own brain overtaxed with this latest influx of info, which she couldn't reconcile with Cole Denning's text message and whatever waited for her at Plotter Kill.

She didn't even remember when Noah clicked off, her head configuring myriad combinations and possibilities. She needed to stay sharp, stay focused. Time could often get the best of Alex and devoting limited mental resources to the farm right now wasn't helping solve anything. She almost had a stable foundation constructed, until she repositioned a tab and the whole damn thing fell apart. Like removing a lower block during a drunken game of Jenga. Even if Wren benefited financially from Benny staying in the hospital, it still didn't explain what put him there. She couldn't connect worlds. Wren and Dan. Meaghan and her crew. They didn't mix. Except through Benny. And Kira. Or maybe it was the other way around? Alex didn't care about wills, projected income, or the best convalescence money could buy. She cared about blood and genetic samples found at the Idlewild Motel; about what really took place on that cold November morning seven years ago. She cared about the mentally handicapped man found bludgeoned and left to die in a culvert, vilified without a chance to defend himself. Because the more she looked into this, the more certain she'd grown of Benny Brudzienski's innocence. And Cole Denning was ready to help answer these questions. Why did Noah have to call right then? She had believed she was speeding toward a solution. Now she felt all twisted around. She should've let the call go to voicemail.

Coming off the 90, Alex caught Rob Roy Road through Rotterdam, entering the preserve via the south side. Unlike last time with Nick, she bypassed 5S, which offered a better view of the front porch and clearer vantage point to weigh odds of an ambush. Problem was this route cut through the boondocks. She lost what little cell service she had, two bars turning to one, one to none, taking all direction with it. Unfamiliar routes delivered her down darker paths. Knotted up, she had no idea where she was going, heart beating faster, palms, neck, forehead damp with sweat. Tall trees loomed stark and foreboding, boxing her in. Her skull still throbbed from the sucker punch at the motel this morning.

A faint moon peeked out of a bank of silver cloud. Behind a

grouping of shagbark, Alex killed the lights, coasting to the edge of a small pond where no wind blew. Elodea and frogbit blanketed murky waters. Alex reached behind her seat and retrieved the baseball bat, holding it low at her side, creeping through the long reeds and skinny trees.

Coming to the clearing, Alex saw Cole Denning sitting on the porch, an old man alone in his rocker on a lazy summer's eve.

The house sat across a large plot of land, empty in the aftermath. A lot of ground to cover. Nothing about Cole or the situation screamed danger. If anything, the moment almost felt too tranquil.

Muddying her sneakers, Alex split bushy bearded weeds and blue stems, soles stuck in the muck as she tried to tread lightly toward the porch on heightened alert. Eider squawked in the bulrush.

The man kept rocking, head turned to listen to the night songs of the country.

As she got closer, Alex offered a half wave. The gesture was not returned.

Alex now saw she'd been mistaken. Cole Denning was not rocking. He was not moving at all.

CHAPTER TWENTY-EIGHT

Whether due to distance or inability to focus, apprehension, inherent caution—the anticipation that something wicked this way waited—Alex had missed the obvious. The first being the Remington, which lay beneath Cole Denning's rocking chair, the expelled red casing at his feet, precariously placed, convenient to find. As she went up the porch steps, Alex scanned the area. Nothing. No one. Immediate vicinity swept clean. The evening birds whispered lullabies in the butternut hickory, owls hooting in the hills. The scene pristine, surreal.

She leaned the bat against the railing, inching closer to inspect the fatal blast. The death was fresh, as if traces of life lingered, fragments of soul humming in the ether. Now that she was standing next to the dead man, she could see his head cocked at a perverse angle, and the entry wound became clearer. The shotgun had been placed under his chin, turning the left half of his jaw to hamburger, popping a hole the size of a tea plate out the top of his head. The other half of his face, the one turned toward her, remained intact. Cole's eyes were wide open, a twinkle of shine to them, slight curl on his lips. He seemed a man at peace.

A blood-flecked, handwritten note sat in Cole Denning's lap. Short, sweet, to the point.

Forgive me Kira for what I've done.

When the screen door flew open, the setup, like the shell and note, felt too staged, the timing and collective gasps too rehearsed, the first in a string of "Oh my Gods" coming a tick too quick.

All four girls walked out, single file, Meaghan, Trista, Jody, Patty, each covering their mouths in horror, before any could've seen the full extent of the damage. Alex eyed the shotgun.

"What happened?" Meaghan asked as the others fanned out.

Patty inched close enough to feign reading the letter.

"What's it say?" Jody said.

"He admitting putting Benny up to it," answered Trista, who remained stationed in the back. The tallest of the pack, she was still farthest from Cole and the note.

Alex brought out her phone. "We should call the cops."

Meaghan came beside her, covering Alex's hand and tucking the cell away. "Before we bring the police into this, let's be sure we're all seeing the same thing."

"Do you see what we see?" Patty asked.

"I see that Cole is dead."

Behind her, Alex heard the shotgun picked up. She looked over her shoulder. "You think you should touch that?"

Jody cradled the Remington, stroking it as one would a pet. Alex noticed the gloves. Jody didn't consider Alex's question, backtracking to the perimeter, standing alongside Trista. With one fist wrapped around the stock, Jody kept her stare locked on Alex as she stuck her other hand deep in the pocket of her padded coat, jostling shotgun shells, rolling them over like fistfuls of stone for the wishing well.

"You see what we see, don't you?" Meaghan titled her head to call Alex's interest.

From the corner of her eye, Alex saw Jody loading the Remington, one shell, two shells.

"When my daddy was alive," Jody said, "we used to go hunting every season." She shouldered the shotgun, pretending to line up a target over the reeds. "Bagged two-hundred-pound bucks in those woods. Venison all winter long. The meat is salty, gamey. But you get used to the taste after a while. My daddy was a real good shot. Runs in the family."

Alex knew what she should do. Stop asking questions, accept their version of events, slink off, surrender, forget she ever heard the names Kira Shanks or Benny Brudzienski. Forget the truth. What did she know anyway? Other than this didn't end with Cole Denning's confession and shotgun suicide on the porch.

There were so many times since Parsons when Alex hadn't been sure if she wanted to live or die. Nights that dragged on till long after the party was over, and she'd find herself sitting in an unfamiliar bathroom of a house she did not know, alone, coming down, sobering up, looking for an outlet to charge her phone so she could call a friend who wouldn't come pick her up as she tried to convince herself she'd had fun. Mornings spent blocking out the sunlight with cheap, stolen sunglasses, pushing against the grain, heading to sleep while the rest of the world headed to work, long walks punctuated by big trash compactors crushing garbage and the grating sounds of everyone else's progress.

Alex had no vested interest, no skin in the game. She could tell these girls what they wanted to hear, offer enough resistance to make it sound plausible, let them think they'd convinced her to see the light, swallow a little pride, no problem. She'd swallowed worse. But she couldn't make words of contrition, however insincere, come out of her mouth, no matter how hard she tried.

Prolonged silence makes people talk, give themselves up, anything to fill the void.

"You know Sharn is full of shit," Patty said. "He never got over Trista."

"Shut up, Patty."

"What? It's true. Poor little rich boy. When he got tired of slumming he went running back to his life on the hill, spreading lies, acting superior because he can fly first class to Spain any time he wants."

Meaghan glowered across the porch. Mentioning Sharn meant they knew he and Alex had talked. It tipped hands, blew cover stories. And as long as hands were tipped, Alex was betting the over. She stared at Cole's limp, lifeless body, now turning blue in the pale moonlight, noting the resemblance.

"I met Cole's father at the Idlewild today." If talking to Sharn upset them, what would snooping around the Idlewild do? Like Blue Lou Boyle, this was a game of show and tell. The girls didn't need to tell Alex anything; they'd already shown her everything.

"You shouldn't have come back here," Patty said. "You had your fifteen minutes. Are you really trying to milk a few more? How pathetic can you get?"

"How long you think you can keep this up?" Alex could've been referring to partying at Plotter Kill, staving off growing up, or covering up murder.

The butt of the gun exploded against the back of her neck, a hard, fast check snapping her head forward, dropping her to a knee. White stars flashed behind her eyeballs. Alex reached into the darkness for something to hold onto, a wall to balance against. Someone swung the stock, zeroed between her eyes. After Sweetwater and Idlewild, Alex was a little quicker, better prepared, reflexes more honed. Or maybe she was just luckier. She juked enough for the blow to clip the side of her shoulder but she laid herself out by the porch steps as though it had been a direct hit. The Louisville Slugger she'd abandoned leaned against the banister, an arm's length away.

"What the hell did you do that for?"

"Oh, come on! She wasn't buying any of this."

"Bullshit!"

"What if you killed her?"

"I didn't kill her."

"You hit her in the head. There's blood!"

"Fuck," someone muttered.

"That looks bad."

"Jesus."

"Everyone just relax."

"We have to call an ambulance."

"You split her skull in two. She's gonna bleed out."

Alex ached but was wide awake. Facedown and eyes closed, she heard everything, feeling the four's panic set in. Took her a second to realize they were scared of her injuries sustained at the motel earlier, a skull that had been split open by a bottle of rye, which made her wonder how hard Cole's father had hit her and how bad the damage really was.

"What are we going to do?"

"We change the plan. Write a new letter."

"How? We can't ply Cole with whiskey this time."

"So we write it on a computer, print it out."

"Can't the cops check that?"

"Check what? Fingerprints on the keys?"

"Time of death?"

"Not within the minute. Listen, it's simple. That bitch accused Cole. We have the text he sent from his phone. She came to see him. No one has to know we were even here."

"Like we weren't at the Idlewild?"

"Who's dragging a body to the river this time?"

"Shut up!"

"They got in a fight. He killed her, felt guilty, shot himself. End of story."

"Maybe she's right."

"No, she's not."

"This is crazy."

"Any crazier than what we did?"

"Shut up! We agreed to never talk about that again!"

"A little late for that, isn't it?"

"Is she still breathing?"

"I think she's still breathing."

"She's not breathing."

"Give me the gun."

In a single surge, Alex pushed herself up and lunged for the baseball bat, grasping, gripping and swinging as Trista pumped the Remington. Maybe Jody knew how to handle a gun, but Trista couldn't shoot straight. Unaccustomed to the force and recoil, she splintered a porch beam ten feet away. The next blast tore out a chunk of ceiling, plaster raining down. The bat cracked Trista's ribs and she dropped the gun, wailing and clutching her side. The boom echoed, scattering evening birds from the trees. Alex swung the bat again, this time taking out a knee. Trista thudded to the porch floor, a sack of wet grain. Patty and Jody jumped on Alex's back, scratching, screeching, clawing, twisting the pile around, knocking into Cole Denning's corpse, which slid from the chair, dragging the whole bloody mess to the ground. On the slick, red wood, the girls pulled hair and gouged eyes, nails raking skin. Only one of them knew how to throw a punch though. Two clean shots, and Alex extracted herself from the scrum, scrambling to reach the Louisville Slugger.

Getting to her feet, Alex stared down the barrel.

"There're no shells left."

"You sure?" Meaghan's hands trembled.

"You ever fire a gun?"

"Shoot her!" Trista screamed from her knees, cradling her cracked ribs, as Jody and Patty fought to free themselves from the dead man whose blood was all over them.

"What did you do to Kira?" Alex said.

"Shut up! Don't say anything, Meaghan!"

"You don't understand."

"Tell me." Alex's voice soft, reassuring.

"Shut up!"

Alex dropped the bat, wood knocking wood. She lifted both hands, holding them high in surrender. "Tell me."

Meaghan kept the shaky shotgun fixed, finger on the trigger. Alex didn't move. No one did. They all stayed that way, frozen in time, as sirens wailed across the pond and through the trees, carried on preserve winds, closing from all around.

"Benny killed her," Meaghan finally said, soft and sad. "I swear to God." Her hands started to shake harder and tears filled her eyes, sobs escaping her lips, until she couldn't hold the Remington any longer and lowered the shotgun, hanging her head, bawling, barely able to get the last words out. "It was Benny. Benny did it…"

This is how the story ends.

Felled twigs cracked underfoot. Bodies emerged from the forest, beams carving profiles, flashlights crisscrossing. A sea of blue flooded the breakers, surrounding higher ground. Static cut through intercoms and two-ways. Officers stomped up the steps, raiding the party house; instructions barked to clear corners and secure the perimeter. Firearms leveled, the police ordered Meaghan to drop her weapon. As she bent forward to place the Remington on the floor, the tears dried up and she locked eyes with Alex. A narrowed stare conveyed silent warning to keep her mouth shut. The threat held no sway.

Alex saw Riley first. For an instant she forgot everything, the years buried between the lanes and the miles, the distance that had grown between them; he'd come to rescue her again. Except he hadn't. She'd done that herself this time.

Then she saw Nick. He'd run around the side of the house trying to reach her. A pair of uniforms held him back, before Riley motioned for them to let him through. Nick rushed to Alex's side. She didn't try to pretend to be stronger than she was. She threw her arms around him. It was over.

New York State troopers and the Reine PD secured the porch. The Plotter Kill party house was now a crime scene.

CHAPTER TWENTY-NINE

Rainwater plopped down in big, fat drops from the telephone line in the early dawn light. Alex tucked away her cell and turned toward the guest bedroom where Nick lay peacefully asleep. She resisted crawling back beneath the covers. She grabbed her things instead, heading through the kitchen, out to the porch, where Linda sat drinking coffee, enjoying the day's first cigarette. Alex wasn't surprised to see Tommy there. Linda had called him from the hospital after Plotter Kill. It had been a crazy night. Panning between them, Alex could see the reconciliation had already begun.

"What did he say?" Linda had overheard Alex's phone call to Riley in the kitchen.

"That Cole Denning confessed in a letter, in his own handwriting, before blowing his brains out. Suicide."

"He doesn't believe that, does he?"

"Doesn't matter. That'll be the official finding."

Riley also explained that Meaghan, Trista, Patty, and Jody had been taken to separate rooms, grilled all night, asked to verify stories, and each repeated the same version. Verbatim. Clearly rehearsed, answers pat. But nothing he could do about it.

"That's bullshit. Trista White took a shot at you."

"And I hit her with a baseball bat. On Jody Wood's property. Evie Shuman reported a break-in at the Idlewild. Which doesn't help. Says she caught an intruder trying to strip copper. Had to use force."

"Her word against theirs," Tommy said.

"So the cops are just letting them go?"

"I told Riley to talk to Sharn DiDonna." In between the mockery and captiousness, Sharn had provided the most credible version to date. He was at least worthy of another interview. Given how much Sharn disliked authority, Alex wasn't holding her breath. "No one has proof of anything."

Whatever happened in that motel room seven years ago was a secret those four were taking to the grave. They'd already proven they were willing to kill to protect it.

"What about everything they said when they thought you were knocked out?"

Alex shrugged and tried to light a Parliament with damp matches.

"Hearsay." Tommy passed along his lighter. "How's your head feel?"

"It's been worse."

"Cole's admission helps Benny, right?" Linda said, still searching for that silver lining. "Keeps him out of Jacob's Island?"

"Riley seems to think so. That's what he said, anyway." Though not an admissible confession, Cole Denning's suicide note at least provided reasonable doubt. Civic leaders would bury the story, the Plotter Kill standoff another black mark to scrub clean, like the trestle's overpass on the way into town, and no one wanted the extra work. Prosecutors wouldn't risk opening that door. Any halfway competent defense team would have a jury hung by noon, which should allow Benny to stay put. Despite Yoan Lee's assertion to the contrary, Galloway offered the best care option. A small victory. But sometimes those are the only ones you get.

"That's it?" Linda said. "Those four get away with it?"

"I called Noah Lee," Alex said. "Told him what happened, handed off what I had." Which, she admitted, wasn't much. "Riley gave me a few quotes. Noah is sending the remaining thousand we agreed on. Maybe he can make something happen." Yesterday's enthusiasm aside, Noah Lee wasn't making anything happen. He'd try. He'd write up something sensational and speculative; he'd get his grade, save his trust fund. His story might run in the Uniondale paper, a handful of people might read it. He might even get to intern at *The Times*, use the case to catapult a career, just like he'd drawn up. But for the rest of them, nothing would change.

"Are you going back to the city?" Linda asked.

"All my stuff is there."

"That's not what I mean."

A sleepy, shirtless Nick appeared in the doorway, yawning, stretching. Alex knew Linda and Tommy were watching her reaction. Last week Alex might've been embarrassed, wouldn't have wanted Linda especially to catch her so unguarded. Today she didn't care.

Alex turned and kissed Nick on the mouth, catching him by surprise. He caught up quick enough.

For the past twelve years, Alex had hated to see the morning come. Strange as it seemed, given events of the past week— beaten, bludgeoned, almost raped and nearly shot dead—Alex felt more hopeful than she had in a long time. Call it a chance to start over, leave behind the parts she wanted to shed, move on. She'd made deals like this before, promises to read more books, eat healthier, pills only on the weekend. It wasn't a question of sincerity this time but accepting that she'd spent enough time trapped underground. There was plenty of fresh air to breathe up here.

Then it was time to go. Tommy hefted himself up. He reached over for a hug, which was more one-arm back pat than full-on embrace. Linda's goodbye didn't last long and the cousins didn't look at each other. It was easier that way, faces too much like their mother.

Nick walked her to her car. They waited silently by her open front door, in the street, beneath the sneakers swaying on the telephone line. She could see him searching for the right words. And it endeared how much he wanted to get it right. When he opened his mouth to speak, she kissed him again. They'd said enough last night between the sheets. This wasn't goodbye. She didn't need guarantees, and she wasn't making any promises. But Alex Salerno had come home, for better or worse.

As promised, Riley waited outside the gates of Galloway, his part of the bargain to get her to go to the hospital last night and get her head checked out. Twelve sutures later, Alex walked away with more questions than answers. Any victory was bittersweet and promised to be short-lived. Even if Riley was right and Cole's letter caught Benny Brudzienski a break, to the town at large Benny would always be a killer. Alex may never learn what really happened in that motel room seven years ago, but of one thing she'd grown certain: Benny Brudzienski wasn't a killer. She had to see him again, tell him that face to face. She owed him that much.

Riley looked better, back to his usual self, well-groomed and handsome, but they didn't speak beyond small talk. Alex had a hard time locating that spark. Maybe it had never been there at all, any connection the by-product of circumstance. No, it had been real. She needed it to be real if she were to leave it behind, grieve proper. And Alex finally felt ready to do that.

On the third floor, one of the orderlies, a young, black kid, greeted them. The boy beamed giddy, like he was bursting with a secret to share.

The orderly brought them to the big man slumped in his chair. Like the other day, Benny's misshapen, lumpy head lolled to the side, vacant gaze locked out the window. Riley held back to give Alex her moment.

She tried to catch Benny's eye, hoping for a glimmer of recognition, an acknowledgment of yesterday's echo.

Alex leaned over and kissed Benny on the top of his head,

before whispering in his ear. "I know you didn't do it. I can't explain how I know that. I just do. In here." She pointed at her chest. "Goodbye, Benny." Then she stood straight and wiped a tear from her eye.

Benny's blank stare remained fixed on the big, black birds gathered on bare, brown branches. His blunted expression showed no signs of comprehension, no indication of understanding.

She knew she'd been asking for too much. Miracle cures don't happen in real life; the comatose don't suddenly wake up excited to hear about new technology or the latest slang. That shit only happens in Hollywood. Real life doesn't end with confessions or the truth.

BENNY BRUDZIENSKI

There are the roads that take you into town and there are the roads that bring you home. I leave the farm and start out to find her. It is getting dark and has been raining for several days. I have not seen her in a long time. I want to give her the book I made for her. I have it tucked inside the bib of my overalls. It has the pictures she gave me, the ones with the pretty words. I added photographs of me too from when I was a regular boy, before I turned into this thing I have become. I do not make it into town before my brother swoops me up.

My brother Wren hates me. He usually brings our other brother Dan with him but today he is alone. Wren blames me for having to quit football, for having to come help around the farm after Mom died. He stares out the dirty truck windshield and will not look at me. Wren usually screams at me. He usually says he is sick of me interrupting his day, wandering off, making him leave the farm to come and fetch me. He says he should be playing football. He says one day he will put a bullet in my head and bury me in the far-away fields, past the silo with the dead chickens. But he does not yell today. He is not taking the road back to the farm.

I try to use my words. I used to be able to do that if I focused all my energy and tried really hard. I have not been able to do that in a long time. I know I am getting worse. I hear Dad on the telephone talking to the men at the bank who want to buy the farm. I hear Dad on the phone talking to the men at the hospital who say it is time I leave the farm and stay with them. I do not want to leave our house. Wren is in charge now. If I can make my mouth say sorry, it might start something good between my brother and me. He will see that we are still brothers and that there is still a person inside me. He will tell Dad to let me stay. But I cannot make any words come, only low gurgling sounds that stay trapped in my throat and make me sound like a mindless beast chewing cud.

"Stop that, Benny. You're making me sick."

There is a darkness behind my eyes. It grows stronger every day. White and light have become harder to see. I feel like I am disappearing.

Wren reaches over and flicks my ear hard with his finger. It stings like a hornet. "I said shut up."

Time goes forward because I know that is how time works, it does not stay in one place, but it does not feel that way to me, and I know I have been here before. How many times have we made this trip? My day feels like a big circle. It has no start. It has no end. It goes around and around, a never-ending loop.

Wren parks at the edge of the woods, across from the motel where I work, on the shoulder where shipping trucks turn around after dropping off deliveries. Wren always makes me ride in the back of the truck. It does not matter if it is raining. Today he had me sit up front. Wren orders me out. It is cold and the wind blows hard, my teeth chatter and makes my bones feel raw. He is taking something off the flatbed. I cannot see what it is at first because the skies have grown darker. Now I see it is a bicycle. A new bicycle. Wren takes it off the truck and sets it down in the mud. It gleams fire engine red through the murky drizzle. It has a banana seat and a pennant flag. At first I am so happy because my brother has bought me a present. He smashed my old bicycle against a tree because I kept wandering off to see her. This gift means he feels something for me other than hate so there is hope.

"I know you can hear me," Wren says. "I know you understand."

I splutter and moan, spittle dribbling down my chin. I want to thank him for my present. The rains begin to pick up and the water pools at my feet. It seeps between the soles of my old boots, soaking my socks. Wren points toward the motel, to a room on the other side, the only one with a light on. It shines, warm and inviting. It is so cold out here. I would like to be inside.

"That's what you want?" my brother says. "Take your turn on the train?" He laughs. It is not a kind laugh. "Have at it. Hell, might make a man of you."

He points down the road, the other way, in the direction away from our farm, away from the center of town, toward the dark places I do not go.

"Take your turn, Benny, you stupid fuck"—he stabs a finger in the middle of my forehead, leaves it there, twisting the tip around my flesh—"and then I want you to get on your little bicycle, and you are going to peddle far, far away. You don't come back to the farm, you hear me? You do not come home. No one wants you there anymore. We have bigger problems. Go find a nice, deep pond to sleep in, go live in the forest and trap rabbits, stick out your fat thumb and catch a ride to hell. I don't give a shit. But you come back to the farm"—he twists his finger harder, deeper, and the friction burns—"you come back to the farm, and I swear to fucking God, Benny, I will gut you like a fish, nail you to the barn wall, and dry you out like jerky."

My brother gets in his truck and spins his tires, spitting mud as he steers off the shoulder and onto the road, speeding into the distance, back to the place where I am no longer wanted.

I shuffle alongside my new bicycle toward the room, its light calling me. I do not know why this room, why now, but I know I have been here before. As I get closer, the music and voices grow louder, and I am filled with fear and dread. I know when I open the door I will find her. I know she will not be alone. I know something bad waits for us both.

People are dancing in their underwear, holding up beer cans and liquor bottles. It is a big party. They are cheering and laughing, celebrating. I do not know why. There was no football game today. It smells like bleach and fire. The air is thick with smoke and sweat like Dad's card games, the holiday parties they no longer have because Mom is dead.

I push forward. Bodies part. I see her lying on the bed. Her arms are twisted above her head, wrists bound with twine and tied to the headboard. There is a wet towel around her neck and a wad of fabric stuffed in her mouth. It is covered with duct tape. I meet her gaze and stare into her eyes. Her expression is hollow, glassed-over and vacant, shattered. She cannot see me.

They shout this is what you deserve. They say this is what you get for taking things that do not belong to you. They punch her in the head, slap her across the face, yank the wet towel around her throat. When they see me, no one cares that I walked in or that the door was unlocked. They say don't worry about the retard, and someone lock the goddamn door. They are all lined up to take their turn, all these people from town who laugh at me, the boys from the Price Chopper, the girls behind the Farm Shop. They laugh at her too. They spit on her and call her names as one man slips off and another climbs on.

I recognize him. It is Mrs. Shuman's son, Cole. He works at the motel too. Cole throws parties in these rooms because he is older and can buy beer. He does not take long. When he climbs off, they pat him on the back and hand him a bottle. When his eyes meet mine, he does not look like these other people. He is not laughing. He does not look happy or proud of himself. He knows what he did is wrong.

Whatever has happened in this room, an evil has taken over. I can feel it. A portal has opened that can never be closed. I know there are demons. I have seen them. The devil is real.

A hand slaps my back. Someone says let the retard take his turn. I hear those girls laughing. It is the meanest sound I have ever heard.

I do not have to be here. I have a choice. I can fix this. I can make it right.

Dad always said I could crush the life out of a cow if I wanted to. I never knew if that was true. I never wanted to try and find out.

Until now.

The first bones crack easy enough. His arms are small. They snap like tiny bird bones. I feel them splintering, tendons snapping like coils wound too tight in a lawnmower. I throw him against the wall. They come at me, one by one, and two by four. I fight them all off. I have the strength of a dozen men. I fling body after body, man after man, until the screaming stops and all I can hear is the heaviness of my own breath.

I make it to the bed, pull the ties, and free her. Then come the bottles, the fists and the fury. The more the mob attacks, the stronger I become.

I lift her up, hoist her over my shoulder, making for the door, pushing people out of my way. I will carry her to safety. Something hard and heavy strikes my legs. The book I made for her with all the pretty pictures slips from my bib. I lose my balance and drop to a knee, and when she slides off my shoulder, I see I am too late. She flops on the floor like a chicken with its neck snapped. Her eyes are open and she is breathing but she is too far away now, unreachable. She is gone. Nothing I do can save her. I do not want her to remember this. I bend over her, shielding her bruised nakedness with my big body. They all jump on my back, gouging fingers into my eyes, tearing at my cheeks, drawing blood with their nails. I am an immovable force. I will not leave her like this. I cup my large hand over her mouth and nose and cut off her air supply. Her body shakes, convulses, twitches. It is an involuntary reaction to want to live. It is okay, I say, no one can hurt you anymore.

They are all on me now. When I grab my picture book and stand, I feel like I carry the weight of the world. There are too many of them. As strong as I am, I cannot fight them all. They keep hitting me, swiping jagged glass at my face, punching my ribs and belly. I stumble for the door and feel something sharp enter my side. I pitch bodies off me, crushing them to the ground, stomping hands and feet and faces. I part the seas and make it outside. I climb on my bicycle to peddle for help. I am bleeding from my head and eyes and mouth, from my gut. It is too hard to see in the dark. The streets are wet, winds whipping, sucking all light behind me. I need to get somewhere safe, wait for the storm to pass. I have to tell someone what happened. They have to be punished for what they did. I go back to the only place I can, to the place where we first met, the place where I know I will find her again. I will hide in the tool shed at the football field. I will rest and get better, heal, and then I will go to the police. I will make them understand. I peddle as fast as I can, but the faster I peddle the harder the cold rain stings my eyes and the slower I go, until soon I cannot see anything at all.

The stands are filling up, the skies bright and blue. I have trimmed the grass, picked trash from the weeds, and swept the lot to get ready for the big game. Cars honk their horns and trucks rev their engines. People cheer. The home team runs onto the field and the sidelines erupt. I look up and see her standing there. High above the rest, beneath the big oak tree. She looks down and smiles. I have never seen anything so beautiful in all my life. I want to protect her, wrap her in a box, keep her safe forever.

And I will always remember her this way. Standing on the hill behind the football field, her yellow hair shining like straw in the autumn sun...

ACKNOWLEDGMENTS

First off I'd like to thank Eric Campbell, Lance Wright, and the Down & Out family for signing me. This is the first of three you've agreed to publish. These books are all very special to me. Thank you for giving them a home. I'll bust my tail for you guys.

This book required more research than usual. I couldn't have written it without the help of James Queally and Jason Isolda, who provided their expertise, correcting all the stupid mistakes I made about journalism and geography. Your signed copies (and checks) are in the mail.

When I was in grad school, Jean Campbell wrote this amazing story about the Second World War and the prejudice of a town against immigrants. And although my novel has nothing to do with war, at least public ones, and takes place far away and much later, I'd be remiss if I didn't mention the heavy debt I owe. (Jean, I trust this will come across as homage and not outright theft!)

Thanks to my lovely wife, Justine. As always you give me the time, patience, and understanding that allows me to write and create worlds. You are the true definition of a better half, and I'd be lost without you.

A shout out to my boys, Holden and Jackson Kerouac. Now that you can read, Holden, there is no getting around the fact that you will want to read Dad's books. I just ask that you don't read *Junkie Love* until you are much, much older. I love you, boys. You are the reason I am here.

And much love to my sister, Melissa Greco. There's not many of us left, kid. We got to stick together. I'm not going anywhere, promise.

Thanks to Liz Kracht for your faith, editing, and insight. You pushed me to make this book the best it could be.

A special thanks to Death Wish Coffee, the world's strongest brew. I had three books out this year. It's not a coincidence.

And last thanks to my buddy Tom Pitts. Tom reads all my books, makes sure I don't fuck up shit like calling rifles shotguns. Mostly, though, I don't have many brothers left. Tom picks me up when I'm low, and he is always there to remind me why we survived the hobo life; that there is something better waiting for us; and to never, ever give up. Love you, brother.

Joe Clifford is the author of several books, including *Junkie Love* and the Jay Porter thriller series, as well as editor of the anthologies *Trouble in the Heartland: Crime Fiction Inspired by the Songs of Bruce Springsteen*; *Just to Watch Them Die: Crime Fiction Inspired by the Songs of Johnny Cash*, and *Hard Sentences*, which he co-edited. Joe's writing can be found at JoeClifford.com.

BOOKS

On the following pages are a few
more great titles from the
Down & Out Books publishing family.

For a complete list of books and to
sign up for our newsletter,
go to DownAndOutBooks.com.

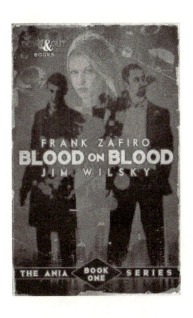

Blood on Blood
The Ania Trilogy Book One
Frank Zafiro and Jim Wilsky

Down & Out Books
978-1-946502-71-1

Estranged half-brothers Mick and Jerzy Sawyer are summoned to their father's prison deathbed. The spiteful old man tells them about missing diamonds, setting them on a path of cooperation and competition to recover them.

Along the way, Jerzy, the quintessential career criminal and Mick, the failed cop and tainted hero, encounter the mysterious, blonde Ania, resulting in a hardboiled Hardy Boys meets Cain and Abel.

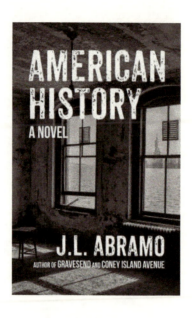

American History
J.L. Abramo

Down & Out Books
September 2018
978-1-946502-70-4

A panoramic tale, as uniquely American as Franklin Roosevelt and Al Capone...

Crossing the Atlantic Ocean and the American continent, from Sicily to New York City and San Francisco, the fierce hostility and mistrust between the Agnello and Leone families parallel the turbulent events of the twentieth century in a nation struggling to find its identity in the wake of two world wars.

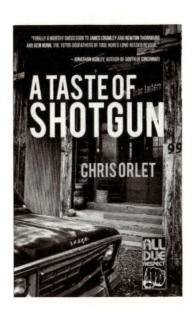

A Taste of Shotgun
Chris Orlet

All Due Respect, an imprint of
Down & Out Books
July 2018
978-1-946502-92-6

A local drug dealer has the goods on Denis Carroll. That shooting at his tavern five years ago? Turns out the cops got it all wrong. Now, after five years of blackmail, the Carrolls have had enough. When the drug dealer turns up dead, Denis is the prime suspect. As more bodies pile up, they too appear to have Denis' name all over them. Is Denis really a cold-blooded killer or could this be the work of someone with a grudge of her own?

In this darkly humorous small-town noir everyone has something to hide and nothing is at seems.

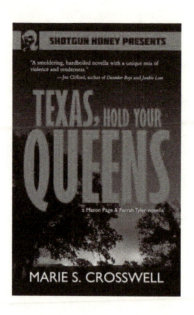

Texas, Hold Your Queens
A Mason Page & Farrah Tyler Novella
Marie S. Crosswell

Shotgun Honey, an imprint of
Down & Out Books
978-1-943402-74-8

When the body of an undocumented Mexican immigrant is found abandoned on a roadside, Detectives Mason Page and Farrah Tyler have no clue how a throwaway case that neither wants to let go will affect their lives.

On the job, Page and Tyler are the only two female detectives in El Paso CID's Crimes Against Persons unit. Off the clock, the two have developed an intimate friendship, one that will be jeopardized when the murder case puts them on the suspect's trail.

Coleman Northwest Regional Library

CPSIA information can be obtained
at www.ICGtesting.com
Printed in the USA
LVHW011717140119
603847LV00006B/673/P